Amarillo by Morning

Hope you're enjoy!
Thanks!

Glen Stephens

AMARILLO BY MORNING

GLEN STEPHENS

TATE PUBLISHING & *Enterprises*

Published by Tate Publishing & Enterprises, LLC
127 E. Trade Center Terrace | Mustang, Oklahoma 73064 USA
1.888.361.9473 | www.tatepublishing.com

Tate Publishing is committed to excellence in the publishing industry. The company reflects the philosophy established by the founders, based on Psalm 68:11,
"The Lord gave the word and great was the company of those who published it."

Published in the United States of America
ISBN: 978-1-61663-884-9
1. Fiction, Westerns
2. Fiction, Romance, Western
10.08-16

CHAPTER ONE

Lukey Flatt's childlike heart burdened him with everyone else's problems. Old Jeniveve Voss fell last week and broke her hip; heavy rains came before big-eared Sam Turnbow got his hay off the ground; Harley Banks didn't get his price for his steers at the auction, blaming it on a "know they did it, but can't prove it" commercial buyer conspiracy; and Lester Shrumm lost ten lambs in one night to a pack of elusive coyotes. Whatever misfortunes intersected the townsfolk collided head-on with Lukey, as their well-being concerned him more greatly than his own.

Unfortunately, life's impartial eyes aimed as equally at the tenderhearted as at the calloused, dealing Lukey a difficult hand. At the age of six, he chased a cat into the street, giving a teenage driver no time to react. He was pronounced dead at the scene, but his older brother's persistence suspended Lukey's leap from the precipice of eternal darkness. Despite gentle tugs from compassionate bystanders, James Flatt administered CPR for fifteen minutes before the ambulance arrived and refused to leave Lukey's side for the one hour transport to the hospital.

The boy lived, but not without suffering consequences. This collision partially paralyzed his right side, damaged his vision, and crushed his left leg. Additionally, he would live the rest of his life with only one kidney, a fact proving crucial to the most heroic story ever repeated in the rural community.

Lukey couldn't recall the incident, but the terrible memory wouldn't allow Jeniveve Voss a moment's peace. The old cat had been her favorite, and she had paid Lukey a nickel that day to catch and return him in time for his medication.

At the age of thirty-five, everyone in town knew and liked Lukey well, employing him for odd jobs. Although his thoughts lacked depth—jigsaw puzzles confounded him—he could mow lawns and rake leaves, slow but steady, for hours without rest, happily taking whatever pay was offered. Money was a mystery to Lukey. He knew those green papers and shiny coins could be traded for food, clothes, and his favorite peppermint candies, but, whether a one dollar bill or a one hundred, their true significance was forever lost. Always sure to finish the jobs he started, Lukey trusted employers to pay him fairly, showing his appreciation with a hug and thank-you. Then he would limp away with a crooked smile, his big, blue eyes shining, magnified by thick, wire-rimmed glasses. His well-soiled straw hat would then smash down his shaggy brown hair, and he would stuff his jean pockets with the money, no more gingerly than if it was a gum wrapper. When accepting donations for fundraisers, Lukey had to be watched carefully, lest he give everything he had earned. Even the deacons at the First Baptist Church purposefully skipped him when passing the plate. Lukey would cast all his bread on the water and go without eating, until the next job came along.

When Bucky Thompson's dog died of old age, the little boy sporadically cried for several days, receiving no consolation from the gifts meant to distract his sorrowful heart. But Lukey's tactics were more effective. More than once he was seen kneeling beside Bucky, his face twisted by compassion, tears streaming his cheeks, as he provided a shoulder on which to cry.

When there was need, Lukey volunteered to help. When there was sickness, he felt the pain of the afflicted. When a local citizen passed away, he quietly mourned the loss for weeks. Which is why, when the benefit dance for the Slaton boy was announced, Lukey stood first in line.

There would be no cover charge. Instead, people were asked to give whatever amount burdened their hearts, making Lukey, with his childish understanding of money, an ideal candidate for accepting donations. Armed with a gallon pickle jar and a crooked smile, Lukey stood just outside the front door of the Corral Club, where he met Deke and Joel, two unfamiliar faces reeking of trouble. Greasy denim, appearing borrowed from a mechanic's wardrobe, covered these two from top to bottom—inappropriate attire for the evening's formal occasion.

"Then I slapped the crap out of him with one of these!" shouted Deke in a boisterous voice accented by too much liquor. He held up a fat fist and explained to Joel how he had beaten a man the night before. His speech offered a variety of obscenities, undeterred by the presence of women and children. "After I beat the hell outta that damn cowboy, nobody else in the place wanted none of me. Guess they figgered if I could whup the biggest of the lot, the rest of 'em better just leave me the hell alone!"

"Yeah," Joel agreed, as usual.

Deke stopped in front of Lukey. "What's the cover, boy?" he asked, reaching for his wallet.

"It's…for my fwiend, Bobby," Lukey explained with obvious simplicity.

Deke glared at him through furrowed brows, as a smile slowly spread across his face. He glanced at Joel and winked. "My fwiend, Bobby?" he mocked. "What the hell's that 'sposed to mean, moron?" He stepped closer, peering into Lukey's eyes. "Damn, boy. You lookin' at me through coke bottles or what? Must be hard up for help around this place," Deke jeered and glanced at Joel.

"Coke bottles," Joel echoed. "That's funny, Deke."

"Bobby needs an opewation," Lukey continued. "We gonna help him buy one. It cost money."

Deke looked at Joel, rolled his eyes, and placed a patronizing hand on Lukey's shoulder.

Joel laughed at the gesture.

"Opewation, huh? So, they picked a retard to take the cash." Deke worked to insult Lukey, but offense was never part of the simple man's character. "Well, in that case, here's my donation."

Deke dug into his front pocket, pulled out a dollar bill, and dropped it on the ground. "Whoops," he faked.

"Thanks, mister," Lukey said and awkwardly dropped to his knees, still hindered by paralysis.

"Got a hitch in your git-a-long, boy?" Deke needled.

He and Joel took the opportunity and ducked through the door.

"A benefit dance," Deke sneered. "How about that? Good thing we wore our Sunday best, huh," he said, wiping his hands across grease-smeared pants.

"Yeah." Joel laughed.

Then Deke barged in, bellied up to the bar, and scanned the crowd with a fierce expression that dared anyone to comment on his appearance.

Deke was as wide as he was tall. In fact, for all practical purposes, it would have been easier to jump over him than walk around him. His puffy, red face engulfed his piglike eyes, and a ring of hair protruded from beneath his collar, indicative of a fur-covered body.

Stubby fingers jutted from his hands, and his head mashed into his shoulders, hiding all signs of a neck.

Joel, on the other hand, was Deke's opposite in appearance. Tall and lanky, his protruding Adam's apple and hook nose spoke of distant kinship to a buzzard. His eyes held a passive, even lazy expression, declaring indifference, as if he held no opinions of his own. Joel was a yes man. He laughed at Deke's jokes and sincerely listened to his stories, for some reason regarding Deke as a type of hero. He would go to battle for the man, perhaps only because there was honor among thieves. This night, however, Joel had hitched his cart to the wrong horse.

"Deke, finish the story. What happened after you hit that dude?" Joel asked and pushed his way to the bar, turning his head up with an exaggerated laugh.

"Well, then I says to him, 'Listen, shit for brains! I'm giving you just three seconds to make like a cow pie and hit the trail!'" Deke glanced about the room, meeting the stares of frowning women in the vicinity.

"I thought the bastard was gonna start crying right there. Shithead fell to his knees and begged me not to hit him again. Thought I was gonna die."

Stick Slaton cut his striking blue eyes toward the bar and fixed them on Deke, wiping beer froth from his heavy, black mustache. In no mood for rudeness and fearing Anna would hear the trash, he turned for a view of the two men, leaning an elbow on the bar. A carnival had moved into town for the rodeo, and these two were doubtlessly its byproduct.

The evening began with Stick tugging at his formidable white collar, which strangled his thick neck. The unpleasant sensation brought to mind his grade school bully, Pug Bond, striving to choke the life from him. A smile highlighted his face, as he recalled that Pug was a preacher now. Stick glanced covertly about the ballroom and quickly freed his throat, releasing the top button with agile fingers. A violent explosion had been building, but blood now circulated once more. He welcomed the relief. "A fish out of water," Stick mumbled to himself.

The townsfolk meant well, but this type of dance was not his cup of tea. They had decided on a formal event in hopes of discouraging troublemakers, persuading them to stay home or behave themselves, at least. Stick was certain, however, that they had succeeded only in adding a manufactured air of conventional etiquette to the trouble that was sure to start. This dance would be no different than any other. It was a breeding-ground for rowdiness.

Stick counted each man in the community a friend. He worked with them, fought with them, dined with them, drank with them, and laughed with them. He knew what they would tolerate and what they would not. One thing was certain: before this night was over, one man would have too much to drink and offend another, and black suits and ties would be ripped to shreds.

The discomfort of formal attire always encouraged a brief evening. Stick was sure everyone was staring at him, and for good reason. His wardrobe consisted mostly of denim.

Like icing on a mud pie, he thought about himself.

Stick glanced suspiciously about the room, attempting to catch anyone harboring a mocking grin. Unexpectedly, his eyes met Anna's. Several suitors had her cornered, but Stick could see she wasn't the least bit interested. They were edifying themselves in hopes of gaining her favor, but Anna didn't put much stock in such things. If any man was to win her hand, it would be with quiet confidence, truth, sincerity, and, above all, integrity. And because such qualities were rare, she would more than likely remain a widow.

Anna politely excused herself from all the attention and weaved her way through the crowd toward Stick. She looked as uncomfortable as he was, but for different reasons. Formalities irritated Stick, like a gate with two locks; but for Anna, it was all the attention—

although, much to her dislike, she was a natural attraction. Her wholesome beauty spoke to a man's soul, not just his basic instincts.

"You look especially handsome tonight, Stick," she stated, and her full lips formed a familiar smile. "I haven't seen you in a suit since…"—suddenly, her eyes shifted thoughtfully to the floor—"since TK's…funeral."

Even though the funeral was ages ago, the memory remained vivid. Stick extended a weathered hand and lifted her soft chin with his index finger. "And you," he said with fondness, "are always beautiful."

Her eyes sparkled at the compliment. "I wish we could just go home," she remarked.

"Yeah. Me too. But the folks were nice enough to do this for us. So I guess the least we can do is try to enjoy ourselves."

Anna nodded in agreement, turned to face the dance floor, and was immediately confronted by a familiar face: Jack Chambers, an old-time cowboy, longtime family friend, and president of the Rodeo Association. He was in his late seventies, a lovable character whom Anna enjoyed. His ten-gallon hat sported a sweeping brim and matched his bigger than life personality. He was small in stature, appearing a bit frail and bent. A white handlebar mustache unfolded with his smile, and his square jaws held a permanent bulge from a lifetime of chewing tobacco. Texas humor was etched into the corners of his fearless eyes.

Anna remembered Jack from when she was a little girl. He had made a lasting impression on her. He was her hero, a man with piercing gray eyes and a grand smile, with vibrant energy and amazing strength, a rodeo champion from the early days. At the age of thirteen, a strong crush made her heart flutter anytime he came around. Now, she laughed about her silly schoolgirl aspirations.

Jack became a pillar of the community in his later years, after he had sown more than his share of wild oats. Involved with the church and youth activities, he always gave of what he had to those in need, though he wasn't rich.

Jack put his left arm around Anna and extended his right hand to Stick, who marveled at the elderly man's still-powerful grip.

"Hey, ol'-timer. Everything all set for this weekend?" asked Stick.

"You bet," answered Jack proudly. "It'll be the biggest rodeo this town has ever had. Cowboys from all over the state have entered. Gonna be some stiff competition in the bull-riding event. Should be a handsome cash prize for the winner. Young fella named Hardy Tillman is favored." Jack winked at Anna. "But...if the world-famous Stick Slaton entered, it'd sure help the turnout." Then, playfully, he frowned. "Second thought, I reckon he's a bit too old."

Abruptly abandoning the small talk, Jack fixed his friendly gray eyes on Anna. "Don't you worry 'bout little Bobby," he said with great compassion. "Things always have a way of working out for the best. Folks 'round here've been doing a lot off praying. If he does end up needing surgery or even a transplant, the money will be there."

"Thanks, Jack." Anna forced a smile. "You sound so certain. I almost believe it. But we don't even have the money for his tests."

"You can bank on it, honey. I've been on my knees for you and that little boy and"—he glanced playfully at Stick and pointed with his thumb—"this sorry ol' uncle of his. I'm just confident that the good Lord intends to take care of it all."

"How, Jack? How can we put so much money together when the ranch barely pays for itself? Stick and I don't have it, and the estate documents wouldn't allow us to mortgage or sell the ranch even if we wanted to. That's the way Sterling wanted it. I'm sure the possibility of something like this never crossed his mind."

"I know, sugar. But you gotta have faith. Why, I'm sure tonight's benefit will raise a few thousand."

Anna's lips tightened with resolution. "Thanks, Jack. You're a good friend," she said and leaned to kiss his cheek. "I'm sorry if I sound like a whiner."

"Thanks, Jack," offered Stick with less enthusiasm. Although he knew Jack believed what he said, Stick thought he was offering false hope.

With a nod to Stick and a wink to Anna, Jack walked away quietly.

Doctor Madison was next in line to visit. A middle-aged, small-town, family doctor, he was always willing to go the extra mile for his patients. He wore a black felt Stetson that accented the gray at his temples. He was tall and thin with big hands, another community pillar. He had vigorously earned everyone's respect and trust by frequently making house calls, a rare practice in this day and age. Doctor Madison was a rancher himself, understanding the related struggles.

"Hey, Doc," greeted Stick while shaking his hand.

"Evening, Stick." He was always formal. Taking his hat in hand, he faced Anna. "I'll be out to see you tomorrow. The latest test results should be here by morning."

Anna nodded, and a troublesome thought worried her brow. The lone wrinkle didn't go unnoticed by the doctor.

"Is there something you'd like to ask?" queried Dr. Madison.

He reminded Stick of an Englishman, without the accent, especially when he smoked his Sherlock Holmes-style pipe.

"Would they"—Anna stepped closer to Doctor Madison—"really let my boy die if … if we didn't have the money for an operation? Would they really do that?"

Doctor Madison's expression was grave. "If they can do anything at all, I'm sure they will. The problem is … this disease is rare. There are very few doctors qualified to treat it."

Afraid of sounding too impersonal, Doctor Madison put a compassionate hand on Anna's shoulder. "You see, normally, when there's a lack of funds, a children's hospital will take someone like Bobby and treat the illness, operate or whatever is necessary, and then coordinate payment according to the parent's or guardian's ability to pay. The problem is that right now, the children's hospitals are overwhelmed with patients. But we can't afford for Bobby to be put on a waiting list."

The doctor glanced at Stick seriously. "Bobby just doesn't have that kind of time. Besides, there are very few doctors at these hospitals qualified to treat him. Regrettably, most standard hospitals and specialists require a large portion of the money to be paid up front."

Doctor Madison struggled, being the bearer of bad news. "You might already be aware of this, but even though this disease is rare, it has the same effect as other kidney diseases. Hundreds of others like Bobby fear the same dreadful conclusion. The organ doesn't function properly, and subsequently, they're in desperate need of a donor."

The doctor shook his head sadly. "Unfortunately, there aren't enough donors to go around. So how do they decide who gets the organ? Transplants are very expensive, requiring experienced surgeons, a highly trained staff, and sophisticated equipment. Is it fair to give the organ to someone who cannot pay and allow someone who can to go without when the hospital's expenses must be paid? How should the decision be made? Money is often the determining factor."

"Excuse me, Doc." Stick dismissed himself and walked toward the bar, wearing a frown. He was irritated and had heard enough. Stick wasn't one to sit and watch. If something needed doing, he was busy getting it done, the hands-on type. But with this situation, helplessness inundated him. There was nothing more he could do. He couldn't fix little Bobby's problem; nor did he have any good ideas about how to get the needed money. He was left with nothing but overwhelming frustration.

Tommy Grant, the bartender, saw Stick approaching and slid a beer down the bar toward him. "On the house," he stated in the spirit of the benefit. Tom and TK had been good friends growing up. They played tricks on Stick when he was little, as older kids often did to younger siblings tagging along. Tom had grown fat and out of shape. He was bald on top, while long, thin strands of hair covered his ears and collar.

"Thanks, Tom." Stick tilted the bottle upward and took a sizeable pull. He wiped his mouth with the back of his hand, turned to face the crowd, and leaned against the bar. His mood had changed quickly. He was angry, angry at life. It was short and full of blisters.

Suddenly, Deke's bragging and Joel's guffaw caught his attention, and Stick focused on the two unfamiliar faces. Deke shared his offensive verbiage with the whole room. The indecent language added fuel to an already kindled fire. Disrespect for women and children was intolerable, and Stick's teeth grinded together as he resisted a growing urge.

Considering the nature of the event, Stick may have avoided confrontation had Lukey Flatt not entered the picture. "Mister," he said to Deke politely, paralysis causing bad mispronounciations, "would you mind not saying that? This is my fwiend Bobby's party. And he don't like that kind of talk."

A mischievous smile darkened Deke's sinister countenance. "Watch this," he whispered to Joel and stepped toward Lukey.

"How would you like your ass kicked, retard?" Deke drew back and prepared to swing an open hand at Lukey's jaw.

"Hey!" yelled Stick, instinctively rushing to Lukey's aid.

Everyone near the bar turned to watch. Couples stopped dancing. Harley Banks winked at his wife, nodded his head in Stick's direction, and smiled.

"Watch this," he whispered, suddenly ending discussions about the "conspiracy" price paid for his steers earlier that day.

Lester Shrumm, still stewing over the loss of his lambs, stepped on his wife's foot, danced her into Harley, and accidentally pressed his chest against her robust bosom. It was the closest they had been in months. He abruptly pushed himself away and stepped aside for a better view of the dispute. A dark cloud lifted from his face as Stick moved quickly toward the strangers.

"Well now," Lester whispered, as was his habit when situations called for a spectator.

Stick halfheartedly suppressed his rising temper, noting the abundance of suits, ties, high heels, and sparkling jewelry aiming his direction. He forced a cordial tone into his voice. "Look, fellas. Call me old fashioned if you like, but indecency in front of women and children is like beer and ice cream. The two don't mix."

"Okay. You're old fashioned, *damned* old fashioned." Deke emphasized the curse word, and the two men burst into laughter.

A mischievous light flickered in Jack Chambers' eyes. He stepped closer, the mustache spreading across his face. His love for a good fight was superseded only by his love for the Lord. His fists instinctively clenched and came up almost into a boxer's stance as he glanced at Sam Turnbow and winked.

Sam's big ears jumped to attention and focused on Stick like a trained mule. He tossed his empty beer bottle into the trash and positioned himself for a better view.

"Mister," Stick said through clenched teeth. He became immediately aware that his cordial tone had vanished, so he leaned toward Deke and whispered, "The only difference between your foul mouth and air pollution is one burns my ears and the other burns my nose. Either way, I don't like it." Typically a man of action, Stick wasted few words, but a peaceful solution seemed appropriate under the current circumstances. Maybe the loudmouth would get the message and leave.

"Better'n gettin' your skinny cowboy *ass* kicked," Deke belched, sporting a wide grin.

Some men have a special gift packaged with their bad habits. Like flipping a switch, they can shut it off when a lady enters the room. Others don't have the knack. Deke was of the latter group.

Normally, Stick avoided trouble, having learned better with age. There were some things, however, he just would not tolerate, namely, rude behavior. Like his pa used to say, "There's a time and a place."

This, as far as Stick was concerned, was neither the time nor the place for a foul-mouthed braggart; and frankly, Stick wasn't in the mood to hear it. It didn't matter that Deke outweighed him by a hundred pounds.

Stick threw an irritated glance around the room and found all eyes fixed on him. He hated talk. Actions always spoke louder than words; but considering the audience, he reluctantly chose diplomacy. Taking a deep breath, Stick exhaled slowly and sneered. "Let me put it in easier terms. You stop flapping that gutter mouth or I'll stop it for you."

There would be no avoiding the fight. Stick could see it in the eyes of both men. And Stick was the hands-on type.

It was Joel with whom Stick decided to deal first. A swift right cross to the beak caught him off guard, forcing him to the sidelines. Stick knew that if either of these men were a real challenge, it would be Deke, and he didn't want Joel interfering while they were engaged. A firm poke in the nose often subdued a surly attitude.

Deke didn't waste a second. He was ready for the fight and had intended to throw the first punch, only Stick had beat him to it. The fact that Joel had been struck first was a pleasant surprise, allowing just enough opportunity. He jabbed the point of Stick's chin, then pounded his midsection with a forceful blow. However, Stick just stepped back and grinned. He was lean and hard, and Deke's pudgy fists were ineffective.

Jack Chambers dodged as if the blows were aimed at him, bobbing and weaving, blocking with one fist and jabbing with the other.

Fights were a common scenario for Cactus Falls, Texas. Since childhood, Stick had fought or wrestled often just to break the monotony—only then it was for fun. Now, thanks to a stint with military Special Forces, he had experienced his fill of it. Still, the Dekes of this world couldn't be allowed to run roughshod over whomever they pleased. While most carnival folks were decent enough, their nomadic lifestyle attracted riffraff. This familiar scene revisited every year when the rodeo came to town.

Stick stepped in, jabbing. His knuckles split the brow over each of Deke's eyes, and blood trickled down the fat man's face. Stick ducked a right cross and came up with an uppercut, forcing the wind from Deke's lungs. The big man gasped and doubled over, and Stick tenderized his nose with a lifted knee. Deke stumbled backward, then, with blind fury, charged ahead like a mad bull. But Stick easily avoided the attack, rolling to his left and slamming Deke on the ear as he passed. The force drove him to the ground, where he remained.

The fight lasted no more than a few seconds, but a crowd had quickly gathered. Already, men were patting themselves on the back, proud of their local hero. Lester Shrumm suddenly kissed his wife, putting a light in her eyes that promised an encore after they got home. Harley Banks shook Sam Turnbow's hand and offered to help him get his hay off the ground.

Someone shoved a beer in Stick's face, and once again, he took a long drink. He felt better. The fight relieved some frustration. The right shoulder seam in the arm of his black suit had ripped, and he blindly inspected the damage with his left hand. He locked eyes once again with Anna—only this time her look was different. A blend of emotions shadowed her face, as if she struggled to sort through a conglomeration of entangled thoughts. Her appearance troubled Stick.

Lukey Flatt limped over to Deke, knelt awkwardly beside him, and placed a compassionate hand on his shoulder. "Mister, are you okay?" he asked.

Anna had overheard some men of town talking about Stick's toughness and quick temper, but she counted it mostly for exaggeration. Now she wasn't so sure. He seemed to enjoy the fight. He was so quick; so confident; so strong; and, she thought, so terrible. Her instincts suggested that Stick was capable of fierce indignation, but until this moment, he had carefully concealed it from her. She was curiously aware of a fresh admiration, an excitement that left her fearful and distant. Stick had beaten these men as if it were play, all the while wearing a strange sort of tight-lipped and angry smile.

Anna suddenly realized she was staring at Stick, and she quickly averted her eyes. It was time to go. Anna turned and made her way to the door, avoiding the rambunctious crowd.

Stick watched her leave and then looked thoughtfully at the two men who were being helped to their feet. He had most certainly disappointed Anna, a thought leaving him in sudden pain. Not physical pain. No. It was something else—grief. But why?

CHAPTER TWO

"Them carnival boys got what they had coming, son," offered Lester Shrumm through the window of Stick's pickup. "If you 'uz to yawn, that big 'un 'd steal the tobacco right out of your mouth. Liars and thieves the whole lot." Shrumm turned, shouting an order to his Australian shepherd. "Bring 'em 'round, Josey."

The dog jumped from the back of his flatbed truck, crouched, moved toward a group of sheep, then leaped forward and barked a warning. The sheep rushed through a gate, and Shrumm swung it closed. He glanced over his shoulder and offered Stick an explanation for his being at the auction barn.

"Coyotes in the back pasture. Figured I'd better sell these ewes before they wind up like my lambs. Did pretty good this year, though. Almost made a profit."

Stick smiled, put his old truck in gear, and pulled away from the sale barn. The sun was dropping low in the vast sky, sparking a desire for the comforts of home. Although he enjoyed listening to each of the old cowboys tell his version of last night's fight, he had more important things to do. More chores needed tending before dinner. Besides, the stench of the barn was almost unbearable. More than a thousand head of cattle had been sold that morning, and the mud, mildew, and manure created a putrid odor.

From the cradle to the grave, life was a mere series of conflicts, and last night was symbolic of them all. The optimist meets each challenge with hopes of a brighter tomorrow, while the pessimist grows more calloused with each battle, knowing that only death will bring an end to the war.

Stick was neither an optimist nor a pessimist. He saw things as they were. He enjoyed confronting each antagonist that life sent his way. Without them, the state of his being would be nothing more than boring.

Stick was a winner. He knew well the thrill of victory. And as yet, there was only one antagonist he had failed to defeat. He was his own worst enemy, self-destructive. The detailed craftsman side of him stood as an architectural angel on his right shoulder, directing him to do great things, while the darker side, the wild hare, stood as a devil on his left shoulder, destroying its counterpart's progress.

Stick had faced a variety of opponents. Sometimes it was the elements of nature, or survival in the business world. In his younger days, it was the North Vietnamese. Last night, it was a man.

At times, Stick was convinced he had been born a hundred years too late. If only he could turn back the pages of time, back to a day when things weren't so complicated. He didn't consider himself stupid, but then, everything did seem rather complex. He liked things simple. Perhaps, given another shot at life, he would take better aim.

But on second thought, his restless spirit prevented him from being content with anything—for any prolonged length of time, that is. So, had he another chance, the outcome most likely would've been the same. His irresponsible nature had left him without a family and would no doubt do so again.

It was twenty years ago this month when Becky, his wife, had left him. Maybe it wasn't meant to be. After all, she had basically the same problems as him. You might say they were just alike. Both were always searching for something, something to fill the void in their lives. But, after a very short while, all ventures became monotonous and they grew bored.

Stick loved the road. His curiosity was a nagging thirst, quenched only while traveling. Questions like, "Who?" "What?" and "Where?" were ever present in his mind. And these questions where easily answered with a little more pressure on the accelerator. Curiosity might offer him the same fate as the cat, but a man couldn't help the way he was made. Yes, satisfaction lay somewhere in the purple haze of the horizon.

His nature to drift was the perfect host for rodeo life. Neither, however, sat well with Becky. She grew weary of the fast lane, weary of him. And then, one day, she was gone. He knew he had only himself to blame. Although much the same, they were incompatible, and it was his discontentment with life that made him try marriage in the first place.

Looking back, there were no permanent landmarks of complacency to be found. He would never be content, never happy. For twenty years he had meandered on his father's ranch, these last ten spent fighting a call to a distant land to care for his sister-in-law and nephew. A wild invitation drifted on the breeze, insisting, enticing, whispering his name. More than once, he found himself straining to hear the ghostly breath while gazing intently toward the faded hills. How many lonesome and restless cowboys had done the same?

Stick had inherited half the ranch after the death of his father, and his brother had received the other half. Now he was partners with Anna, his brother's widow.

He still called the place his father's ranch. Perhaps subconsciously, he thought it best not to own anything, as everything he had owned before had somehow slipped from his grasp. Like water through his fingers, once Stick touched it, it became intangible. But was man really meant to own anything? After all, he's here today and gone tomorrow. No. Stick had concluded that ownership was no more than a product of human pride. One could own only what he would take with him when he passed away; otherwise, he was just leasing. He loved the old home place, but if he was to call it his, Lady Luck might take it too.

At forty-two years of age, Stick harbored the itch of discontentment, and no matter how hard he scratched, it persisted. Each time this itch distracted him, he subconsciously dropped his right hand to the silver and gold buckle at his waist. His index finger would move along the top of the oval shape to feel the words "World Champion Bull Rider" etched into its surface. He would then slide his finger across the impression of the cowboy, whose arm flew high in the air as he straddled a wild bull. Then he would touch his name at the bottom: Stick Slaton. A distant glimmer would appear in his penetrating blue eyes, eyes that stood prominent against his sunburned skin. A slight smile would show at the corners of his mouth. Instinctively, his thigh muscles clenched as though he were straddling the bull on his last ride.

The buckle and the old Ford pickup he drove were among the few things left from his rodeo days—including, of course, the memories. And now the memories haunted him more often with each new day. Perhaps they were responsible for the itch.

Stick was unstable but didn't know why. Maybe it was one of those heritage things, a legacy handed down from past generations, choosing occasionally to rear its ugly head. At any rate, he felt he couldn't trust himself. You might even say he was paranoid. It seemed he always came to wrong conclusions and made wrong decisions, but once a decision was made, he stuck with it. Right or wrong, if he made the bed, he slept in it.

Maybe paranoia had something to do with his refusal to ever plan anything. Or maybe it was because he liked being spontaneous. At the moment, he was certain of only one thing. The thirty-four hay bales in the back of his truck had to be unloaded before dark. Then, if time allowed, he had to shoe the horses.

Stick's reflective mood concluded with thoughts of Lukey Flatt and caused a smile to light his face. *You're the lucky one, Luke—simple, honest, no expectations, no ambition, just enjoying life.* He shook his head sympathetically. *But a perfect target for assholes.*

Stick had been driving through the ranch for half an hour, but it would be another ten minutes before he reached the entrance. A county road divided the ten thousand acres almost perfectly, leaving no more than a few acres difference between the two halves. Stick's father had donated the right-of-way to the county. It gave people access through the ranch and provided the Slaton's a paved approach to their home. Sterling Slaton bordered the road with a fence made from old drilling pipe. He painted it white, making an attractive addition to the countryside.

Stick pulled his sweat-stained, black, felt cowboy hat low over his eyes, warding off rays from the burning Texas sun. Heat waves danced on the pavement before him, forming a mirage of water, which vanished as he neared the ranch entrance. Birds quickly swooped to the asphalt behind him, catching seeds as the wind blew particles of Sudan hay from the back of his truck. Stick pulled the blue bandana from his neck and wiped sweat from his brow and then tapped his index fingers against the steering wheel to the beat of the radio's country music.

Suddenly, another remnant of the past claimed Stick's attention. He grinned and leaned toward the passenger-side window.

"Hey, Willy Boy!" Stick yelled to an old Brahman bull.

The bull nonchalantly lifted his head and gazed after the truck as it passed. Afterward, he resumed pulling the knee-high Bahaia grass that covered the field. Long needles protruded from his nose, attesting to his sampling of the prickly pear.

The pasture was plagued with cactus and mesquite trees, but Stick had cleared a small portion of it with a machete and plenty of elbow grease. After scattering Bahaia seed and fertilizer, the meadow became a useful hay field.

Willy Boy was partially responsible for the buckle at Stick's waist. By chance, Stick had drawn his number at the finals, and Willy Boy had performed admirably but failed to sling Stick from his back. Afterward, Stick purchased him from the owner, using part of the prize money.

The bull had been two years old at the time, just experiencing his prime, but Stick expected to pass by any day now to find buzzards circling the field. Patches of white hair and bald spots on Willy Boy's back reminded Stick that he wasn't getting any younger himself. Yet, he still hadn't found his purpose in life.

Having been preoccupied with the past, Stick suddenly found himself bumper to bumper with a fiery red convertible, its driver appearing intently interested in the beautiful ranch land. Long, blond hair reflected the brightness of the sun as the wind tossed it about. The license plate was personalized with the letters *I C U*.

Male or female? Stick wondered.

Unnaturally attractive hair sometimes grew from an awfully ugly ol' boy, so he didn't jump the gun and offer his best smile.

Led by curiosity, he attempted to pass, but the truck's leaking muffler grew increasingly louder upon acceleration.

"Aw shoot!" Stick exclaimed. "I've got to get that thing fixed." It had already cost a traffic ticket over in Johnson County.

Annoyed by the noise, the car's driver cut provocative eyes at Stick, revealing the beautiful face of a young woman. Stick tipped his hat, and her frown changed immediately to a seductive smile.

The years of hard work and "few worries" had treated Stick well. Age only served to enhance his rugged appearance.

Wonder if the rest of her matches the top half. He chuckled. *Reckon her trail is marked by a string of broken hearts. Oh well. Too young for me,* he admitted, although he was especially appreciative of the change in scenery. After all, it was a lonely road. He had driven it many times without passing a single vehicle in either direction.

A little more pressure on the accelerator, and he passed the sports car only to find himself approaching the entrance to the ranch. Stick veered into the drive and slid to a stop, jamming the stubborn shifter into neutral. The emergency brake argued a few times before it stayed put, and the door complained with its usual rusty creak as Stick stepped out to open the gate.

To his surprise, the sports car followed him into the drive and waited just behind his pickup. As Stick walked to the iron gate, the young lady leaned from the convertible and studied the steel beams overhanging the drive. Large white letters dangled beneath, and she read them aloud: "Diamond S Ranch."

Without opening the door, she slid up the back of her seat and sat on top, peering at Stick over the windshield. "It's beautiful. Do you work here?"

"Yes'm. They let me shoe the horses," Stick jested and smiled in a way proven to charm women.

The young lady made a quick appraisal of the artistic rock work that formed the entry and coupled that with the cost to build the pipe fence. She concluded the owners must be rich.

She was a romantic. The fact is, she had been fantasizing about the day when some handsome cowboy would sweep her off her feet. She was like her grandfather, a bit melodramatic, and her parents constantly reminded her of the fact. She felt they purposefully destroyed her dreams with reality and common sense. But she would show them someday. She would meet her cowboy and settle down on a beautiful spread of her own. It was her lifelong dream.

"Someday, I'll have a place like this." The thought resounded aloud.

"Wouldn't doubt that a bit," replied Stick, considering her beauty.

"My name's Shelly, Shelly Tanner. What's yours?" She had never been shy. Instead, she was outgoing and was beginning to perfect the use of her feminine wiles. She knew how to get what she wanted and wasn't opposed to using her God-given assets.

"Stick Slaton," he replied over his shoulder. "Pleasure to meet you."

Stick unlatched the gate. He didn't see much sense in being overly friendly with her, considering the age difference. *Couldn't be over twenty-two years old,* he thought.

"Did you say Stick?" she asked with a raised brow.

"Yes'm. That's my handle." Sometimes he wished TK hadn't given him the name, as if often required explanation.

"That's kind of unusual, isn't it?" she posed.

"Yeah. Reckon so," he agreed. "It's my nickname. I've had it a long time."

A minute was ample time for Shelly to become infatuated with the strong, silent, and very handsome cowboy. She watched his youthful stride as he opened the gate and returned to his truck. She knew, of course, that he was older than her, but she was not one to make a mountain out of a mole hill. Why should she let something like age stand in the way?

His mannerisms excited her—everything from the bandana tied loosely about his neck to the customary way a cowboy working a sale barn stuffs his jeans into the top of his boots. He was definitely the genuine article. It didn't matter that she loved black mustaches, a shade of gray at the temples, or flashing blue eyes; she loved cowboys in general. But the fact that Stick Slaton had all these qualities didn't hinder the attraction. His blue denim shirt fit tightly around muscular shoulders, an attribute comforting to her. After all, a woman wanted to know she could depend on her man's strength.

This cowboy, on the other hand, didn't seem as interested in her. His truck grinded and grumbled, as it shifted into gear and drove through the gate, all while she attempted conversation. He didn't seem rude, just busy. *Or can it be that he isn't interested?* She quickly dismissed the thought, knowing men in general. *Maybe he is married.* She hadn't spotted a ring, though.

Maybe his boss is expecting him, she thought to herself as Stick got out of his truck and walked back to close the gate.

"Well, guess I'll see you around," she said. Then, waving, she slid into the seat backed out of the drive.

Stick smiled again and rubbed the black stubble on his face. "Maybe so," he said to himself as he watched her drive out of sight. He hadn't seen the girl before, but evidently, she wasn't going far.

He returned to his truck and drove toward a big, two-story, white house nestled in a stand of Spanish Oaks on a distant hill. On the way to the ranch house, several men loaded hay onto a flatbed trailer from a nearby field, and Stick waved as he passed, smiling at a few yelled comments concerning last night's brawl.

Across the drive from these men, another ranch hand drove a tractor pulling a hay cutter, avoiding several rusted oil rigs that had long since quit pumping. Stick blew his horn, and the cowboy waved, smiling as the old pickup continued up the grassy hill toward the ranch house.

Stick loved these old cowboys. He understood their restlessness. That's why he didn't mind so much when one disappeared for a few weeks now and then. They were honest and worked hard when they were there, and that's what mattered to Stick.

Anna, on the other hand, never understood it. But then, she had married his brother, and TK and Stick were like night and day. TK was stable, responsible, and always content. He drove to church on Sundays, loved to stay home, worked the ranch during the day, and sat by a crackling fire at night. Anna was perfect for him. But now she expected the same from Stick. It had been over eight years since the accident, but she seldom left the ranch.

Stick thought her to be exceptionally beautiful. She had a dark complexion, as though of Spanish descent, and her long, black hair accented deep-brown eyes. Her skin was soft and unblemished, and she stood taller than most women. Most often sensibly dressed for comfort, the rare occasion like last night's fundraiser revealed her natural curves and slim waist. Although she was the same age as Stick, she looked much younger.

But to Stick, these qualities were not what made her beautiful. She had motherly instincts and always displayed innocence and other feminine qualities that Stick enjoyed in women.

It was beyond his comprehension why she had not accepted invitations from the gentlemen in town. There had been many within the year or two following TK's death; but after a while, they quit asking. If only TK hadn't died, little Bobby would have a Pa, Anna a husband, and Stick a stable brother to help run the ranch.

If. It seemed to Stick that he used this word more than any other in the English language. If this. If that. If things were different. If the oil hadn't played out. If Pa was still here. Why was he always confused about his life? Why did he have so many unanswered questions?

Stick believed he should have everything under control. After all, he was forty-two years old. Why wasn't he happy? Could he be experiencing a midlife crisis?

His life was one big midlife crisis—nothing new, just an age-old problem churning inside like a volcano preparing for the impending eruption. The itch was becoming unbearable.

Suddenly, as Stick rounded a bend in the drive, he met a black Lincoln town car moving toward him. Recognizing it as Dr. Madison's, Stick knew the results of Bobby's tests were in. The doctor eased the car to the side and rolled to a stop. He lowered his window, and Stick pulled alongside.

"Evening, Stick," he greeted in a despondent voice.

"Howdy, Doc. What's the news?"

"I'm afraid it's not good, Stick. His left kidney is infected with a disease called afomeranephritis. He'll have to receive an operation soon. Without it, he won't make it a year. He can live on one kidney, but if the disease spreads, a transplant will be imperative. I've already checked with the children's hospital. They can't help us at this time."

Stick was prepared for the worst, so the news wasn't a total shock.

"But he seems fine, Doc."

"Yes," Dr. Madison agreed, "but right now, the disease is confined to one kidney. His health will slowly decline. First, you'll notice his energy level decreasing and then discoloration of the skin. Afterward, he'll become nauseated and lose his appetite, resulting in substantial weight loss. There might be traces of blood in the urine and some pain in his side."

"How much are we looking at?"

The doctor squinted one eye as if punching a calculator in his mind. "Probably ninety to a hundred thousand," he guessed. "And that's only if a transplant isn't necessary."

Stick shook his head and sighed. "Where are we going to get that kind of money?" Ranching had never offered the luxury of a benefit package and health plan.

"Sorry, Stick. I hate being the bearer of bad news," Dr. Madison said with compassion, "but you'll have to find it somewhere. And the sooner the better. It's his only hope." He began to roll up the window.

"Thanks, Doc. We'll make do," Stick said with encouragement in his voice and then started his truck in motion.

CHAPTER THREE

S tick forced the worry aside, and his thoughts quickly changed to the chores that lay ahead as he approached the stables. He wasn't one to dwell on bad news. He stopped the truck near the large, sliding doors at the west end of the barn and got out, examining the once-bright-but-now-fading red paint of the large, wooden structure. "Hmph." Stick shook his head thoughtfully. "Just like everything else around here. Looks like I'll be putting a coat on you before long," he said and then entered the sliding doors.

A dozen pigeons flew out through the loft door. He liked to watch them, but they made a terrible mess on the hay. They preferred to roost in the rafters, showering the top bales with their droppings. Stick stopped at the feed bin on his right and lifted the lid off of a fifty-gallon drum half full of horse and mule feed. It always smelled sweet, so he inhaled deeply and scooped a coffee can full, replacing the lid.

"Hey, Keepsake!" he yelled. "You in here?"

Stick smiled when he heard a horse whinny from the other end of the barn. "Time for some new shoes, fella."

Stick pulled a halter off the stable gate and walked up to an Appaloosa gelding that waited impatiently, hammering a forehoof against the stall. The horse affectionately nuzzled Stick's chest as he slipped the halter over his head.

"Guess you're about ready to get out of here for a while, huh? Reckon that load of hay can wait."

Again, the horse whinnied, and Stick led him out of the east gate and tied him to the corral. He put the feed in a wooden trough, placed an armload of hay on the ground in front of Keepsake, and began taking off the old shoes.

"Uncle Stick!" The small voice came from inside the barn. "Uncle Stick, where are you?"

"Out here, Bobby!" Stick answered without rising.

Stick dropped Keepsake's left rear leg to the ground and straightened the kinks in his back. He turned to face an eight-year-old boy running toward him from the barn.

"Hey, cowboy." Stick greeted him with a smile.

Bobby jumped into Stick's outstretched arms and hugged him. Stick wrapped his strong arms around Bobby and closed his eyes as to savor the child's embrace. He couldn't help but consider the worst. The boy's condition was very serious, and the horrible truth was that he might not always be around. A lump swelled in Stick's throat at the thought.

He loved this boy as if he were his own. Bobby was Stick's idea of the perfect kid. He was polite, well mannered, and minded his elders. His mother taught him to respect others and work hard. Anna was strict and deserved all the credit for her son's good raising. It just didn't seem right, the cards that were sometimes dealt to the young and innocent.

Bobby favored Anna in looks. He too had a dark complexion with black hair and brown eyes. But on the inside, he was more of a cross between his dad and Stick. He had a restless energy like Stick that didn't go unnoticed by Anna. Although she never complained, Stick knew she frowned on the negative influence he had on the boy.

Bobby's dad had died soon after he was conceived, so Stick was the only father figure he had ever known. As one would expect, he wanted to be just like his Uncle Stick when he grew up, and this scared Anna more than anything.

"Mom's got the table set. She told me to find you," said Bobby.

"Yes, sir. You tell her I'll be in just as soon as I finish up with ol' Keepsake here." Stick knew well that if he wanted to be on Anna's bad side, he had only to be late for dinner.

"Yes, sir," said Bobby as he turned and crawled under the corral fence. Then, jumping to his feet, he ran toward the house.

Stick turned to the horse. "Okay. Let's get finished up here before Anna starts to hollering."

Stick worked quickly and methodically, making every move count. The job was familiar—one he could do in his sleep—but today his sore knuckles made the work tough. However, the horse, also familiar with the work, cooperated perfectly, and in a matter of minutes the last shoe was in place.

Suddenly, Stick's sixth sense told him that he wasn't alone. He rose slowly and rubbed his back. His great grandpa was full-blood Comanche, from whom he guessed he'd inherited his instincts.

"Looking for me?" came a voice from behind him.

Startled, Stick whirled to find an old man smiling at him through very young eyes. He was wearing faded blue jeans and a checkered shirt with blue suspenders. An old straw hat sat on his head, and he chewed a blade of grass.

"Dusty, I swear, if I was totin' iron, you'd be buzzard bait right now. You're sneakier than a church house mouse," complained Stick.

"What're you so jumpy about, son? You been dating somebody's girl? I've been standing here no less than thirty minutes."

Dusty was known for his exaggerations. They were part of him. Besides, they added spice to his storytelling. He was no liar, but many times Stick had sat at his feet as a child and listened to his larger-than-life stories of days gone by, attempting to identify the embellishments.

"Didn't think you were ever going to get that hoss shod," Dusty needled.

Stick rolled his eyes and untied the halter from the corral fence.

"Here," said Dusty as he reached for the halter. "Let me give you a hand. You've been busier than a barefoot boy in an ant bed. Anna won't let us eat till you get to the table, and I'm hungrier than a bitch wolf with ten suckling pups in the dead of winter trying to get up a—."

"A forty-foot snow bank while dragging a number nine trap," Stick interrupted. "I know." And he did know every one of Dusty's quotes by heart.

"That's right!" added Dusty, always having to have the last word.

Dusty took the halter and led Keepsake into the barn while Stick climbed the corral fence. At the top, he sat momentarily and watched the old man enter the barn. He loved the old rascal. He loved the way that white handkerchief always hung from the rear pocket of his worn-out jeans, the way his red long-handles showed through holes at the knees, and the way he always stopped to kick dirt out of the split sole in his right boot.

"Dusty is the only man I know that can chew a pack of tobacco and never spit," Stick's pa used to say. "And he doesn't even take his plug out for dinner."

"Dusty was old when New Orleans was a blueprint," TK once said of the old man. "He was here first, and then God built these Texas hills around him."

Dusty had been with Stick's father, Sterling Slaton, from the beginning. They were "pards." Their paths crossed when they were young bucks, and they'd been together ever since—that is, until Sterling died. The two had weathered many a storm, and Stick inherited his father's fondness for the old man.

Dusty's gray-colored eyes had a way of piercing right through Stick. When he was a boy, Dusty always knew what was going on inside his head, and even now the old man probably knew him better than Stick knew himself.

Dusty had a serious side to him, but Stick had only seen it once. When Sterling died, that permanent smile went away, and even the laugh wrinkles at the corners of his eyes disappeared. Stick wondered if he would ever see them again.

Dusty never cried. At least Stick didn't know about it if he did. Finally, one day, he just snapped out of it. Stick felt it had something to do with little Bobby, but he had never asked. Some things a man just doesn't share with anyone but his Maker.

"Uncle Stick, Mom's getting mad!" yelled a small voice from the house.

Stick jumped off the fence and walked under the stand of Spanish oaks shading the yard. Several hens left the crickets they were chasing and darted out of his way, and He entered the side door of the house where Anna worked in the kitchen. The tantalizing aroma of fried chicken teased his nostrils, causing Stick to suddenly realize just how hungry he was.

"Don't tell me. Let me guess. Fried chicken, mashed potatoes, gravy, black-eyed peas, and homemade bread," Stick said with his eyes closed.

Anna stood near the kitchen sink, stirring a pitcher of tea. She smiled and handed Stick a glass of ice, pouring it full of her famous sweet tea. Anna had a servant's heart, and cooking and tending to others brought her great joy. To her, it was a privilege.

"It's getting cold," she said and walked into the dining room.

Stick trailed behind her, and Dusty came in through the rear entrance, rubbing his palms together. The dining room was as one would expect from observing the outside of the house. An extravagant walnut table sat in the center of the room, and a grand chandelier hung just above it. The walls were walnut paneling trimmed with white pine, crafted in four-foot squares and coated with walnut stain. The flooring was polished hardwood, all a contradiction to the reputation of ranching, but a perfect reflection of the temporary prosperity granted by oil.

"Anna, this here looks good enough to eat," Dusty said while surveying the table. "My belly's been complaining my throat's been cut."

Bobby had already seated himself at the table and had a napkin stuffed down the neck of his shirt. He held a fork in his right hand, aiming it at a drumstick on the platter in the center of the table as if looking down a rifle barrel.

"Bobby, put that fork down," said Anna sternly. "When your Uncle Stick and Dusty get washed and seated, you may start eating." Secretly, she wished that Stick would take more responsibility in disciplining the boy. But she couldn't expect him to. After all, Bobby was only his nephew.

"Yes, ma'am," Bobby returned and set the fork on the table next to his plate. He watched the men wrestle over the faucet at the kitchen sink.

Anna took her seat at the table, and the two men followed suit, using their pants to dry their dripping hands.

"Mom, can we eat now? I'm starving," said Bobby with puppy dog eyes trained on her.

Stick reached over and tousled the boy's hair. Bobby reminded him of his own childhood, and it was Stick's opinion that sometimes Anna was a bit too strict with him. The boy needed a father, someone to pull him away from his mother's apron strings.

"Just as soon as you give thanks," she said.

"Yes ma'am," Bobby said and bowed his head. "Thank you, Lord, for this day. Thank you for the time to play. Thank you for the birds that sing. Thank you, Lord, for everything. Amen."

The grownups echoed their usual amens, and Bobby stabbed the drumstick with his fork. Stick picked up the platter of biscuits, took one, and passed it to Dusty.

"Only one?" asked Anna. She was quick to notice when someone wasn't eating their share, and Stick was always good for three or four biscuits.

"Uh, yes'm. I'm eating kind of light these days," answered Stick with a guilty expression.

"I've noticed. You've lost weight too," she observed with genuine concern.

"Heck fire," exclaimed Dusty. "If he loses any more, he'll have to walk twice to make a shadow. Bet he can run between raindrops as it is."

Stick cut his eyes at Dusty, letting him know that the comments weren't appreciated. Then he turned to Anna like a child caught with his hand in the cookie jar.

"Aw. I was saving this, but I might as well let the cat out," he said, about to offer an explanation.

Stick took a deep breath, knowing what Anna's reaction to his next statement would be. Why did she make him feel like a kid waiting to be punished? Immediately, his thoughts flashed back to a day when his pa sent him to cut a hickory switch. Anticipating the impending calamity grieved him more than the painful stripes. It taught him to face adversity and get it over with so he could breathe easy again.

"I'm riding in the rodeo tomorrow," he blurted.

Dusty stopped eating and dropped his fork as though struck by lightning. He looked at Stick through wide eyes, and his face became a road map of wrinkles. He swallowed his last bite, grinned, and cut his eyes at Anna, waiting for a reaction. She too stopped eating but stared sorrowfully at her plate. Bobby's eyes roved back and forth from Stick to Anna with uncontrolled excitement. This was the greatest news he had ever heard.

"Don't you think you're a little…old for that?" she contended quietly without looking up.

"Old?" Stick protested in jest. "Well…probably so," he replied, subconsciously dropping his right hand to the belt buckle. "Reckon I'll find out anyhow."

Bobby wanted to side with his uncle. He had great respect for his mother but didn't want her to win this one. He had heard some of the old men in town talking about Stick's rodeo days. People still enjoyed their hometown hero's reputation. A great sense of pride came to town the day he won the title. Anxiously, he held his breath to see how Stick would react to his mother's scrutiny.

Stick felt bad about upsetting Anna. He wanted to break and run. He didn't mind responsibility but didn't like having it forced on him. *Well, I've gone this far,* he thought. *Might as well spill the whole sack of beans.*

"If I do good, I might hit the circuit again, maybe even win little Bobby a buckle," he finished with a great sigh of relief.

"Oh boy!" Bobby exclaimed as he jumped out of his chair. "Mom, did you hear that?"

Dusty raised his bushy eyebrows and gritted his false teeth, knowing Anna's feelings about the subject. Then a sheepish grin crossed his face as he too felt the excitement. Quickly, he cut into the conversation in order to sidetrack Anna.

"Heck fire! I remember that time when you and ol' TK kept riding the same—." Dusty cut himself short, realizing that he'd said something he shouldn't.

Stick pushed black-eyed peas around on his plate with his fork, while Anna sat quietly, staring at her food. Dusty was disgusted with himself, and it was evident in his eyes. Bobby continued to chew his food, enjoying the tension. It had been a long time since he had experienced this much excitement.

Why are grownups so hard to figure out? Why do they quit having fun when they get out of high school? They make such a big deal out of everything! Bobby just couldn't understand his mother. She cried a lot, although he would never tell her he knew it. But he didn't have a father, and he didn't cry about it all the time. Why did she?

"I'm getting worse than an old widow woman," Dusty mumbled to himself, "talking when I ought to be listening."

Suddenly, his mouth flew open, and he cut his eyes at Anna again. "Uh, I didn't mean…old widow woman…I…what I mean is…" he stammered and looked across the table for help, only to see Stick fighting laughter.

"Why are you grinning like a baked possum?" he demanded of Stick. Then he glanced softheartedly at Anna and tried again. "I'm sorry. I didn't mean—."

"I know, Dusty," she interrupted. "That's all right."

For another moment, the four of them sat quietly, eating their dinner; then Stick broke the ice.

"Hey! I hear there's a good band playing in town tonight. Anybody want to go?" he asked with a raised brow and searched Anna's face.

Anna looked inquisitively at him and managed a smile. He thought her to be exceptionally beautiful when she smiled, though it seemed that her smiles were few and far between.

"After last night?" she asked.

"Sure. Why not?" replied Stick.

"I really shouldn't," she answered. "I don't feel very comfortable in those kinds of places." The benefit was Anna's only night out in years.

"Anna," pleaded Dusty, "you two go and have a good time. Me and Bobby here will hold down the fort."

"Well," thought Anna out loud, "I guess I would enjoy getting away for a little while. I mean, without being pressured." She knew Stick would go with or without her. He was at home on the dance floor, but she couldn't rest when he was away at night. Perhaps she could keep him out of trouble if she went along.

"Great!" exclaimed Stick. "It's a date then. Pick you up at seven."

The cloud of adversity lifted, and everyone began to enjoy their meal with newfound enthusiasm. Stick discovered that he was looking forward to the evening ahead. This would be something different. He would teach Anna how to have a good time. Hurriedly, he polished off the last of his food and excused himself from the table.

A short while later, Stick was standing in front of his bathroom mirror, having just finished a shower. A towel was wrapped around his waist, revealing a muscular body and hairy chest. He made one final stroke across his chin with a razor and wiped the remaining lather from his face. One quick examination and he concluded that he looked his best.

Steam clouded the air and fogged the mirror as Stick analyzed his obscure reflection, drifting thoughtfully over the eight years that had elapsed since his brother's death. Never before had he done such a thing with Anna. The two of them were so different. Despite her beauty, he really wasn't attracted to her. Or was he? Why did he feel such excitement about going out with her?

Occasionally, he caught her regarding him in a strange manner. It was as if she studied his character in a way he didn't understand, only to be left puzzled by some deep thought.

Stick was accustomed to seeing her in the cotton robe she habitually wore until midmorning. Even after waking, Anna looked good, but she was more a sister to him than anything else. Yeah, she should marry someone like Chester Kosse from town. He would ask her in a New York minute if he thought she would accept.

Stick unwrapped the towel from his waist and threw it at the dirty clothes hamper. The bathroom was like the rest of the house: immaculate. When Sterling Slaton built it, he was well-to-do. His attitude was "easy come, easy go," so while he had money, he spent it. He would worry about the hard times when they came.

A sunken tub was located opposite the lavatory, and deep blue marble tile covered the floor and walls. Like the dining room, a chandelier hung from the ceiling. Stick wiped fog from the mirror and pulled a yellow Western shirt from its hanger behind the door. He slipped it on and climbed into a new pair of jeans. After slipping on his snakeskin boots and tucking in his shirt, Stick twirled his black hat, dropped it in place, and stepped back to examine himself. Satisfied with what he saw, he slapped on aftershave, smiled, and walked out.

Stick descended the stairway leading from his bedroom to a large, Western-style den. A wagon wheel chandelier hung from the center of the room, elk horns rode over the rock fireplace's cedar mantle, and a black bear rug rested on the floor between two easy chairs, one of which held Dusty. The old man puffed on what remained of a cigarette, as was his habit after dinner.

"Well, ol' timer, what do you think?" Stick asked, spreading his arms out to offer a full view.

Dusty broke from a trance and examined Stick. He was in a tranquil mood but allowed his humorous character to surface. "Where you preaching?" he asked. "You'll do, I reckon," he offered more seriously. "Remind me a little bit of myself when I was your age. Course, I didn't have to get all duded up to look good. Some people just have it naturally."

Stick accepted this as a compliment and seated himself on the ottoman across from Dusty. While taking time to light a cigarette, he couldn't help but notice an expression of disgust cross Dusty's face. His slip of the tongue during dinner obviously still troubled him.

"I wouldn't worry about it, Dusty. TK's dead, and she's got to face the fact that he's never going to be around again. We all miss him, but we've got to get on with our lives. We can't go around walking on eggshells all the time. And she can't keep living in the past."

Dusty sat quietly, mulling over Stick's opinion. Finally, he took a long drag on his cigarette, lifted his leathered chin, and blew smoke toward the ceiling.

"Yeah. I reckon you're right, son. But I love that little gal, and I hate to see her hurting like that. It seems that I'm all the time opening my mouth about TK when I know good and well I shouldn't. Heck fire! It seems like just yesterday you and your brother was riding the circuit together."

Dusty smiled, took a final drag on the cigarette, and mashed it into the ash tray in his palm.

"Me and your pa never missed seeing you boys ride," he continued. "Them was the good ol' days, back before the oil played out. When you boys was growing up, there was money enough to hire all the hands we needed. Hmph. We had time for fun back then."

Stick nodded slowly in agreement. The dimly lit chandelier lamp reflected in his eyes as he smiled.

"Think you got a chance at another buckle?" Dusty asked, changing directions.

Stick rarely smoked, but of late, it had become a ritual while sitting with Dusty in the den. He, too, disposed of the cigarette after a final drag. Carefully, he considered the question.

"Well, I'm in just as good of shape now as I was then, I suppose. And I'm a good bit wiser. But I hear the competition is a lot tougher now," answered Stick. "I know it's a long shot, but with a little luck, maybe I'll win some money to help pay for Bobby's operation."

"Maybe so, son. I figured that's why you're doing it. But you're right. It's a long shot at best," agreed Dusty. "It's a hard road with lots of bumps and bruises and broken bones. I'd say that—."

Suddenly, Anna entered the room, interrupting their conversation. She wore an appealing, low cut, and slightly revealing dress, a dress that neither of these men had seen before. She had completely transformed herself. If she was attractive before, she was radiant now. The glow about her face was evidence that she felt beautiful too. Stick and Dusty looked her over and exchanged glances.

Dusty stood up and took off his hat.

Anna spun around to display herself. "Well?" she asked.

Dusty stepped forward with a playful gleam in his eyes and extended his right hand. Expecting a gentleman's kiss, Anna offered him her hand. Instead, Dusty gave it a mild squeeze and granted her a hardy handshake.

"Uh, howdy, ma'am. Uh, I'm Dusty, and this here hombre is Stick. If you're lost or something, we might be able to hep you," he jested.

Anna frowned and turned to Stick for help.

Stick stood quickly, took off his hat, and made a sweeping bow. "Pleased to meet you, ma'am," he greeted, playing along.

"Oh, will you two cut it out? You'd think neither of you had seen a lady in a dress before," said Anna, pretending to be angry. She knew very well that her appearance was quite out of character and that neither of them had seen her like this. Of course, she had worn her Sunday best at the formal last night, but never before had she revealed so much of herself to anyone other than TK. She had taken special care with her makeup and touched just the right amount of perfume about the nape of her neck.

There was something peculiar about this night, as if she had subconsciously anticipated this moment for years. She was surprised to find herself experiencing a school girl's excitement. Why? Was she just glad to get away from the house without the single men from town worrying her? Or was it something else? She did feel beautiful, and the expression on Stick's face was very encouraging.

"Anna," Stick said seriously as he stepped forward, "you're a mighty pretty lady."

"You've told me that before, but do you really think so?" she asked shyly.

"Prettier than a goggle-eyed perch," Dusty added.

The generous fuss that they were making was more than she could take. "Thank you," she said, turning her back to them. "I've decided that maybe it was time I started to enjoy myself a little bit."

The screen door slammed loudly, and Bobby ran into the room.

"Uncle Stick," he yelled with excitement. "I think that ol' brindle cow's going to have her calf to…"—stopping abruptly, he stared at his mother—"…night," he finished.

Bobby's smile faded. He was awestruck. Slowly, he shifted his wide eyes toward Stick and then Dusty before settling once again on his mother.

Instinctively, Anna wrapped a shawl around her shoulders.

"Mom, you look like a movie star!" Bobby exclaimed.

Anna felt a blush come to her cheeks. This was beginning to be too much. If she didn't leave soon, she was afraid she would have to change clothes. "Thank you, Bobby," she replied.

Stick sensed her discomfort, smiled, and offered the crook of his arm. "Shall we go?" he asked.

Anna took a deep breath, nodded her head, and slid her arm inside his.

They walked out of the room, and Stick shouted over his shoulder. "Ya'll don't wait up."

CHAPTER FOUR

Hardy Tillman was a head taller than the average modern-day bull rider. He came from a well-to-do family and was accustomed to getting his way, which was evident even in the way he carried himself. He had an irritating way of looking down his nose at people that offended anyone with an ounce of pride.

He unbuckled his spurs from his boots and stepped into the backseat of his truck. Unlike most cowboys, Hardy used a sharp, six-pointed star spur with long, knifelike blades, which he cruelly employed on each bull he rode. Money couldn't buy happiness, as Hardy well proved, and his deep discontentment drove him to inflict great pain on others, even animals, as a type of revenge for being born.

His parents were rarely at home during his school years. Profits from their east Texas mineral rights came in faster than they could spend them. As a result, he found himself at home, being raised by the live-in housekeeper. It was his opinion that the wranglers who worked the ranch took greater interest in him than his folks did. The employees often came to his high school sporting events, such as football and track, but his folks never watched him play.

At twenty-one years old, Hardy was half the age of Stick Slaton. He had no idea Stick was a world champion bull rider, nor had he even heard of him. Even if he had, he wouldn't care.

Hardy had everything money could buy. What his parents lacked in patrimonial skills they attempted to reconcile with gifts, as this soothed their slightly tarnished consciences. He had all the best equipment, including a personal gymnasium, therefore was in great condition. At an even six feet tall, he weighed one hundred and ninety pounds. His grip was like a vice, his muscled shoulders like tempered steel, attributes which accounted for his numerous first-place buckles.

That he was a great athlete one could not argue. But if you had a mind to debate the issue, he would gladly oblige. Hardy Tillman was his own number-one fan, as only his intelligence superseded his oversized ego. Hardy was very smart, knowing precisely when to jump, when to hang on, and when not to ride at all. As a result, he had sustained great health over his five years of bull riding.

Hardy had recently taken first place at the Jasper County Fair and Rodeo, The ride adding twenty-five hundred dollars to the seventy-five hundred he had already won, making him the earnings leader for the Professional Rodeo Cowboy Association. He was the favorite to win this year's world champion title, and often declared, "the title is as good as mine."

Hardy's good looks attracted cowgirls in every town, and, for this reason, a pack of cronies followed him everywhere, benefiting from the money he spent and squabbling over the girls he rejected. But Hardy enjoyed the crowd, tolerating these leeches as long as he always remained the center of attention. The one sure way to get on his bad side was to attract attention to yourself.

Phil McGrawe and Bull Hawthorne had been traveling with Hardy for three months. They were from his hometown and had attended school together; although now they were fed up with him. A person could only take so much of this egotistical prima donna.

Life on the road could be very boring, and though Hardy thought himself above them, he enjoyed their company. Phil held intelligent conversation when he wasn't drunk, times few and far between, and was easy to boss around. He took orders without question, just as long as Hardy supplied the alcohol.

Bull was an enormous man, and Hardy used this to his advantage. When they entered a town, Hardy made it a point to locate his competition, immediately initiating the mind games. Most often he belittled them or attempted to steal their women, anything to distract them from the upcoming ride. This was Hardy's idea of fun, and he excelled at it.

Afterward came Bull's part: intimidation. Commonly, Hardy's opponent simply backed away from the big man, while other times they exchanged a few fruitless words. Rarely did a competitor possess the nerve to fight Bull. Regardless, this distraction provided the competitive edge Hardy wanted.

Neither Phil nor Bull could be labeled good-looking, posing no real threat where females were concerned. Usually, they lagged behind, accepting handouts and performing tasks Hardy considered himself above.

Phil was behind the wheel of Hardy's brand-new, dual-cab, one-ton pickup. Bull was riding shotgun, and Hardy was stretched out in the backseat. They pulled out of Jasper, Texas, on their way to Cactus Falls.

The metallic black truck stayed polished at all times. The color matched Hardy's hat and his heart. Hardy had no respect for material possessions due to the availability of money. As a result, he always had the very best of everything but was quick to replace anything that was even slightly tarnished.

Hardy folded his hands behind his head, smiled, and closed his eyes. "You ain't hauling this rig through the Indy Five Hundred. I gotta get ready for the next ride, so take it easy."

Phil gripped the steering wheel, started the engine, and glanced at Bull, pretending to ignore Hardy's order. He enjoyed driving the new truck, and it gave him a feeling of significance to chauffeur the next world champion bull rider, but he didn't appreciate being talked down to. Bull, on the other hand, didn't seem to be bothered by Hardy's attitude. In fact, he didn't care about anything other than the money Hardy spent on him.

"How far to the next show?" Hardy asked with his black hat tilted over his eyes.

"About two hundred and fifty miles," returned Phil.

"Wake me up when we get there," ordered Hardy. "I'll be about ready for a steak." He needed the break. The three had gotten very little rest in the last thirty-six hours. Normally, Hardy was in bed before midnight on the night before a ride, but a pair of beautiful green eyes had caused him to make an exception.

His right ankle was somewhat swollen. The crowd-pleasing dismount he was famous for had almost cost him. At the sound of the buzzer, he used the bull's upward thrust to catapult himself into the air and clear of the bull's path. This time, however, he landed wrong and went to his knees. The bull seized the opportunity, and Hardy ran for his life.

He was ready to get off the ankle for a while and catch up on his rest. And he was hungry for a steak.

"You got it," answered Phil as he licked his lips and glanced at Bull.

The two of them smiled at each other. Then Bull slid down into the seat and tilted his hat over his eyes. Phil turned the radio on and settled in for the long drive.

Gradually, the countryside turned from tall pine trees to smaller live oaks and then hills covered with cedar and valleys filled with mesquite. The prickly pear cactus was in bloom, and yellow flowers covered the rocky ledges near the road. An occasional deer stood near the barbed wire fence that bordered the highway as if trying to decide whether or not to cross. Long-eared jackrabbits darted into the cedar breaks. At one point, Phil could see what must have been a hundred miles toward the west. The sun was disappearing beyond the horizon, and the yellowish glow slowly gave way to a purple haze. A flock of turkeys flew across the road just in front of him, no doubt on the way to their roost.

Phil had dreamed of living in this kind of country. The cattle were fat, the country was rugged, and the sunsets were beautiful. Someday, when his ship came in, he would move to this place. Suddenly, an idea popped into his head. If that spoiled brat in the backseat won at the National Finals, maybe he would share some of the prize money. After all, Hardy threw money around like he had a key to Fort Knox.

It was the least he could do. Hardy should pay him back for all the time he spent pretending to be his friend. The truth was, Phil knew Hardy to be a conceited know-it-all who thought himself better than everyone else.

When they were kids, Hardy always ran the show. Everything always had to be his way. Even when they played games, Hardy fabricated the rules as he went along. He had bullied his way through high school and was throwing his weight around still. Even Bull Hawthorne was being manipulated by him, but he was just too dumb to know it.

Phil found himself getting very aggravated with the situation he was in. He wasn't dumb like Bull. He didn't need Hardy or his money. Sure, it might help him get the ranch he wanted, but was it worth it? Phil decided that he had better put a little more thought into the relationship.

He had taken Highway 71 west from Austin and was within an hour of Cactus Falls. Deep in thought, the hours had flown by without realizing it. Two emerald green objects appeared in the darkness ahead, reflecting the truck's headlights. Suddenly, a deer came into focus, and he realized that he had been looking at its eyes. The animal was standing in the middle of the highway. With amazing quickness and agility, he swerved the truck and slammed on the brakes, sliding sideways and narrowly missing the deer.

Phil smiled with great satisfaction at the way he handled the truck as it slid to a halt.

Not a scratch on it, he thought to himself proudly.

"You knothead!" complained Hardy from the floorboard in the back. "You mashed my hat!"

Phil and Bull turned to see Hardy sliding himself back onto the seat and staring solemnly at his flattened hat. They watched as he popped it back into place and brushed off the dust. Then he placed it on his head, turned the dome light on, and leaned forward to examine himself in the rearview mirror.

"How about being a little more careful!" he grumbled to Phil.

The darkness concealed Phil's frown. *One of these days,* he thought to himself.

Now wasn't the time. He would just bite his lip for the moment, but the day would come when Phil wouldn't take any more. So he pressed the accelerator and drew closer to the distant lights of the city.

Bull Hawthorne knew that Hardy Tillman looked down on practically everyone. People thought him to be dumb, and he knew that. But very little went by unnoticed. It was all right with him if people underestimated his abilities. After all, the element of surprise had won many a battle.

Bull heard the way Hardy talked to Phil. It was obvious to him that Hardy had little respect for either of them. Bull knew that Hardy would've spoken to him in the same manner, were he not so big. Maybe Phil wasn't what you would call a close friend, but he was good company, and he didn't seem to mind the driving. It irritated Bull for Hardy to be so abusive.

Bull remembered when they were in high school. He played guard on the strong side for the football team. Hardy, who was a quarterback, received all the glory for their district championship. He was in the limelight before and after every game. Not once did Bull hear him credit the fearless front line for the magnificent advances he made. Nor did Bull hear him say he had all the time in the world to pass the ball because of the way the line held off the defenders.

Many times, Bull had seriously considered letting the defense through so they could pound Hardy into the turf. But his loyalty to the team wouldn't allow it. So, Hardy ran through the openings that Bull provided, never failing to plant his shoulder or elbow in the small of Bull's back as he passed.

Bull didn't hate Hardy. Matter of fact, they had some pretty good times together. But the truth was, they were little more than associates—not friends. He doubted Hardy would ever have a close friend. So, for now, he would take advantage of the money Hardy threw around and the female company he attracted.

Bull didn't own a watch. He was cursed with an infirmity that stopped those he wore for any length of time. But the bank sign read eight o'clock when they rolled into Cactus Falls. He was definitely ready for the steak Hardy had mentioned earlier.

Hardy felt the pickup slowing as it approached a bridge towering over the Colorado River on the outskirts of town. He awoke and sat up in the seat.

"You're a real good driver, Phil," Hardy commented.

"Thanks," replied Phil, surprised by the compliment.

"Yeah. You managed to hit every bump in the road," Hardy added sarcastically. "Good job!" Bull couldn't resist chuckling to himself. Sometimes, Hardy was comical with his insults. Phil, of course, didn't think so.

"Well, we're here," said Phil, sneering.

The town was situated in a great valley. Hills covered with cedar, live oaks, and mesquite surrounded it. A dam on the Colorado provided the town with a beautiful lake that backed up past the city limits. The highway entered the city at a higher elevation, and the bridge rose some one hundred feet above the water.

It appeared to be a ranch community. Feed mills, saddle and tack stores, building supplies, and other rural-type markets lined the highway. A steakhouse called the Feed Lot sat on the right-hand side of the road, near the traffic light.

"Pull 'er in right here," ordered Hardy.

Phil carefully eased the pickup into a parking space, and the three men stepped out. After stretching their limbs to restore circulation, they made their way through the front door.

Bull and Phil immediately eyed the menu hanging on the wall while Hardy went right to work on the waitress. He flashed her his best smile while the other two found a seat at a table nearby.

The waitress was redheaded, young, and very attractive. She wasted no time filling three glasses of water and getting it to their table.

"In town for the rodeo?" she asked.

The question was intended for all three, but she was watching Hardy. Phil glanced at Bull and rolled his eyes.

"Yes'm," returned Hardy while blatantly looking her over.

"Let me guess," she continued. "Bronc rider, right?"

"Wrong," Hardy said, smiling.

"Steer dogging?" she asked.

"Nope," Hardy answered.

"Okay. I've got it," she exclaimed. "Team roping?"

"Strike three, you're out," Hardy said playfully. "I ride bulls." He was getting bored with the girl but knew her type. She was aggressive and pretty but certainly not innocent. He would take care not to insult her.

The girl's eyebrows rose. "You're kind of big to be a bull rider, aren't you?"

"Maybe. Maybe not," said Hardy, "But I tell you what. Why don't you come to the show tomorrow night and see for yourself? By the way, what's your name?" he asked.

"Helen Rollins," she answered, "but my friends call me Red."

The girl was definitely attracted to Hardy. Phil could see the wheels turning in his head. It was almost like clockwork the way Hardy used every situation for his own benefit. Phil knew exactly what Hardy would do next. It wasn't that he could read his mind; rather, he knew Hardy's motives and, therefore, knew his intentions.

Sure enough, Hardy's next question proved Phil's speculation accurate.

"Are there any good bull riders in this town?" asked Hardy.

"You bet there are," bragged the girl. "We've got Allen Palmer, Trent Summers, Pudge Foley, and Stick Slaton."

"Yeah. I've heard of Palmer and Summers," agreed Hardy. "They're good all right, but what about the other two?"

"Pudge is just getting started," said the girl. "My dad said he's got the right stuff, so I guess he's pretty good. Stick Slaton used to be real good. He was a world champion twenty years ago. I overheard two guys this morning saying he's riding this year."

"Twenty years ago!" exclaimed Hardy.

He turned to his partners and laughed. Hardy held no respect for age, experience, or wisdom. His feelings were that nothing could beat youth and nerves of steel.

"Did you hear that, boys? This guy was world champion twenty years ago. And he's riding in this rodeo. Sounds to me like my competition is going to be Palmer and Summers," Hardy added and winked at the girl. "Where do you think I might find these boys tonight?"

"Well," she said thoughtfully, "there's a live band playing tonight at the Corral. They'll probably be there."

"How about you?" Hardy asked. "Will you be there?"

Red Rollins was a girl who was easily infatuated with a handsome face—especially on a cowboy. This cowboy had an air about him. He was self-confident and sure, almost arrogant, but she liked a take-charge kind of guy.

"I get off in an hour," she said.

Hardy looked deep into her eyes. "That's when the fun starts," he returned. This was a game to him, a game he had mastered before graduating high school. He knew that she was hooked and all he had to do was reel her in.

"Okay," she answered. "I'll be there."

"Good," Hardy said coolly. "Now how about sending us three sixteen ounce T-bone steaks, French fries, hot bread, and iced tea."

"You got it!" she said excitedly.

The girl wrote the order down on her pad and went into the kitchen. Hardy looked at his two companions and proudly raised one eyebrow.

"Well, boys, looks like we're going to the Corral Club tonight. Maybe we'll meet the competition."

Both men knew this meant trouble. Phil would much rather avoid it, but the better Hardy's chances for winning, the better his chance to get the money he wanted.

Bull was ready for some trouble. He had been quiet for long enough. He didn't especially like Hardy's tactics, but at least the night life wasn't boring when he was with him. He didn't know anyone in this town, and nobody knew him. It was time to let his hair down.

"After we eat, we'll get a room," stated Hardy. "I want to clean up a bit before we go. Besides, we might not be in any shape to find one afterward."

The three of them laughed. Phil knew that that meant Hardy was paying for the booze, and booze was his weakness. He was young and strong. If he had a problem with it, well, he had plenty of time to deal with that later. Bull was the one he was worried about. The man had a mean streak in him that alcohol brought straight to the top. Phil didn't like being around him when he was drunk. Someday, he was going to hurt someone.

Red brought the steaks, and they attacked them like starving hyenas. Even Hardy seemed to forget his sophistication when it came to his stomach. No one said a word until the meal was finished. They didn't even bother to tell Red thank you as she refilled their tea glasses.

Bull could easily have eaten another but was careful not to mention it. If Hardy wished to be generous, it would be his idea, not because someone asked for it; Bull wouldn't push his luck.

Red brought the ticket, and the three pushed away from the table. Hardy pulled his wallet out and filtered through his bills. He handed her fifty dollars and smiled.

"This is for the steaks," he said.

Then he pulled out a ten-dollar bill and gave it to her. "And this is for the prettiest waitress I've ever seen," he added.

The girl blushed, and Bull and Phil looked at each other, shaking their heads. Hardy thought he could buy anything, and it was likely that he could. One day, however, he would find the happiness he bought was counterfeit—although one thing was for sure: he'd certainly left an impression on Red Rollins.

"See you tonight at eleven," he said matter-of-factly.

"Okay," said the girl eagerly while staring at the ten-dollar tip. It wasn't the largest she ever had, but it was impressive. Her mind was racing. If she played her cards right, this cowboy might be her ticket out of this place. He was tall, good-looking, confident, and apparently had money.

"By the way," asked Hardy, "where's a good hotel in this town?"

"Go through town, past the last traffic light, and you'll see it on the right. Can't miss it. If you turn left at the light and go about five miles, you'll see the Corral Club on the left," she added.

Hardy nodded. "See you there."

The three left the cafe and piled into the truck. Phil stared out the window into the night sky. There was a strange sort of electricity in the air—nothing visible, just a feeling. Something in the July air warned Phil of an impending plight with destiny. He couldn't put his finger on it, but something was up.

A chill suddenly went up his back, and he shivered. His grandma would have said that someone stepped on her grave. Since he was a kid, he had sort of a sixth sense about things. He had learned to trust that feeling, but what did it mean? Maybe it was just the fact that they were in a strange town.

As he drove the pickup toward the motel, he couldn't help but wonder if maybe they shouldn't just stay home this night. If nothing else, he would try to be careful.

"Hey," queried Bull, "what's up? You look like you seen a ghost."

"Aw, nothing," Phil answered. "Something I ate."

"Boys," Hardy said, ignoring the two, "we're going to have fun tonight."

All Hardy had to do was release his natural charisma, and they would follow him straight into battle. Manipulation was an art, and Hardy took pride in his ability to figure out his subjects. A smile of satisfaction appeared on his face. They were putty in his hands.

I hope, thought Phil.

CHAPTER FIVE

The Corral Club was lit up like a south Texas prison. Tall pole lights distributed a yellowish glow, and the highway sign flashed neon lights around its borders, reading, "Welcome to the Corral." Magnetic letters advertising the name of the band read, "Hoss Taylor and the Western Gents." The word *Corral* was written across the front of the building in bright red, neon letters. A smoky haze encircled the club.

Stick Slaton was seated behind the wheel of his late brother's Eldorado Cadillac, staring at the sign's neon lettering while Anna sat nervously in the passenger seat. They watched as people exited their vehicles and entered the club.

"Stick, are you serious about going on the road again if you do well tomorrow night?" asked Anna.

They had been there several minutes, but both seemed hesitant about going through with the date. Something just didn't feel right. Stick thought about his brother. He had such great love and respect for him. Maybe that was it. Maybe he was worried about what others might think. He glanced at Anna and couldn't help noticing how her eyes shined. Her opal earrings shone beautifully against her olive skin. She was beautiful. His brother was lucky, but then, he deserved someone like Anna. At that moment, he knew the answer to her question.

"Yeah. I miss the road, Anna. You know me. I never could sit still for very long. Guess I inherited that from Pa. Anyway, if I do, it'll only be for a year."

He wanted to share his thoughts about what could be done with the prize money, but he knew Anna all too well. Her good sense and conservative mindset would say he was chasing rainbows and counting chickens before they hatched. Besides, he knew from experience that the majority of cash won would be eaten up in expenses. Rodeo wasn't cheap.

"Oh, Stick!" she exclaimed. "I wish you wouldn't."

Stick detected a tremble in her voice. He looked deep into her eyes and saw wholesome innocence and pure honesty. They were not just intangible character traits but so real they could be touched. Never before had he known any woman like her. She was not deceptive, manipulative, or anything false. She was simply beautiful and refreshing, and she never tried to control him. Sure, she was emotional, but she attempted to control her emotions so as not to use them to get her way. Stick saw fear somewhere in the glistening stars that danced in her eyes—not obvious fear, but a trace, like the way one sees the wind. It was just there.

"Are you afraid of running the ranch by yourself?" he asked. It was something he hadn't considered.

"Stick, I'm afraid for you," she said sincerely. "Anything could happen to you. And I don't need an invalid for a partner. And what about Bobby? He loves you. He watches your every move. Surely you can't just leave him."

"I love him too, Anna, as if he were my own son," Stick replied. "School won't start for a while, and he'll be able to make some of the shows with me."

"No," she said firmly. "I'm sorry, Stick, but I don't want him getting used to that kind of life."

"Yeah. I guess you're right," he agreed. One Stick Slaton was bad enough. It wouldn't be right to corrupt his nephew too. Besides, Stick didn't want to get into another argument with Anna. For one thing, she was usually right, and he didn't enjoy losing. For another, even when a woman was wrong, it was best left unmentioned. It was time to change the subject so their fun didn't end before it started.

"Anna, let's try to have a good time tonight. Relax, forget about everything else, and concentrate on enjoying yourself. Okay?"

"It's been a long time. I don't know if I can," she replied. "Last night was something I did out of duty. Tonight, well, it's different. This all seems so strange to me."

"Look," Stick nodded in the direction of the parking lot. "There's Chester Kosse's truck. He likes you, Anna. Why don't you give him a chance?"

Stick winked at her, but she didn't respond. The suggestion hurt her feelings, although he didn't understand exactly why. He just didn't understand women in general and figured he never would.

Chester was the local certified public accountant. Stick wasn't one to stereotype, but Chester fit the occupation. He was a real nice guy, but he was boring. All he ever wanted to talk about was tax returns and whatever new laws the IRS came up with.

He was Stick's age, and they had attended high school together. Chester was voted most likely to succeed, and he received class salutatorian honors. In those days, Chester was witty and fun to be around. Somehow, the years made him lose focus on the spice of life. He had no idea how boring he was.

He too had been married. Ironically, Chester's wife left him because of his boring lifestyle while Stick's had left him because of his impulsiveness. Stick shook his head and smiled. He considered his brother again. Theirs had been the perfect marriage, and look what happened. Here was a beautiful woman destined to spend the rest of her life alone, because no one could fill TK's shoes. She wouldn't even consider another man.

Stick was angry at life and the curves it threw other people. Why couldn't, just once, things work out right? Was there some hidden force sent from some unknown place specifically to plague honest people? Was there a wicked little demon hovering around him and others alike, determined not to allow them fulfillment in life?

"Who knows?" pondered Stick out loud.

"What?" asked Anna. She too had been deep in thought.

"Uh, let's go," replied Stick, and he opened the car door.

The two of them made their way through the parking lot and entered the front door of the club. Smoke belched out as the front door swung open. Stick offered ten dollars to the attendant, and both of them received a stamp on their wrists.

"Enjoy yourselves," allowed the doorman. Stick didn't recognize him and assumed he was with the out-of-town band.

Stick nodded and held Anna's hand as he wormed his way through a large group of people. The roar of the crowd was almost deafening. The band members were tuning their instruments on stage and, as of yet, hadn't begun playing. The floor was slick from spilled beer and mixed drinks, and the smell of whiskey brought a frown to Anna's face.

The place was full of people Stick didn't recognize. Obviously, the rodeo had brought them in. Suddenly, he passed a table where two familiar faces glared directly at him.

One of the men had a long, hook nose that was freshly broken. A bandage stretched across it and caused his eyes to cross. His oversized Adam's apple jumped upward and plunged down again as he swallowed. His eyebrows were raised high on his forehead when he nodded at Stick.

The second man had one barely visible pig eye. The other was swollen shut. His face sported many bruises, and his bottom lip was busted.

Stick stopped for a moment and studied the two. He couldn't resist twisting the dagger just once in passing.

"Howdy, boys," he greeted. "Hope there won't be any trouble here tonight."

"No, sir, Mr. Slaton," answered Joel while Deke shook his head. "Matter of fact, we ain't even drinking. We blew a week's pay last night."

Stick smiled and started to offer them a few bucks but decided to leave well enough alone. He already knew what they were like when they were two sheets to the wind. His sore knuckles reminded him of that.

Anna watched, surprised by a strange sense of sympathy for the two. They were afraid of Stick, and he was so calm, so sure of himself. She knew what it was like to be afraid.

The dance floor was located in the center of the club with the stage against the back wall. Tables were situated on the other three sides, and the bar was located opposite the stage. Several waitresses carried trays high above their heads, miraculously weaving their way through the crowd without spilling a drop.

Stick found a long table with Chester Kosse, two business men, and their wives seated at one end.

"You folks mind if we join you?" Stick yelled above the noise of the crowd. This would be an excellent opportunity to get Chester and Anna together.

Chester immediately jumped to his feet with obvious surprise. He pulled a chair for Anna and stared as though she was a turkey on a platter and he was on a peanut butter and jelly diet. She smiled politely and accepted the chair. Chester seated himself but struggled with an attempt to regain his composure. He had not seen her like this before, a fact that left Anna feeling more uncomfortable than ever.

"Welcome to the Corral Club," said the lead singer in the band. "How about some Silver Wings?"

The crowd applauded, and the band cranked up. Stick caught Chester's eye and nodded toward Anna.

The accountant glanced at her and quickly downed his drink. "Okay," he mouthed indiscriminately.

"I'm going to the bar," yelled Stick. "I'll be right back. Can I get you anything, Anna?"

Anna shook her head, and Stick made his way through the crowd. She watched as he disappeared, suddenly feeling abandoned. He was a source of strength for her. She was never afraid for her safety when he was around, although sometimes she feared for him.

Stick enjoyed visiting with the locals as much as he did the dancing. This night, however, it was a little crowded for him. He normally found a place at the bar and told stories or "swapped lies," as the cowboys called it.

As he approached the bar, Stick recognized two young men he was especially fond of. They were in their early twenties and were true cowboys, working hard for a living and accepting charity from no one. Their fathers had raised them that way, and the boys had been best friends since early childhood. Wherever one was seen, the other was certainly nearby.

Allen Palmer was slightly older than his friend, Trent Summers. Allen was of average height and had clean-cut, sandy hair; blue eyes; a muscular build; and wore a white, straw cowboy hat.

Trent Summers was slightly taller than Allen but somewhat slimmer. He too had sandy blond hair and wore a white, straw cowboy hat. His eyes were green, and the two could have passed for brothers. Both had friendly faces that made one warm up to them immediately.

Smoke lingered heavy above the bar, as well as the people around it. Stick approached his two friends, and broad grins greeted him.

"Hey, ol'-timer," called Allen. "I hear you're riding tomorrow."

"My goodness, word sure travels fast. Yep," answered Stick. "Think I'll show you young fellers how it's done."

Stick shook hands with the two and motioned to the bartender for his usual.

"Heard you had to straighten a couple of them carnival boys out last night over at the ballroom," stated Trent.

"Aw. They're all right," Stick replied. "They just had a little too much to drink. That's all. I don't think they'll be a problem tonight."

"There's someone else who needs straightening out tonight," added Allen. His irritation was obvious.

"Hey, I'm not in the straightening-out business," Stick answered.

"Yeah, but this guy is enough to get you started," Trent entered. "He came over here, bragging, a while ago about how he was gonna be the next world champion bull rider. I swear I thought he'd break his arm patting himself on the back that way."

"Sure aggravated me," added Allen. "Reckon I might've straightened him out myself if that big galoot hadn't been with him. That guy was standing behind him just grinning at us."

"He said we didn't stand a chance," Trent added. "Said he was the new breed of bull rider and he was way ahead of us part-timers. Said he had it down to a science. Said he had all the newest equipment to build the right muscles. Who ever heard of that?"

"I'd like to jack his jaws," added Allen.

"He stood right here in front of us, looking down his nose," continued Trent, "like he was God's gift to bull riding. Said he'd bet a thousand dollars a piece that he could outride us."

"I'd like to soften his noggin," added Allen.

"I ain't got that kind of money or I might've taken him up on it," continued Trent.

Stick smiled and patted the two young men on their shoulders. This wasn't his first rodeo, and he knew what was taking place.

"Boys," he said, "this feller is getting your feathers ruffled so you'll forget about the ride and start thinking about him. Your heads have got to be screwed on right if you're gonna stay on top for eight seconds. If he can distract you, he's won before you ever get started. What's his name anyway?"

"Hardy Tillman," answered Trent.

"I'd like to slap him silly," added Allen.

"Hardy Tillman," pondered Stick as he rubbed his chin. "Yeah. I've heard of him. Jack Chambers said he was favored to win."

"That's him over there," said Allen, pointing toward the dance floor. "Look at him. I'd like to take him down a notch or two."

Stick could see Hardy sitting at a table with a red-headed girl, who he recognized from the café in town. She was talking to him, and although she was very pretty, he didn't seem to be interested in what she had to say.

He was wearing blue jeans; a blue Western shirt with a white collar and cuffs; elephant skin boots; and a black, felt cowboy hat. His eyes roamed continuously about the dance floor as the girl maintained the conversation.

"Heard he's leading in prize money won," mentioned Stick.

"Yeah. He just won first over in Jasper. I think he's netted around ten thousand altogether," commented Trent.

"Well," said Stick, "one ride in the right rodeo will win that much." He didn't want to discourage his friends.

"He looks too big to me," Trent said. "I bet he's at least six feet tall and probably two hundred pounds."

"I'd like to take some starch out of his britches," added Allen.

Suddenly, Allen and Trent saw Stick's expression change. With a frown on his face, he stepped quickly around them and rushed through the crowd, staring straight ahead as he went. He passed Deke and Joel, and they watched as he hurried by.

Stick was no stranger to trouble. He knew better than to go charging in, head on, without first taking a good look at the situation. It wasn't that he was afraid, but his pa did not raise a fool. Sterling Slaton had taught him long ago to be careful.

"If you have a run in with some jug head," he'd say, "don't follow him out the door. Go out the back way. You never know what notion he might have in his head. Could be waiting for you outside with something water won't wash off."

Stick had learned to listen to his pa. The man had taught him a lot. He was a good judge of character, and many was the time he told his sons not to trust a particular person. Maybe it was the way they acted or maybe it was the way they looked, but sure enough, they would confirm his suspicions with some act of dishonesty.

Now was no time for Stick to be forgetting anything he had learned. A giant of a man had Anna by the arm, trying to drag her to the dance floor. Although Stick was half his size, he had to fight the urge to run in swinging. Instead, he stopped a few feet away from the table and surveyed the situation.

Chester Kosse noticed Stick's arrival. He shrugged his shoulders, and Stick glared at him. Chester didn't feel as though he had a snowball's chance in hell in defending Anna, but he knew that Stick wouldn't accept that excuse. He had rationalized in his mind that this was none of his affair. After all, Anna had not come to the dance with him. No. It was Stick Slaton's place to defend her.

One glance told Stick the big man had friends. There were a set of interested eyes observing from the sidelines. Stick didn't recognize the man, but was sure he shared a relationship with the gorilla antagonizing Anna. He made a mental note as he appraised the situation.

"Come on, darling. Let's dance," insisted Bull in a drunken slur as he tugged on her arm.

"No, thank you, I said," returned Anna. "I don't know you."

"Well, I can fix that, honey!" shouted Bull. "My name's Bull

Hawthorne, and this here's my partner, Phil McGrawe. Now, let's dance." Bull was used to being turned down, but tonight he wasn't going to take it. He had decided that the women had come here to dance and that was just what they were going to do.

"No. I'm sorry, but I don't feel like dancing," she refused. "Please let go. You're hurting me."

"Phil, ain't this the purtiest Mex you ever seen in your life?" he asked, ignoring her request.

Phil was slightly drunker than Bull, but he could never take advantage of a woman. Still, if Bull wanted to do it, well, that was his business. The alcohol had him feeling out of sorts—not mean like Bull, but reckless.

"Yep," he said. "I ain't never seen a purtier Mex in my whole life." The caution he had felt after dinner was all but forgotten.

Anna suddenly jerked her arm free and pushed away from the table. She stood and tried to walk away, but Bull was persistent.

"I said I want to dance!" he demanded.

As he reached for her arm again, Stick stepped in between them. He pushed Bull's hand away and smiled.

"Not tonight, cowboy. She's with me, and we're heading to the house," said Stick. Then he took Anna's hand and pulled her toward him. "Let's go, Anna," he said. He knew once trouble started, it wouldn't just stop—especially where alcohol was involved. The only way out of this was to fight or leave. Considering that Anna was with him, the only thing to do was leave.

For a big man, Bull was light on his feet. With catlike reflexes, he moved quickly toward Stick, and with the skill of a boxer, he slung an accurate backhand to Stick's head.

"Back off, cowboy!" he yelled furiously. "The night just got started." The attention they were getting from a growing crowd served only to fuel the fire. Bull had been humiliated.

Stick whirled and stared cold and steady into Bull's eyes. With his left hand he wiped blood from his brow.

"Go to the car, Anna," he ordered without taking his eyes off Bull. The only alternative was to fight, and Stick had seen bigger men fall.

"You come too," Anna pleaded. There was a critical fear in her voice that grabbed Stick's attention.

Stick had great respect for Anna. His father had taught him well. Women were the weaker vessel, and it was man's responsibility to look out for them. For that reason, Stick turned to Anna and nodded his head.

Bull took this opportunity to swing a left cross to Stick's nose, knocking him to the floor. "I said the night just got started, cowboy!"

Anna covered her mouth with both hands to muffle a scream. She rushed to Stick's side, and a dangerous grin appeared on his face. One look, and Bull knew he was a man to be reckoned with. Bull's size didn't intimidate Stick.

"Leave him alone!" Anna screamed. Tears formed in her eyes as she frantically took Stick by the arm to pull him from the floor. He was strong, but she thought it physically impossible for Stick to defeat this man.

Bull smiled and held his fists in a boxing stance. He would have some fun with this. Maybe, just maybe, he had found a worthy opponent.

"Come on, ol'-timer. Let's see what you've got," he dared.

Stick looked again at Anna, and got to his feet. He took her hand and walked toward the door while Bull and Phil laughed loudly behind them. As Stick exited the club, his eyes burned with vengeance. A large crowd of onlookers who had gathered to watch the fight began to disperse, showing their disappointment.

Joel and Deke stared wide-eyed at one another. Deke thoughtfully rubbed the whiskers on his chin, and Joel shrugged his shoulders. The two men stepped to the exit and watched as Stick opened the car door for Anna. "Every dog has a master," Deke whispered and smiled.

"Reckon he ain't as tough as he thought he was," Joel added. Satisfaction changed their moods. "I got enough for one round. Let's have a drink."

Stick drove the car out of the parking lot and onto the highway. Anna had never before seen the scowl on his face. She felt like thanking him for what he'd done but decided against it. So, for the moment, they sat quietly.

Anna had the urge to put her arm around Stick, to comfort him as though he were a child. She thought of him as a youth in some ways. He had a restless energy. He wasn't totally irresponsible, but she didn't trust him completely. He was like a wild animal that had a mind of its own. She wasn't afraid of him; she simply had to consider his unpredictable nature. *Respect* was the word she wanted to use. She had to respect him as one would respect a stallion—not from fear of being intentionally hurt but using precaution to avoid accidents.

He was a man with a restless spirit, a man that wouldn't be tied down. He was a man with a child's curiosity about life and a child's energy to enjoy it. He was so different from his brother. Stick was everything she was not. So why did she care so much about him? Was it a motherly instinct?

What did Stick think about her? Did he really think she was pretty? Was she the reason he wanted to go away? She wished she knew what he was thinking.

She looked at him for a moment and watched as blood trickled from the cut above his eye and met another stream flowing from his nose. Suddenly, she couldn't take it any longer. Tears began trickling down her face, and she cried softly. Taking a tissue from her purse, she gently wiped the blood from Stick's face.

He glanced at her, and his hard expression quickly softened as he noticed the tears.

"I'm sorry, Anna," he apologized. "I never should've left you alone."

"It wasn't your fault," she returned. "I shouldn't have gone there in the first place. I knew better."

Perhaps she was right. But Stick thought she needed to get out more and meet new people. She needed a man to take care of her and little Bobby. He wanted only what was best for her, and he said as much.

"You've been using the ranch for a shell to hide under ever since TK died," he added. "I just want you to be happy."

Stick turned the Cadillac into the driveway of the ranch and stared at the gate for a moment. He read the sign above the entrance and thought about his pa. Sterling did everything big. He didn't know the word *small,* and he'd never settle for halfway.

He wasn't a perfectionist. He just thought big. And what was wrong with that? Sure, it might have led him to an early grave, but he enjoyed life. Still, Stick missed him and wished that he was there with them. He remembered the glow of his pa's cigarette as he sat in the dark, next to Stick's bed, sipping on a Scotch and telling Stick things he recalled about the past, the times when he and Dusty were young.

Anna shifted her gaze from the Diamond S sign above the gate to the floorboard as her eyes again filled with tears. She knew that Stick was right, but it was hard for her to focus without TK. A woman wasn't meant to be alone.

"Stick, I know you're right," she said. "I do need to get out more often, but those kinds of places aren't where I belong. I need someone stable in my life, someone I can lean on, someone I can trust. I guess I'm not very strong. I'll try to change and be more outgoing, but—."

Emotion wouldn't allow her to continue.

Stick looked at her and gently brushed away the tears with the back of his hand. He wanted to hold her, to comfort her, to make her troubles disappear. He found himself wishing he was more reliable. But if there was one thing the years had taught him about himself, it was that he was anything but reliable. No. She deserved more, much more. At least now she knew she needed a man in her life.

"That's my girl," he encouraged. "All you can do is try. Someday, the right man will come along." He was sure of it.

Stick leaned over and kissed her forehead, then got out of the car and opened the gate. Anna watched the long shadow made as Stick strode in front of the car's headlights. He swung the gate open and returned to the car.

He drove through the gate without stopping to close it. This didn't go unnoticed by Anna. She studied his face in hope of learning his intentions.

The lights on the distant hill told Stick and Anna that Dusty was waiting up for them. Stick knew that he would. He was worse than an old mother hen.

Dust clouded the air behind the car as they continued toward the ranch house. Then it settled slowly, coating the cactus and the mesquite trees that grew along the drive. Instead of pulling the car into the garage, Stick drove in front of the house. Dusty was sitting on the porch swing, smoking a cigarette and staring at the stars. He took one final drag and thumbed the cigarette into a flowerbed lining the porch and then walked over to the car and opened the door for Anna.

Stick didn't make an effort to get out, and Dusty noticed the blood under his nose.

"What's up?" queried Dusty. He already had guessed, but he hoped for the story.

"I'll be back later, Dust," Stick returned. "I've got some unfinished business back in town."

"Uh huh." Dusty nodded. He had seen that look before—once or twice on Stick, but many times on Sterling. To him, that look meant trouble was around the corner. He felt sorry for whoever was responsible for putting it there.

Dusty watched as Stick drove away in a cloud of dust. He had just about decided that he would follow Stick into town when he looked at Anna. Tears flowed down her face as she watched Stick's taillights disappear. Dusty thought it better to stay and console her.

"He's going back, isn't he?" asked Anna.

"Yes'm. I reckon so. I don't know what happened, but I'd say there's gonna be hell to pay," he answered. He knew Stick well, and it was his guess that the town would have plenty to talk about tomorrow.

"Dusty, I'm afraid for him," she cried. "There were three men. The big one hit Stick, but it was the tall one who instigated the whole thing. I'm sure Stick didn't see him. He watched from across the dance floor. The third man stood at our table and talked to the big man just before he tried to make me dance with him. I think they planned the whole thing."

"What makes you think that?" Dusty asked. He was becoming worried.

"Well, the tall one came to my table and asked me if I came with Stick. He said he thought Stick was an old friend of his. When I told him I did, he asked if Stick was a bull rider. I told him he was riding in the rodeo tomorrow night. Then he just smiled, turned around, and walked off. There was something about him I didn't like, and I think he sensed it. He was very conceited. I think he expected me to fall for him."

Dusty stared into the night sky and rubbed his chin. There were a million stars dotting the heavens. The air was dry. There was a slight breeze. Suddenly, a falling star crossed from east to west, disappearing a million miles away.

"What did this fella look like?" he asked.

"Well," she said, "he was tall, like I said. He was very good-looking. And he wore a black, felt hat. He was very smooth, kind of cool, like a crook."

"Yep," said Dusty. "Sounds like they're setting him up all right." But why? He had no idea.

"Oh, Dusty," cried Anna. "That big man will hurt him. What are we going to do?"

"Nothing, I reckon," he answered. "If he needs some backup, he's got friends. But I doubt he'll need it." Although the odds seemed to be against him, Dusty knew Stick would be cautious.

On the outside, for Anna's sake, Dusty appeared confident in Stick's ability to handle the situation; but inside, he wondered. Did Stick know he was playing against a stacked deck? He only hoped so.

"Stick ain't no greenhorn, Anna. He'll be all right. Let's go on in the house and get some shuteye." Dusty knew though that he'd be getting no sleep this night—at least not until Stick returned.

Anna turned and walked through the front door. Dusty followed her but stopped at the entry and took one last fearful glance in the direction Stick had gone, watching a distant set of taillights dimmed by a thick cloud of dust.

Stick pulled into the parking lot and got out of his car, thinking about the man inside. Had he not insulted Anna by his insolence, Stick would have been less determined to seek justice. The bruises he had received would heal, but the man's rudeness demanded accountability. Stick could not walk away from such arrogant behavior. His conscience would not let him. Stick's father had been a military man and had taught him much about wartime strategy. One thing he remembered was he should always know his enemy. If you didn't have time to learn about them, then you must be prepared for anything.

Stick would have to settle for being prepared for anything, for he certainly didn't know him. He did know his type, though. *But who was with the big man? Does he have any hidden weapons? What are his strong points? What are his weaknesses?* A dozen questions crossed his mind.

The answer to the first question was probably, "Two others." Stick figured that the big man named Bull was the same fellow that was with Hardy Tillman when he harassed Allen Palmer. He also figured that the one named Phil was with him by the way Bull had addressed him.

He doubted that Bull carried any hidden weapons. He was the type that took pride in his physical strength and his ability to overpower his opponent. No. He was confident that the man would use nothing but his fists.

His strong point would be his strength, and Stick knew he would have to keep his distance. One grasp by his massive arms could crush Stick's backbone like a twig.

His weak points would probably be his drunkenness and his slow reflexes. Most big men were slow, but there were exceptions to every rule. Bull wasn't naturally slow. Stick had seen that when he received the cut over his brow. Hopefully, by now, the alcohol would have had time to take effect.

Stick pulled his hat down on his head and re-entered the club. Allen Palmer saw him step through the door, and a great smile appeared on his face. He tapped Trent Summers on the shoulder and nodded toward the entry.

Trent looked in that direction and saw his friend standing just inside the door, allowing his eyes to adjust to the dimly lit building. Immediately, Trent started laughing and reached for his wallet.

"Okay," he said. "But I didn't think Anna would let him out of her sight."

Allen held out his hand, and Trent slapped a ten dollar bill in his palm.

"Well, he ain't no coward," answered Allen. "Him and his brother were in 'Nam together. They were in the same battalion of Green Berets. I doubt that Anna even tried to stop him. She knows him well enough. I knew he'd be back."

Stick searched the crowd and finally spotted his adversaries talking to two women from the carnival. He made his way through the crowd unnoticed and stood near the men. He watched them for a moment and then stepped closer. Allen Palmer and Trent Summers drew near, certain trouble was brewing. Both were prepared to lend a hand if necessary.

Bull wrapped his arm around a hefty, middle-aged woman and pulled her close. Phil was standing slightly behind and to Bull's right with the other woman. It was he who spotted Stick first. He slowly tapped Bull on the shoulder and nodded toward Stick, and Bull turned to see him standing at arm's length. The smile on Stick's face unsettled him. He pushed the woman away and stared at Stick.

"What are you doing back here, Smiley?" he demanded. "I thought you ran home with your tail between your legs." He began to put on a show for his female companions.

"Obviously, you shouldn't be trying to think," said Stick calmly. "You need a lesson or two on manners."

His quiet, matter-of-fact style disturbed Bull. *Why isn't he afraid? Everyone else is.*

Slowly, a circle of people formed around the men. Bull felt like showing off, and this was a great opportunity.

"And who's going to be my teacher?" he asked, raising his voice so all could hear.

He turned toward Phil as if to say something but lashed out suddenly with a left backhand. Stick expected as much and ducked. He then stepped quickly to the left and inward, driving his fist into Bull's ribs. The blow came as a total surprise, and the impact forced the air from his lungs. Bull doubled over, and Phil rushed in swinging.

Stick had calculated every move. He thought Bull would start the fight, and he figured Phil would join in afterward. Although his momentum left his back exposed to Phil, he sidestepped as if he had eyes in the back of his head. Then, twisting, he lifted his leg so the heel of his boot struck Phil in the kidney. He learned the move while in the Marine Corps, a roundhouse kick. Phil crashed into a table and onto the floor.

Stick turned and caught Bull with a swift uppercut to the point of the chin before he had time to recover from the first punch. Then he jabbed him in the throat. Bull rocked backward and fell to the floor, gasping for air. Stick had disabled men before with the same punch. Bull rolled over, attempting to get to his feet, and Stick took off his hat and wiped his brow. With a slight smile, he looked across the room into the wide eyes of Hardy Tillman and winked. Hardy's nostrils flared.

Hardy hadn't really drawn any conclusions about Stick Slaton, but had he done so, he was sure he would have underestimated the man. How could anyone be so cool and calculating? It was obvious to Hardy that his opponent was shrewd and certainly no tenderfoot. He suddenly found himself smiling at Stick—not a smile of contempt but more of admiration or respect. The feeling was unfamiliar to him. No matter. This man was an enemy and would have to be treated as one.

In the moment Stick looked at Hardy, Bull quickly jumped up and moved behind him. Suddenly, Stick felt a pair of huge, hairy arms squeezing the air from his lungs as they lifted him off the floor.

Hardy almost felt sorry for his counterpart. He had seen more than one poor soul caught in the death trap. In another moment, Stick Slaton's ribs would be in such trauma he'd not be able to ride for months.

Stick's arms were pinned to his side, and he was unable to free himself from the remarkably strong grip. Phil struggled to his feet, saw his target, and charged in to deliver a fatal blow. His face was red with anger.

Stick's move, once again, was quick and deliberate. He lifted his right leg and slammed the heel of his boot onto the crown of Bull's foot. The big man gasped in pain. Feeling the hide scraped away, he loosened his grip. Stick jammed his elbow into Bull's side, broke free, ducked, and rolled away as Phil came crashing in, using the crown of his head as a battering ram. Bull tumbled again to the floor, cursing, and Phil dropped as though he'd slammed into a brick wall.

Stick watched the two men lying, exhausted, on the floor and struggling to breathe. It appeared they'd had enough. He adjusted his hat and pulled a roll of bills from his pocket. Another glance suggested the men were finished. Stick palmed the money and walked toward the bar. Allen Palmer met him with a joyful smile and slapped him happily on the back.

"Look out!" yelled Trent.

While Stick was approaching his friends, Bull managed to get to his feet. He was moving like a freight train toward the small of Stick's back. Unlike Phil, Bull's charge connected. Stick was hurled headlong into the bar, causing the roll of money to fall from his hands. Suddenly, he was angry. Until this point, he had enjoyed the fight, but now he was ready for it to be over.

He jumped to his feet with glaring eyes and jabbed at Bull's face, one blow after another. Bull was weary and gasping for breath, and his knees trembled. His eyes rolled back, and his giant frame began to sway. His massive arms seemed heavy, too heavy. With all his might, Stick slammed a left cross to his nose, and Bull fell, motionless, to the ground.

Deke and Joel were in the crowd. Subconsciously, Joel's hand went to his sore nose as Stick delivered the final blow. Deke cringed as Bull's body hit the floor. The steel of Stick's knuckles was fresh on their minds.

Stick turned, expecting another run in with Phil. He, however, still lay on the floor where he had collided with Bull. Suddenly, Stick wanted to go home. The two carnival women passed by with expressions of disdain, having wasted their efforts. Stick tipped his hat to them and walked to the door. It was late.

Behind, in the large crowd, one pair of eyes had seen the roll of bills fall from Stick's hand. It lay near the bar, underneath a stool, and she approached, purposely dropping her purse next to the cash. Without attracting attention, she slipped the roll of money into her purse and stood up. She stepped over Phil, who lay moaning on the floor, and headed to the door, watching as Stick pulled from the parking lot. A smile crossed her face, and she leisurely walked to her car.

Hardy Tillman sat quietly in the corner of the bar, considering his opponent. A red-headed girl sat next to him, wondering what he thought about her. Slowly, the smile of confidence returned to his face, and he put his arm around the girl.

Stick's money sped toward town in a fiery red convertible. Shelly Tanner was an unusual girl. Being an only child, her grandfather had no one else to teach—no grandson to tell stories to or show card tricks or play chess with. So he taught her. And she learned well. The roll of bills in her purse represented an ace in the hole, a queen in her newly established game of chess. After all, that's what life was to her: a game of chess. And Stick Slaton's heart was the opposing king.

This will be an easy victory, she thought to herself, *but one promising a thrill.*

CHAPTER SIX

The morning sun peeked over the horizon, and somewhere, a rooster crowed. A few rays of light filtered through the curtains into Stick's room, as dust particles floated on the sunbeams, stirred into a frenzy by the morning breeze.

Slowly, the doorknob turned, and the door creaked open. Bobby walked to the bed, where Stick slept completely covered by a sheet, and he contemplated whether he should shake the snoring lump or not.

"Uncle Stick," he whispered. "Uncle Stick."

"Uncle Stick," he called again, this time louder.

A lump shot up near the foot of the bed and lingered, so Bobby, with a puzzled expression, yanked the sheet off the pillow to find his uncle's feet where his head should have been. He laughed.

Stick shoved the cover from his face and searched the room with hazy eyes, smiling as he located Bobby. Still in his pajamas, a pair of handguns hung at his waist. A red cowboy hat sat low on his head, folding his ears downward.

"Morning, cowboy," Stick greeted.

"Morning, Uncle Stick," said Bobby. "Mom says she's fixing to give your breakfast to the hounds 'cause it's almost time for lunch."

"She did, did she?" queried Stick. The boy could always lift him out of the worst moods.

"Yes, sir, she did."

Stick rolled over and touched his feet to the cool floor, rubbing his eyes clear of sleep. He smashed down his unruly hair with the palm of his hand, cringing as he disturbed a painful knot just above his temple. Bobby watched his every move and noticed the cut on his brow.

"How did you cut your head, Uncle Stick?" he asked. Then he climbed onto the bed and touched the sore spot with his index finger. "Does it hurt?"

Stick looked at Bobby and smiled. He knew Bobby idolized him. It was obvious by the way he looked at him. Stick could have told him black was white, and Bobby would've believed it. All little boys should have a hero, and Stick was Bobby's. But with being a hero came a great responsibility, and that was the one word Stick feared most of all.

"Naw. It doesn't hurt much," answered Stick. "Besides, cowboys ain't supposed to cry."

Stick drew closer to Bobby. He didn't want to be obvious, but he was sure he detected slightly darkening rings around the boy's eyes and a somewhat yellowish discoloration of the skin.

"What happened to you?" Bobby asked with concern.

"Well," said Stick, smiling, "it's like this. I hit some ol' boy right square in the fist with my head." He pulled Bobby's hat down over his face and laughed.

Stick got out of bed, straightened his stiff back, and stretched his sore muscles. Afterward, he interlocked his fingers, turned his palms out, and stretched the stiffness out of his knuckles. he slowly massaged the back of his neck.

"Reckon my head ain't the only thing that connected with his fist," said Stick under his breath.

"Yeah," said Bobby. "I bet you that other guy looks a whole lot worse."

Stick smiled and winked at the boy and then slipped his hand under his hat and tousled his hair, as was his habit.

"You run along and tell your mother not to throw away my breakfast. All right?"

"Yes, sir," answered Bobby, and he jumped off the bed and ran out the door.

Stick took a deep breath, smelling the inviting aroma of hot coffee, bacon, and homemade biscuits. It brought a smile to his face. Nothing could replace the comfort that gave him.

Anna was the best cook he'd ever known. Not only did she love to cook, but she loved to watch a man eat. Stick was always sure to raise a fuss over every meal.

He quickly donned a light flannel shirt, pulled on his jeans, and stepped into his boots. The smell of the food made him realize just how hungry he was. As Stick was headed out the door and down the stairs, he pulled a comb from his pocket and ran it through his hair.

Stick hoped Anna was still wearing her apron and working in the kitchen. He loved to see her there. The sight always added a soothing sense of comfort, reminding him of when he was a young-ster. He could remember his mother standing in the same kitchen, wearing an apron, her hair up in a bun.

He remembered how she would always make him proud of him-self when he would bring rabbits and squirrels or a catfish from the river. She acted excited and told him what a good provider he was. It made him feel special, important. He would dress the game and give it to her, and she would admire it in front of him. Then she would cook it for dinner and tell everyone what a good job he'd done.

TK was more like her side of the family than he was the Slatons. Somehow, everyone knew he would turn out all right. For that reason, Stick's mother didn't give him as much attention. Instead, she worried about Stick. He was just like his pa, and that was a matter of great concern to her. So, as a result, she fussed over Stick, leaving people with the thought that he was her favorite.

He wished she would have gotten to see him and TK in the rodeo. He thought she would have been proud. Stick and TK were close, and that was important to her. As it was, she died before Stick was a teenager. Having gotten pregnant at a later age, she and the baby died of multiple complications. The ranch hands had found her in the barn, and everyone assumed she must have fallen. No one really knew, but Sterling was never the same afterward, losing his desire to stay home. Instead, he became addicted to work and poured the remainder of his life into building a future for his boys.

Anna was busy putting away jars of homemade preserves when, suddenly, there was a knock at the kitchen door. She walked over and opened it.

"Good morning," greeted Anna pleasantly. She loved the mornings and was always in a good mood at this time of the day.

"Hi. Is the owner of the ranch here?" asked a beautiful, young blond.

"Yes. You're speaking to one of them," answered Anna. She wondered what on earth could have brought this young lady all the way out to the ranch.

"Oh…uh…well, is the man who shoes your horses here?" she asked. "I think his name is Stick."

Anna opened the screen door to invite the girl inside. Suddenly, Stick stepped into the room with Bobby at his heels. He was tucking his shirt tail into his pants and didn't notice the girl.

"Anna, you can just go ahead and fix my lunch too," he said. "I'm hungry enough to eat both this morning."

The girl seemed bewildered as she looked first at Stick, then at Bobby, and back to Anna. Nervously, she fumbled around in her purse and pulled out a roll of bills.

"Told you I could wake him up, Mom!" exclaimed Bobby proudly.

The girl stared blankly at Anna and shoved the money into her hands.

"Uh…I'm sorry," she said and hurried away before Stick could see her. Certain that Stick was married, she believed she was about to make an absolute fool of herself.

"What was that all about?" asked Anna softly. She looked from the money in her hand to the girl as she hurried away.

Curious, Stick stepped close to Anna and saw the roll of bills, realizing it was his. Immediately, he remembered it falling from his hands at the club.

"Where did you get that?" he asked.

"Some young lady just handed it to me," she replied. "And she certainly left in a hurry." The statement came out with a curious but sarcastic air.

Stick rushed out the door in time to see a red convertible sports car disappear around a bend in the drive. He smiled and rubbed his chin as he remembered Shelly Tanner.

He walked back into the kitchen, and Anna confronted him, holding the roll of money. "I suppose this is yours?" she asked.

Guilt was written all over Stick's face. *How did she end up with the money? Was she there last night? Did she witness the fight? Evidently, she had.* Stick looked at Anna and shrugged.

"I don't know how she ended up with it. I guess she must've been there last night and picked it up after I dropped it," he explained.

"How did you…? Never mind," said Anna, deciding it was better that she didn't know too much. Besides, she knew how uncomfortable Stick became when she asked questions. He didn't like the pressure, and she had learned when not to get too personal.

Anna gave the money to Stick, and she walked to the door. She stared through the screen for a moment. Somehow, the young lady bothered her. But why?

Stick considered Shelly Tanner for a moment. *Why did she drive out to the ranch? Why didn't she just give me the money last night? I don't remember seeing her around before yesterday. Was she just passing through? And why did she leave so quickly?*

Anna returned to her work but noticed that Stick was in deep thought. She knew he was thinking about the girl. She could read it on his face. *How well does he know her?* Stick had never lied to her before. She didn't think him to be capable of lying. He had led her to believe that he really didn't know the girl. *Is he interested in her?*

She shrugged away the thought and set breakfast on the table for Stick. He pocketed the money and sat down to eat, and Anna returned to the kitchen to finish her work. Bobby sat down next to Stick and tossed down a glass of chocolate milk.

"Anna," said Stick with a mouthful, "I'm going into town. I have to pick up some sweet feed for the horses and a couple of sacks of range cubes for the cows. Do you need anything?"

Bobby's face lit up, and he watched his Uncle Stick. It was obvious that he wanted to go, and this didn't go unnoticed. Stick winked at the boy to acknowledge his permission.

"I need some crumbles for the chickens," she replied from the other room. "They won't lay eggs on hen scratch unless I let them out to chase crickets. Then I can't find where they nest."

"Okay," Stick said, glancing at Bobby. "I'm going to take Bobby with me."

"All right," she agreed, "but you two stay out of trouble."

Bobby's face beamed with excitement. He loved to go places with Stick because it made him feel grown. Maybe Stick would get him a real cowboy hat.

Stick wiped his plate clean with a biscuit and popped it into his mouth. "Let's go partner," he said to Bobby with his cheeks bulging.

Bobby jumped from the table, and the two of them went out the back door through the kitchen. Dusty met them at the door, leading Stick's Appaloosa gelding.

"I saddled ol' Keepsake," he stated. "If you're going to pen those steers in the back pasture, you'll probably need him. That country is steep. Me and your pop had a cabin back there. We had to look up the chimney to watch the cows come home."

"Thanks," said Stick, taking the reins. He led the horse into a trailer that was hitched to his pickup truck. "We're going into town first. Thought a couple of sacks of range cubes might help me pen those rascals."

Dusty rubbed his chin thoughtfully. "Reckon I could use some more chewing tobacco myself. Mind if I tag along?"

"Hop in," said Stick. "The more the merrier."

"Anna!" Dusty yelled toward the house. "I'm going with them!"

Before she could respond, they jumped into the truck. Stick started the engine and pulled away just as Anna made it to the screen door.

"Since when does it take three of you to buy a little feed?" she asked. She knew they expected trouble from her, and she didn't want to disappoint them. Her mother had told her, "Men get a kick out of thinking they are getting away with something," and Anna found it to be true.

Stick had left the front gate open the night before, and he pulled through it and onto the highway. Little Bobby sat between him and Dusty.

"Well, Bobby, I can't wait until tonight. Can you?" asked Dusty.

"No, sir. Me neither," exclaimed Bobby.

A nervous grin appeared on Stick's face. He hadn't realized it before, but having Bobby at the rodeo was going to put him under a different kind of pressure, different than he had experienced in the past. He had a reputation to live up to, and he didn't want to let this little boy down. Bobby expected him to win.

He had been busting some green stock, but other than that, he hadn't practiced riding at all. He could remember the technical points as though it was only yesterday. But was that enough? Was it like riding a bike? Was it something you never forgot? What if he failed? What if he had lost his touch?

Suddenly, a gloomy feeling came upon him. He was afraid—not of the ride, but of failure. After all, he was forty-two years old.

"Yep," continued Dusty. "It'll be like old times, when you and ol' TK was riding. Hey, you remember when ya'll kept drawing the same bull?"

A glimpse of the past appeared in Stick's mind, and he began to smile.

"First night you had him," continued Dusty. "Second night, TK had him, and then vice versa on the third and fourth nights. Heh! Heh! Ya'll dern near tied on points scored. Weren't no one else could come near you. If TK would've had that wild style of yours, you probably would've tied. As it were, the Slaton boys took first and second."

"Yeah," said Stick. "That ol' bull won me fifteen hundred dollars. TK won seven fifty."

There wasn't anything Dusty liked better than talking about the past. In fact, the older he became, the better things used to be. He took pride in the fact that he could "swap lies with the best of 'em." He had put a lot of miles on his skinny frame and was proud to tell people all about them. But now he sat quietly, thinking about TK. The silence of the moment intensified their nostalgia. They missed him.

"Uncle Stick," said Bobby, breaking the silence, "would you tell me about my dad?"

Stick snapped back to the present and sobered quickly. He thought for a moment and then looked to Dusty for help. Stick had known this day would come and had even rehearsed what he would say. Now the choice words he carefully planned to use were forgotten. His mind raced. Where should he start? Dusty turned his head and stared out the window, offering no assistance.

Bobby had caught him off guard. Where were the edifying

phrases he had memorized? What were they? Nothing came to mind. Bobby's timing was off.

Stick planned this to happen at a much more jovial time, a time when they could somehow joke about TK. He had hoped to talk about TK's sense of humor and the funny things that happened to him. But now the time wasn't right.

The most wonderful eight-year-old boy that Stick had ever known was sitting beside him, wanting to know the dad he had never seen. Stick looked into his innocent eyes and swallowed hard. It was one thing to remember TK quietly, but it nearly always brought emotions to the surface when he spoke of him. This time, however, it was necessary.

"What would you like to know?" Stick asked.

"Well," answered Bobby in a small voice, "I already know that he was a good bull rider. But what else did he do?" His words trailed away quietly. He was reluctant to ask the next question but driven by a need to know. "How did he die?"

A sudden dreadful mental picture brought pain to Stick's heart. He could see TK's lifeless body as vivid as the day he found him, although neither he nor anyone else had spoken of it since. Again, Stick looked to Dusty for help, but the old man stared straight ahead, silent and distant. Suddenly, Stick's forehead became a mass of wrinkles, and he felt himself giving in.

"Son," Stick began, "your daddy was the best man I ever knew. He was my big brother, and he taught me a lot. He was always looking out for me." Stick fought to control his voice. He cleared his throat; then, after determining where this story should start, he began.

"Dusty, you remember that ol' Dragoon Colt forty-five pistol that Pa gave TK?"

"Yep," returned Dusty. "Ol' Sterl used to carry that thing everywhere he went. Had his name carved into them ivory handles: Sterling T. Slaton."

Stick took his hand off the wheel and slipped his arm around Bobby. He pulled him close and looked again into his eyes. "Your daddy saved my life once," continued Stick in a soft voice. "I reckon it was that what finally killed him."

This was something Dusty had never heard all the way through. Sure, he had heard bits and pieces but never the whole story. He raised one brow and looked curiously at Stick. "What do you mean, son?" he asked.

Stick set his eyes on the horizon and concentrated on the past. "TK and I never talked about it. I guess it was, I don't know, personal maybe. It was just something we never shared with anyone else. But it's time the story was told."

"Well, you knew we were in the same battalion of green berets back in 'Nam."

Dusty nodded and looked at Stick through squinted eyes as if, with a more clear view, he might read what was on his mind.

"And you knew he was wounded."

Dusty nodded again, and Bobby listened fearfully.

"Right before we were discharged," continued Stick, "me and TK and eighteen other guys volunteered for a mission to help search for some of our buddies trapped behind enemy lines. A chopper crashed in the jungle, and there was no communication."

"We found them all right, but it was too late. Every one of them was dead."

Stick frowned as he remembered the pain of the gruesome sight.

"We radioed in for a chopper to pick us up, but before they could, we had to cross back over enemy lines. The Charlies were thick as flies, and it wasn't long before they had us pinned down in a clearing."

Stick began to relive the vivid memory. Bobby saw fear come over his face, and the reality of the incident became apparent.

"Every few minutes one of us would get hit, and it wasn't long until there was just a handful of us who were still healthy." Stick squinted as though he were looking for something somewhere in front of them. "We couldn't see them. They were out there, hiding in the jungle, invisible-like. We'd fire every time we heard a shot or saw smoke from a rifle, but I don't think we ever hit anything."

He sat quietly for a moment, staring at the road ahead. Sweat beads suddenly appeared on his forehead. He could hear the explosions and rifle fire in his mind.

"We just couldn't see them. But TK, he was cool. He always kept his head when the going got tight. He was a thinker. Me, the adrenalin would start flowing and I'd want to charge the whole lot of them."

Bobby stared wide-eyed, and Dusty listened intently, wondering why Stick had chosen not share this story in the past. Maybe it was good that he had saved this one for TK's son. Stick wiped the sweat from his brow as he relived the trauma.

"TK radioed in for air support. The flyboys were shorthanded and sent only one chopper. It wasn't long before we heard it coming." Stick smiled. "When he dropped that napalm, I could've done a double back flip. He let them Charlies have it, and then he sat down right where we were. Man, that guy had guts. By that time, there were only five of us who could still walk. We started loading the dead and wounded. Then we climbed on board. I felt the chopper lift off just about the same time the North Vietnamese broke through the clearing again. They started firing at us, and I took a round in the side."

Stick looked sadly at Bobby and then Dusty.

"TK was hit in the head."

Tears began to form in Bobby's eyes, and he stared at the floorboard. Dusty realized why he hadn't heard the story. It was too painful for Stick to remember.

"I saw TK fall backward, and I remember thinking that if I lived, life would never be the same. In that brief moment, I thought about Pa and wondered how to tell him. Then a hand grenade landed in the chopper. I shoved TK out the door. I guess we were about twenty feet off the ground when I jumped. The chopper blew just a second later. It crashed with everyone else on it."

"Well, I figured TK was dead and the best thing for me to do was to play dead. They came in, and I heard one of them roll TK over with the toe of his boot. Then they walked over to me. I felt them staring down at me. It seemed like they stood over me for an eternity. Then one of them hauled off and kicked me in the side. The blow knocked a grunt out of me. Well, I knew I was done for, so I just opened my eyes. I found myself staring down the barrel of an automatic rifle, and I knew I was about to cash in my chips."

The whites of Stick's eyes turned red as the emotions surfaced. A shudder went through Dusty, and he shook his head. Bobby sniffled and tried hard not to cry.

"He had that rifle pointed right between my eyes, and I saw his finger starting to squeeze the trigger. I remember the way he was smiling through them yellow teeth. All of a sudden, I hear a familiar voice yell, 'Hey, Charlie!' Then, blam! I hear a shot, and the gook falls on top of me with a bullet hole in the center of his forehead.

"Well, I didn't know what had happened, but while I was grabbing for his rifle, I heard another shot, and another gook hit the ground. They started running into each other, trying to find cover. I looked over, and I'll be a son of a gun...there was TK with Pa's ol' Dragoon colt forty-five smoking in his hand."

Stick slammed his palm against the steering wheel with enthusiasm, smiling proudly through cloudy eyes as he relived the emotional victory.

"I've never seen anything like it. TK was so cool, steady as a rock. I started firing, but before I could get the other three with the rifle, one fired another round at TK and hit him in the shoulder.

"Smoke was so thick from the firefight and the burning chopper that I could hardly see. But I looked over at TK, and he was just laying there, grinning at me. He says, 'Look like you seen a ghost,

Stick.' I just crawled over to him and hugged him hard as I could. I can't honestly tell you if we were laughing or crying.

"A few minutes later, another chopper came in and picked us up. The bullet shattered TK's shoulder and, as you know, Dusty, it never got well. The muscle deteriorated, and his arm shrunk down to the size of my wrist. That shot to his head just bounced off somehow. We figured it must've been a ricochet. TK just chalked it off to heredity. He said, 'The Slatons have the hardest heads in Texas, and that covers lots of ground.

"Anyway, about eight years ago, one of my colts got stuck in the mud at the stock pond by the old windmill. He was a year and a half old, so he was pretty good size. Well, TK spotted him and waded in to pull him out."

Stick reminisced quietly for a long moment, struggling to continue. His clenched knuckles turned white over the steering wheel.

"What happened?" Bobby asked, needing to know.

"If he'd just came to me for help," Stick finally exclaimed. "He must've slid his good arm underneath the colt to pry him loose. I guess it must've lost its balance and fell over on TK. If his arm hadn't been crippled, he might've been able to free himself."

Stick turned sad eyes on Bobby. "Dusty and I found him a couple of hours later. He was dead, and the horse was near drowned too.

"I started to shoot that horse right then and there. I would have, too, if it hadn't been for Dusty. He talked me into keeping him. He said that it wasn't the horse's fault and if TK thought enough of him to risk his life, I ought to keep him. He said that that colt would be a reminder for me and that I would think of TK whenever I looked at him."

Bobby's head was bowed in sorrow. He sniffled, and Stick knew he was crying. He pulled him close to his side and held him tight.

"You want to know what your dad used to tell me when he'd see me crying for some reason or other?"

"Yes, sir," said Bobby with tear-filled eyes.

"He'd say, 'Rich'—that was before he named me Stick—'Rich,'
he'd say, 'cowboys ain't supposed to cry.'"

Bobby raised his head and dried his eyes with the back of his
hand. If that was the way his dad saw it, then that's the way it
would be.

"Uncle Stick?" asked Bobby.

"Yes, sir?" Stick answered in a sympathetic voice.

"What did you do with that horse?"

"I can tell you that one," answered Dusty, smiling. He couldn't
resist telling part of the story, and getting the last word was a tri-
umph. "He named him Keepsake."

Suddenly, Bobby turned and stared out the rear window. He
could see Keepsake's head lifted into the wind. For a long moment,
he studied Keepsake as if he was seeing him for the first time. The
horse's beautiful mane waved in the breeze as they traveled down the
highway. The gelding was more beautiful now than ever, and Bobby
was glad Stick hadn't destroyed him.

A smile came to Stick's face, and Dusty gave a wink of approval.
Some memories were extremely painful, and Stick didn't like having
to relive them again. But he was proud he had shared the story with
his brother's son.

"Uncle Stick," said Bobby with his eyes still glued to Keepsake,
"when we get to town, can we get me a real cowboy hat? I think a
real cowboy ought to have a real cowboy hat. Don't you?"

Stick smiled and pulled him close again. "Yes, sir. I reckon a real
cowboy ought to have a real cowboy hat."

Dusty nodded in agreement and proudly slapped Bobby's knee.
The boy was special to him. Dusty knew Sterling Slaton better than
any man alive, and this boy was his spitting image—not necessarily
in the way he looked, but more in his mannerisms and expressions.
Somehow—God only knew—Stick had ended up with Sterling's
wild side and TK his stable side. Now, a generation later, Bobby had

the characteristics of both. Dusty hoped and prayed that the boy would live and that he would be around to see it.

Bobby didn't talk a lot or ask a lot of questions like most kids. Instead, he did a lot of listening. There were times when a person hardly knew he was around. For this reason, grownups didn't seem to mind him tagging along.

Stick crossed the bridge and glanced at the Colorado River. Speed boats, ski boats, and tour boats dotted the water below. The clear water lakes of the area attracted numerous tourists during the summer months, and Stick was always glad to see them gone. He didn't like crowds, and he preferred the cooler months. He enjoyed deer hunting. And besides, he slept good on cold nights, and the cattle seemed to handle the cold weather better.

He remembered the town when it was barely more than a gro-cery/post office/feed store. The old men would gather in the back to play dominoes and hide out from their wives for a while, telling jokes and swapping lies. They argued and fought with one another, but any one of them would have given the other the shirt off of his back. And there were times in each of their lives when it was almost necessary. Stick was young then. Now it was different.

He drove the pickup into a newly opened group of stores on the left side of the road. Included in the plaza were a pharmacy, a jewelry store, a gift shop, and a Western wear store. He parked in front of the latter, and Bobby's face lit up.

"Can I pick it out?" he asked excitedly.

"Get after it!" exclaimed Stick, and he opened the door of the truck. Bobby slid out after him and ran into the store. Dusty pulled the red handkerchief from his back pocket and wiped the sweat from his face. He followed Bobby, and Stick checked on Keepsake.

He took three sugar cubes from his shirt pocket and slipped his hand between the rails of the trailer. Keepsake carefully nibbled them from his palm and whinnied softly. Stick patted the horse on the rump and suddenly remembered his brother's laugh. It brought a smile to his face. He shook his head and set his thoughts aside. Then, glancing toward the store, he followed the others.

He had barely gotten a foot in the door when Bobby ran up to him already wearing a new straw hat.

"Uncle Stick! Uncle Stick! What do you think?"

Stick tilted the hat back and pulled both front and back downward onto his head. "Now that's some fancy lid you've got there, partner."

Bobby turned and pointed. "That nice lady over there got it for me."

Shelly Tanner stood behind the counter, putting on a girlish act of embarrassment. Some people could make themselves cry, others could make themselves laugh, but Shelly could make herself blush. Although Stick didn't seem to notice, to Dusty, she was an open book. He read between the lines and realized the two had already met.

"What's the big idea?" Stick asked in a playful voice. His intention was to tease her for leaving the house so abruptly.

Shelly, however, mistook the question. She thought him to be angry with her for showing up at his house, possibly upsetting his wife.

"I...I'm sorry," she mumbled. "I didn't know you were—."

"You ought to be," Stick interrupted. "I didn't get a chance to thank you." He smiled at her, and she realized immediately that he wasn't angry.

"I thought your wife might be angry," she returned. "I didn't want her to get the wrong idea." She raised one eyebrow and smiled, purposely leaving a question as to her sincerity.

Dusty had seen that expression before. To him, she was the beginning of trouble. It was obvious that the girl had eyes for Stick and she didn't really care if he was married or not. He was ready to get out of there while the getting was good and was just about to suggest that very thing when Stick continued with the conversation.

"Well, you might be right about that," he said. "My wife might get mad about a pretty young lady like you showing up on my back doorstep. What do you think, Dusty?" Stick winked at him in an unsuccessful effort to get him to play along.

"Yep. She's right all right," agreed Dusty halfheartedly. The tone in his voice let Stick know that he was getting bored with this. Stick was enjoying himself, though.

"Yeah. I'm sure of it. If I had a wife and you showed up on my back doorstep, she'd get mad." Again, he charmed her with a wide grin.

"If? You mean you're not married?" she asked, genuinely surprised. A slight lifting of her spirits could be detected.

"I mean, you met my sister-in-law this morning," he answered. "She's been my partner since my brother died."

Shelly was enchanted with Stick, and for a brief moment, their eyes locked, held by attraction. Stick became suddenly uncomfortable as he felt Dusty's scrutinizing glare. The old man had one hand on his hip and rubbed his whiskers with the other. He was beginning to feel as though three was a crowd.

"I see you found Bobby there a right handsome hat," Stick said, trying to avert her attention. He knew that Dusty would interrogate him later. The old man's sense of humor was ruthless, and Stick was sure he would never hear the end of it.

"Yes. He's a nice boy," she said, pretending to be interested, although unable to shift her eyes from Stick's face. "He told me that he needed a hat to wear to the rodeo tonight."

"Yeah, and that ain't all he told her," added Dusty with sarcasm in his voice. "He said that he needed the new hat to go with the new belt buckle that his uncle was going to win for him." Dusty used special emphasis on "his uncle" to remind Stick of his age.

"He did, did he?" Stick asked, ignoring Dusty's apparent intention. He only hoped he wouldn't let Bobby down, as already butterflies turned his stomach. The boy expected him to win, and the thought of getting thrown left him feeling ill.

"So you shoe horses and ride bulls, huh?" asked Shelly with enthusiasm.

"Guess so," answered Stick. "Anyhow, it's too late to back out now. They already took my entry fee." He smiled and reached for his wallet. "Speaking of money, thanks for returning mine to me. How did you happen to end up with it anyway?" He was curious about what she had seen at the dance.

"Well"—she smiled—"I was driving by the club, and I noticed you going in the front door. I, uh…I wanted to…I thought that…well, anyway, by the time I got inside, you were in a fight with two guys. I stood by the door and watched. I guess I was the only one who saw you drop it. By the time I picked it up, you were walking out the front door. I remembered that you worked at the ranch, so I thought it would be a good opportunity to…" She shrugged and glanced at her feet.

"Well, I'm glad you did," he added as he opened his wallet and pulled out the money for Bobby's hat. "Say, why don't you come watch me get thrown on my head tonight?"

"I'd love to watch," she exclaimed, "but I bet that doesn't happen." She refused his money and explained. "Mr. Dusty has taken care of the hat."

"That's just plain Dusty, ma'am," offered Dusty.

"Well come on, just plain Dusty. We better get our feed and get back to the ranch before Anna calls the sheriff after us." Stick glanced at Shelly, and a thought entered his head.

"I figured you to be a nurse."

"Oh? Why is that?" she asked.

"Well, your license plates read 'ICU.' Doesn't that stand for Intensive Care Unit?"

"No," she laughed. "It stands for I…see…you," she said and then fluttered her eyelashes. The personalized plates had given her many opportunities to meet men. She was glad she had spent the extra money for them.

"Uh huh," he said to himself and then turned to Dusty. "You fellas ready?"

"Been ready," answered Dusty.

"See you later, ma'am," said Bobby, tipping his new hat.

"Bye bye," she returned. She watched as they walked away, smiling with great satisfaction. Her foot was in the door with Stick, and it wouldn't be long until he was wrapped around her finger.

CHAPTER SEVEN

The Cactus Falls Rodeo Association had dedicated much time and money toward the success of this year's rodeo. Having recently joined the Pro Rodeo Cowboy Association, this was their first annual PRCA rodeo, with hopefully many more to come. Jack Chambers had created a legacy to immortalize his name.

Flags and banners filled the complex, and virtually every upright pole waved an American or Texas flag. A new sound system had been installed, and two PRCA guest speakers were invited to narrate. The grandstands had just been refurbished, it and the corrals receiving a matching coat of white paint. The carnival was set up just to the west of the arena, where Its Ferris wheel spun almost continuously. A local band performed on stage, the new speakers filling the air with country music.

Children ran to and fro with large clouds of cotton candy. Cowboys and cowgirls rode horses with rhinestone stars reflecting the arena's bright lights.

Stick sat astride Keepsake and watched the spectacle. It amazed him to see people gathering together with such tension and excitement. The sight reminded him of an ant bed after the top of the mound had been kicked away. He couldn't help but smile. People seemed drawn to a crowd like a moth to a flame.

But not Stick. He preferred the solitude of the surrounding hills of the Edwards Plateau, which extended as far south as San Antonio. He loved this country. His eyes had seen many wonders in their forty-two years, wonders most people overlooked. Beauty was in the eyes of the beholder, and his eyes had beheld their share of it. Like the time a mother cougar and her three kittens had nested on the north slope of Comanche Ridge, and Stick watched them for months without telling a soul. Most people would have killed them for fear of losing sheep or cattle, but Stick felt they had just as much right to the land as he did. So, to keep from losing livestock, he hunted rabbits, squirrels, and deer to feed the foursome.

Then there was the time he found an albino fawn. It had been born earlier in the day and lay nestled in a small stand of rye grass. It was rare to even hear of such a sight. People would have paid dearly to own an animal of its kind, but this, too, he kept to himself.

He had seen other rarities, such as bald eagles, wolf dens, trophy bucks, and blind fish in clear water springs that fed from somewhere deep underground. There was a cave halfway up a bluff on the backside of the property with ancient writings on its walls. Once, when making his way into a dry ravine, he found a gold nugget that had been unveiled during recent rains. His interest wasn't in material gain, so he never bothered to keep it. Now, considering Bobby's condition, the find would have been useful. The possibility of returning to the spot in chance of finding more would be something worth considering.

All of these things he kept to himself, things the Almighty had created for his eyes only. If he were to show others what he had seen, the things wouldn't be as special anymore. No. If God wanted anyone else to see them, well, He would have to be the one to show them.

Stick then considered his Creator, something he rarely did. Common sense told him there was a God. There must have been. All the things around him couldn't have sprung from nothing. Church was another story. Stick couldn't understand how some men could stand in front of everyone and make such fools of themselves. They would tell stories about how some man died two thousand years ago for the wrong Stick was doing today. To him, it was no more than a fairy tale and it didn't make a lick of sense.

Anna and little Bobby had tried many times to get Stick to go to church with them. It might have been fine for TK, but the few times Stick had gone, he felt mighty uncomfortable. No. They could worship God the way they wanted, and he would worship the way he wanted.

To him, God was an impersonal force. He was around but really didn't have much to do with what was going on. When Stick died he would get to spend time with Him—but not until then. There was a time when Stick had tried to find Him on a personal basis but God just wasn't there.

Suddenly, Stick snapped to attention as the sound system played "The Star-Spangled Banner," and two horsemen carried the American and Texas flags to the middle of the arena. Every cowboy in the complex held his hat in hand. A member of the band sang, and the crowd joined in.

The grand entry was next, and every contestant and participant was required to parade around the arena. Stick put a white breast collar on Keepsake, and somehow, the horse seemed to know how beautiful he was. He held his head high and pranced with pride. His tail was slightly elevated, and Stick had to laugh.

Stick slowly became aware of the adrenaline in his veins and just how nervous he really was. Hopefully, he wouldn't make a fool of himself. As he rode Keepsake into the arena, he knew Bobby's eyes were on him, pointing him out to Anna and Dusty. The boy would be ecstatic, but what did the townsfolk think?

Allen Palmer and Trent Summers rode just ahead of him, Both in deep concentration. They were unusually quiet, their faces like chiseled granite. Stick tipped his hat and wished them luck, and Trent managed a smile, but Allen was already riding an imaginary bull in his mind.

A moment later, he locked eyes with Hardy Tillman. He looked magnificent on a broad-chested, solid black gelding with a white star on its forehead—a large horse, at least sixteen hands. Hardy's nerves were like steel, and he stared at Stick from across the arena. Stick flashed a sarcastic smile that aggravated the younger man.

The large crowd applauded as the contestants left the arena through the rear gate, located near the press box. Two clowns ran behind the last horse and pulled his tail. One disappeared through the gate and came back carrying a pair of water skis. He put them on his feet. The second clown mounted a horse and rode within an arm's length of the first. A moment later, the crowd was roaring with laughter as the first clown rode the skis around the arena while holding the horse's tail.

"Skiing Texas-style," exclaimed the announcer.

Bull Hawthorne and Phil McGrawe assisted Hardy Tillman with his gear. Bull tied the back of Hardy's chaps while Phil worked the rigging, each showing traces of Stick's knuckles on their faces. All three were in irritable moods.

"Hardy," said Bull, "you ought to run away with this one-horse show." He wanted nothing worse than to see Stick Slaton trampled in the dirt. The man had humiliated him, and he'd not be forgetting it. If only he hadn't been so drunk, he would have crushed the older man.

"Yep," answered Hardy with great confidence. "Write me down for another two grand in prize money." He didn't want his companions to know he was concerned, but Stick worried him. The man had a certain air about him, something that made Hardy lose confidence in himself.

"Phil," ordered Bull, "get Hardy's gloves off the front seat of the truck."

Phil resented being sent on an errand; but, considering Bull's temper and current mood, he decided not to argue.

Suddenly, all three men stopped to watch Shelly Tanner walk by, searching the crowd of cowboys behind the press box in hopes of finding Stick. She felt the pressure of Hardy's eyes upon her and glanced at him. Slowly, he inspected her five-foot-six-inch frame and smiled.

"How about me and you after the show, sugar?" he knew the question was too forward, but he felt reckless.

Shelly was no easy catch, but the cowboy was strikingly handsome. His arrogance was a little too much, although she did like confidence in a man. She smiled and walked away, glancing over her shoulder as she left.

"Ha ha ha!" Bull laughed. "You ran her off, Hardy!" Although he was only joking, he did like to see Hardy strike out.

"She looked back, didn't she?" Hardy asked to make a point.

Phil smiled and went to get the gloves out of the truck. Hardy watched Shelly disappear into the crowd, while Bull worked resin into his rigging. He hoped Hardy would win—not only for the sake of beating Stick Slaton, but also because he became a selfishly motivated philanthropist when he won.

The barrel-riding event had just concluded, and the crowd was applauding the first bronc rider. Hardy knew he needed to shift his attention to the task at hand. Immediately, he began to stretch his limbs and twist his body in an effort to release tension in his muscles. Phil returned with the gloves, and Hardy stretched the rawhide over his fists. He slapped a handful of resin onto the gloves and rubbed them together.

With Shelly at his side, Stick suddenly appeared near Hardy, wearing chaps and carrying his own rigging. He chose to rub a little salt in the trio's wounds by displaying an attitude in contrast to their own.

"Beautiful day, isn't it, boys?" he said cheerfully.

They glared hatefully at him, and Shelly stifled a laugh; then the two continued on their way. Hardy frowned at them, disturbed about having his concentration interrupted. He was suddenly aware that Stick was beating him at his own game.

"Hey, honey," Hardy yelled in an attempt to get even. "Is your daddy going to ride a bull tonight?" Using Stick's age as a knife with which to stab him, Hardy thought, would definitely upset him. He smiled with satisfaction and then yelled, "Good luck, grandpa!"

Stick's eyes revealed a trace of humor. He was beginning to enjoy the competition. He suddenly remembered the mind games that he and his opponents had played on one another in the past. Strangely enough, he possessed a liking for Hardy Tillman. Yeah, he was young, spoiled, arrogant, and couldn't be trusted; but he was good at what he did, and Stick respected that. With experience, he had the makings of a world champion.

If Stick intended to stand in Hardy's way of the title, he had to get his head into the ride. To do that, he must be left alone to concentrate.

"Shelly, why don't you see if you can find Dusty and Bobby in the stands," he said. "I'll see you after the ride."

"All right," she agreed and stood for a moment with her fingers jammed into the hip pockets of her tight jeans. "Good luck. I know you'll do well." She smiled and walked away.

Stick watched as she made her way through the crowd. Her youthful figure was a definite distraction, so Stick closed his eyes and shook his head, trying to clear his mind.

Shelly knew he was watching. She enjoyed the fact that men stumbled when she walked by, so she added an exaggerated sway to her stride for his benefit.

"Ladies and gentlemen!" said the announcer. "My name's Skinny Fuller, and I'm narrating tonight's bull-riding event. Most of you know me. I've been around for quite a few years. Fact is, when I started out, my first name fit better than my last. Now it's the other way around. When the dinner bell rings, I seem to get fuller than everyone else. Folks, bull riding is the most dangerous sporting event of all. Every time one of these cowboys climbs aboard a twenty-five-hundred-pound bundle of meanness and muscle, they take their life into their own hands. They have to be in top physical condition with an iron grip and nerves of steel. They've got to be light on their feet and, if you ask me, a might narrow between the ears. Heh heh. Just kidding, cowboys."

Skinny Fuller was a magnificent bull rider in his day. He never won the title, but made it to the finals five years in a row. Afterwards, he worked rodeos for two years as a clown. He was known to have a great sense of humor, and everyone loved his jokes, so finally someone from the PRCA asked him to narrate the bull riding events. His face was familiar to anyone involved with rodeo. At fifty-eight years of age, he was a rodeo legend.

The year Skinny started announcing was also the year Stick won the title. Before that, Skinny had kept bulls from goring both Stick and TK on numerous occasions. They knew him personally and were good friends. He attended both Sterling's and TK's funerals.

"Coming out of chute number two, we're happy to present to you an up-and-coming new bull rider. This is his second year in the PRCA, and he made it to the finals last year as a rookie. By the way he's riding, we'll probably see him there again this year. Put your hands together and give Hardy Tillman a big Texas welcome. He's riding Nitro."

Stick stepped up on the fence and threw one leg over, watching Hardy get situated on the bull as the crowd applauded. Nitro looked to be three quarters Brahman. One horn protruded in front of his face, and the other angled toward his lower jaw. Both horns had been cut off on the ends but remained dangerously sharp.

One thing Stick knew from experience was no matter how a bull's horns were shaped, the bull knew where they were and how to use them. He had seen cowboys put their hands inside the chute only to draw them back broken after the bull jerked his head to the side. It was no accident when the bull's horn mashed them against the rails.

The horn that turned down would be worth remembering. If Hardy was to get hung up, the bull could use it to puncture his lungs. The other horn would only be dangerous if the bull was facing him.

Stick watched as Hardy's comrades helped him tighten the rigging. The crowd was quiet, anticipating the perilous ride. Hardy slid forward and pounded the rigging with his free hand, ensuring a tight grip. Then, he leaned back and nodded.

The gate opened, and the crowd went wild. The bull exploded out of the chute, and Hardy lifted his left arm above his head. The bull leaped into the air, landing hard on his front hooves, his rear colliding with the back of Hardy's head. Then the bull whirled sharply to the left and ran to the center of the arena, bucking hard until the eight-second horn sounded.

Hardy pulled his hand free and used the upward thrust of the bull to catapult himself into the air. He landed on his feet but winced with pain as his sore leg absorbed the shock. Two clowns immediately crossed between him and the bull, attracting its attention while Hardy made good his escape.

The crowd applauded, and Hardy bowed low. Although he lasted the eight seconds, his frown testified that he wasn't satisfied with the ride. Disgusted, he kicked a mound of dirt before climbing the corral fence.

Hardy loosened his rawhide glove straps with his teeth, shedding the gloves.

Stick stepped down from the fence and crossed over to Hardy. "Not bad," he offered.

"I did my part," growled Hardy. "But that bull is rodeo wise. He's been ridden too much. He didn't do his part."

"Luck of the draw," Stick added and stepped away to find a place to concentrate. He prepared himself by visualizing the ride in his mind, creating different scenarios and making conscious decisions about each. If the bull whirled right or left out of the gate, he would react instinctively rather than take the time to think. All cowboys had to be mentally prepared if they hoped to ride. Staying on for eight seconds was not a matter of luck.

"And the judges give Hardy a seventy-nine!" exclaimed the announcer. "Good ride, cowboy!"

The crowd displayed their appreciation, and Hardy took his hat off and waved.

Bull slapped him on the back, and Hardy smiled. "Judge was good to you, Hardy!" yelled Bull above the roar.

"Yeah. I couldn't make that bull mad!" explained Hardy. "I raked him hard as I could. He's got high mileage." It aggravated him when he drew a bull that was wise. They seemed to know the cowboy was only a temporary nuisance.

Skinny announced the rides of several more cowboys. Allen Palmer scored a 78, as did Trent Summers. Pudge Foley was disqualified for touching the bull with his free hand. Other cowboys were bucked off, and two scored 75s.

Stick was picked to ride last, a position he enjoyed having because he knew the score he had to beat. The only hindrance with being last was, if he wasn't careful, he could get cold while waiting for his turn. Stick was a veteran, though, and he used every opportunity to stretch.

Hardy Tillman was in first place, Allen Palmer and Trent Summers were tied for second, and the others were out of the picture. Stick was somewhat handicapped because he wasn't familiar with the bull he was riding. This was the animal's first rodeo, so he hadn't the opportunity to observe his pattern.

A bull's bucking pattern was almost like a signature, typically making the same twists and turns each time the chute opened. Most cowboys memorized the moves each bull made, knowing which direction they would most likely need to lean.

"Our last bull rider is another local," announced Skinny. "He's coming out of chute number three. I've known this cowboy for a long time, longer than he cares for you to know. So, while he's getting ready down there, I'll give you a little background on him." Skinny smiled to himself. He intended to have a little fun at Stick's expense.

"I've had the distinct pleasure of announcing his rides over twenty years ago. He was world champion. He and his brother took first and second in twenty-three rodeos that same year. Let's have a big round for Richard 'Stick' Slaton."

The bull Stick straddled was a spotted Brahman cross with a large hump and horns protruding straight out about twelve inches. Both were dangerous for anyone in any direction. The bull snorted several times while Stick tightened the rigging, behaving very unfamiliar with the treatment. "He's a green one, fresh out of the pasture," yelled a cowboy from somewhere behind Stick.

Suddenly, the bull bolted forward, trying to go over the top. Stick dropped the rigging and grabbed the top rail on either side of the chute, lifting himself off the bull's back.

As the bull settled down, a cowboy gave Stick his rigging, and he made another attempt to tighten it down. The bull was nervous, slowly working himself into a frenzy.

"For those of you who don't know it," announced Skinny, "it was Stick's brother who gave him that name. He accused Stick of putting glue on his britches because of the way he stuck to the bull's back. He's riding the Terminator."

Stick suddenly felt the rush of a familiar feeling, as a controlling force settled his nerves. It was like coming home. A motivating alteration was beginning to envelope every fiber of Stick's body. It wasn't something he fully understood, but it came on him each and every time he straddled a bull. He became like an extension of the animal. It had been a long time, but suddenly, he knew he was still a master of this dangerous sport, if truly it was a sport. He could feel the strength in his arms. He was thinking clearly. He was confident. He felt good.

Stick had the rigging in place and pounded his fist to assure himself of the grip. Then, as a second thought, he double-wrapped the leather around his hand.

"Them pokers are sticking straight out!" yelled a cowboy who saw Stick make the extra wrap. "You hang up, and he'll punch more holes in you than your granny's pin cushion."

Stick ignored the advice, slid forward, and leaned back. He held his left arm high in the air.

"Hey, Stick! See you got your lucky number!" yelled the cowboy working the gate. The number thirteen was taped to Stick's back.

Stick grinned and nodded, and the cowboy pulled the gate open. The bull sprang into the air and came down on all fours. He bounced twice and landed on his front hooves, almost vertical to the ground. Stick felt himself sliding toward the bull's head; so he jammed his spurs into the bull's side, pushed with all his might, and leaned against his back.

Suddenly, the bull whirled to the right. One, two, three circles, bellowing all the while. The bull was furious. He catapulted himself high into the air and twisted, and Stick felt his grip break loose. The rope started to slide, and he fought the urge to grab it with his free hand. The bull jerked forward, and suddenly, Stick's hand was out of the glove. He felt himself falling backward. Then the bull's rear drove a wicked blow to the back of Stick's head, knocking him forward. The forward shift allowed him to catch the rope and regain his grip, but it was too loose to offer support. Instinct took over, and his waist became a well-oiled hinge. He rose and fell, twisted and turned, floating with the bull's fluid motion like a green leaf on a wind-tossed limb.

The buzzer sounded, and the crowd roared. The clowns darted back and forth in front of the bull, allowing Stick an opportunity to slide off to the right and roll. Once clear of the bull's hooves, he broke for the fence.

It was a wild ride. Stick's form wasn't typical, but sheer determination was enough to give him a high score. Certainly the biggest majority of professional bull riders would not have made it. To lose grip, maintain position, and regain control was something unheard of and would definitely be appreciated by the judges.

The crowd shared their enthusiasm as Stick climbed the arena fence. He couldn't keep from smiling. He loved everything about rodeo: the crowd, the lights, the danger, and the competition.

"Stick Slaton scores eighty-four points," exclaimed Skinny as Stick lifted a leg over the fence. "That ride wins him first place and two thousand dollars. Give that cowboy a big hand, folks."

Hardy Tillman savagely kicked the dirt and glared in Stick's direction. He knew Stick deserved to win, but why couldn't he have drawn that bull? How did Stick Slaton manage to stay on? Could he himself have ridden the bull if he had drawn him? Hardy had watched a million rides, but never had he seen a bull work so hard to throw a man. Yeah. Stick Slaton was a man to be taken seriously.

Dusty's chest swelled with pride, and he lifted Bobby up to his shoulders for a better view. People standing nearby patted them both on the back as if they had ridden the bull themselves.

To have a hometown cowboy win the first PRCA bull riding event was uplifting for the whole community. Everyone shared their version of the ride with the person next to them. They were proud that Stick belonged to them.

Anna stood next to Dusty, her face beaming with excitement as she watched little Bobby. His eyes were glued to Stick, who was sitting on the top rail of the corral. Stick was his hero, the one he wished to be like. The sparkle in Anna's eyes instantly faded as she realized what Stick's winning really meant. He was going to be leaving, which would break Bobby's heart.

Shelly had spotted the three of them just before Stick's turn to ride. She made her way through the stands and sat on the row below them. She introduced herself formally to Anna, who forced a smile and a, "How do you do?"

Anna found herself harboring a desire to be unfriendly to the young lady. Was it jealousy? She thought not. The girl was too forward, aggressive. She was pretty, she was young, and she was not the least bit shy. Anna figured her for someone who was used to getting her way, someone who would use all of her feminine attributes to accomplish her goal.

Shelly picked her way down the stands, as the crowd applauded and Stick waved his hat. Anna knew Shelly was making her way to him, and another twinge of dislike clouded her thoughts. The girl was so attractive, and Stick was so young at heart. She would be to him like a shiny new penny to a child. What if she captured his heart? She was not right for him. Stick needed someone stable in his life to offset his carefree extremes.

It was not like Anna to dislike anyone, especially for no good reason, and she quickly regretted her improper thoughts. She would not interfere. Whatever would be, would be. Her opinion of God was different from Stick's. She believed God directed the steps of men, and she trusted Him with every aspect of her life. She would trust Him with this also.

"Excellent ride by forty-two-year-old Stick Slaton," shouted Skinny Fuller over the loudspeakers.

A frown came over Stick's face, and he glanced toward the press box at the mention of his age. He placed his hat back on his head and jumped to the ground. He entered the alley behind the press box, making his way toward the stands. Unexpectedly, he found himself face to face with Hardy Tillman, along with Bull Hawthorne and Phil McGrawe. For a moment, their eyes locked. Then Stick grinned and looked each of them square in the face.

"Good ride, grandpa," said Hardy sarcastically.

"Thanks," returned Stick cooly. He sidestepped them and continued on his way. "See you at the finals, sonny," he said without turning around.

Hardy stared at him and thoughtfully rubbed the back of his neck. Then he nodded in agreement. "Yeah. You probably will," he said to himself.

For the first time, Hardy considered the possibility of losing. He was younger, stronger, and had just as much nerve, if not more, than Stick Slaton. So why was he worried? Surprisingly, Phil answered the question for him.

"That guy is a natural," he admitted. "I saw him lose his grip on the rigging, and he still stayed on. It was like…he became part of that bull."

"He ain't much!" snarled Bull while rubbing his sore jaw. "I might just take him out of the competition myself." Bull's hatred for Stick was clear. Never before had anyone made a mockery of him, but now he felt as though people were secretly laughing everywhere he went. No. He wouldn't rest until he had obtained sweet revenge.

"Well, just in case you don't take him out, I want to double up on the number of shows we make. The more chances I have to win, the more chances I'll have to stay ahead. Check the PRCA roster, Phil," Hardy ordered. "I want a different show every night. If we can't make it driving, we'll fly."

Phil nodded and glanced at Bull, who was still staring after Stick. Remarkably, they were no longer enjoying themselves. Phil trusted his instincts, and they told him that Stick Slaton was not one to lose—even in a match against Bull Hawthorne. Sure, Bull blamed his loss on the liquor, but Phil had a notion that Stick hadn't shown them the full extent of his capabilities during the fight.

Shelly Tanner met Stick halfway between the arena and the grandstands. She jumped up and down and clapped her hands with excitement as they approached one another.

"What a wonderful ride!" she exclaimed and threw herself into his arms. She wrapped her hands around his neck and kissed him on the lips.

Her forwardness took Stick completely off guard. He dropped his rigging and held Shelly by the shoulders. After the kiss, he held her at arm's length and smiled.

"Glad you enjoyed it," he said, laughing.

Stick shifted his gaze to a group of people standing behind her. Anna stood next to Dusty, who carried Bobby on his shoulders. The three of them witnessed the kiss. For some unconscious reason, Stick looked directly at Anna, who quickly averted her eyes.

"Good ride, son," said Dusty, "but pardon me if I don't kiss you."

"Thanks," returned Stick. "Say, why don't we go into town and grab a bite to eat and celebrate? How 'bout it, Bobby?"

"Yes, sir!" he exclaimed. "Can we eat pizza?" It wasn't often they ate out. But when they did, Bobby preferred pizza.

"You bet, cowboy!" agreed Stick. Then he lifted Bobby from Dusty's shoulders and set him on his own. "Let's go."

Just a short while later, they were seated around a table, waiting for their order.

The pizza parlor was unusually crowded, a spillover from the rodeo and carnival. Many of those in the crowd had seen Stick win the bull-riding event, and several stopped by to congratulate him, while others simply patted his back in passing. "Here you go, partner," said Stick as he slid a small box across the table to Bobby.

Bobby's face lit up, and he reached for the box. He quickly pried the top off and pulled out a beautiful silver and gold belt buckle. A cowboy riding a bull was molded into its center. "PRCA Champion," was written at the top, and, "Cactus Falls, Texas," was written at the bottom.

"She's all yours, cowboy."

Bobby's expression gave Stick a thrill. He loved to see the boy get excited.

"Wow!" exclaimed Bobby. "Thanks a lot, Uncle Stick!" He studied the buckle at length, only taking his eyes off of it long enough to smile at Stick, who, in Bobby's mind, was the greatest uncle ever to live.

A moment later, the pizza was delivered to the table. Bobby still eyed the buckle, too excited to even set it down and eat. "Hey, cowboy," said Stick to get his attention.

"Sir?" answered Bobby.

"I want you to wear that buckle and think of me every time you put it on. I'm going to be gone for a little while, and I don't want you to forget me."

Bobby's smile faded, and a look of apprehension took its place. "I could never forget you, Uncle Stick. But where're you going?" he asked with concern.

"Well, I'm going to be on the road for a while." Stick found himself struggling while having to explain. It hadn't occurred to him that Bobby didn't understand that he would be leaving.

"Can't I go with you?" Bobby asked softly.

Stick glanced at Anna, who stared solemnly at her plate. "Well, not this trip, partner. But maybe your mother will take you to see me ride."

"But why do you have to leave? I don't want you to go," he said sadly.

"I won't be gone that long, and I'll call you on the phone." Stick promised. He was beginning to wish he had never said anything. He felt terrible for adding heartache to the boy's declining physical state.

"I love you, Uncle Stick. I want to go with you," Bobby persisted.

Stick looked around the table, noticing mutiny in everyone's eyes. He was sure that it was only his imagination, but what was he to do?

Tears formed in Bobby's eyes. He stepped down from the table and walked around to Stick, throwing his arms around him and holding him tight. His painful expression was almost unbearable. "What if you don't ever come back?" Bobby asked with his face pressed against Stick's side. "I'm afraid. You might not come back. Don't go."

Stick didn't claim to be a genius, but he was smart enough to know what was going on inside the boy's head. Bobby had lost his real father, and now he was afraid of losing the only father figure he had. Stick held him tightly and kissed him on top of the head. "I'll be back. Don't you worry about that."

"Well, I think it's about time that we were going," said Anna, both sad and angry. She didn't understand Stick. How could he do this? She felt that the only way to relieve the tension was to take Bobby home.

"Remember," said Stick as he tussled Bobby's hair, "cowboys ain't supposed to cry."

"Yes, sir." He sniffled. Bobby held his mother's hand, and they walked away from the table.

"Dusty," she asked, "would you drive us home? I believe Stick has other plans."

Dusty nodded his head sadly and got out of his chair. "See you later," he said to Stick.

Stick solemnly gestured an acknowledgment with his hand, but emotions welled up in his throat and kept him from speaking. He loved Bobby and the ranch, but this was something he had to do. He found himself completely torn between the two, and he knew that Anna didn't understand.

"Think I'll have another beer," he mumbled. Then he turned to Shelly. "What do you have up your sleeve for tonight?"

"Why don't we go back to the rodeo grounds," she suggested. "The dance will be starting by now. It'll get your mind off of things."

"Shelly," he said seriously, "about that. I'm twice your age. You ought to have those pretty blue eyes set on some lucky young cowboy, like that Hardy Tillman."

"But they're not," she said seductively. "They're set on you." Something told her that Stick was weakened by the moment, and she intended to take full advantage of it. He needed someone right now, and she just happened to be there.

"Well, you should look in another direction," he demanded in a weak sort of way.

Shelly began to act sad, as though her feelings were hurt. She knew Stick wouldn't be able to handle hurting another person, not tonight. "I thought you felt the same way I do."

"It's not that. I like you...very much, but it just wouldn't work."

"You'll never know unless you try," she insisted.

Stick looked deep into her sparkling blue eyes. It was against his better judgment, but she was so young and attractive that he felt himself giving in. "I did try. Years ago," he said to himself more than to her. "Besides, I'll be leaving soon."

"I'll be here when you get back," she returned. The tone of his voice suggested to her that she had already won the battle. Besides, he couldn't out-argue her. Her parents had tried many times, but she always managed to twist words around to work in her favor.

Stick sat quietly for a moment, considering the whole situation. "Oh. What the heck," he exclaimed. "Let's go dancing."

Sometimes Shelly even amazed herself. She smiled with satisfaction, growing increasingly confident in her ability to get her way. Stick stood up and fumbled through his wallet, dropping several bills on the table. He stood and pulled out Shelly's chair, helping her rise, and they headed for the dance.

Chapter Eight

The dance floor was a large, concrete pad nestled in a stand of live oaks. The night was clear, and a welcome breeze rustled the trees. A soft glow from the full moon made area lighting almost unnecessary. Bats from a nearby cave darted in and out of sight, dining on bugs attracted by the lights.

It was late. The band was growing tired when they started their second encore, but the restless crowd just wouldn't allow them to leave. Everything from beer bottles to tobacco plugs were thrown on stage. At 1:00 a.m. the dance floor was still just as packed as it had been at 10:00 p.m.

Stick held Shelly close as they swayed to the beat of a slow song. They had become very familiar with one another in the last few hours and stared deep into each other's eyes. An intense physical attraction pulled them together.

Shelly had carefully calculated her every move, using her feminine qualities as an attorney used the law. She could be deceitful without telling lies, sometimes misleading a person with a mere raised eyebrow. A smile at the right time, a frown, or a pouty lip was all it took.

Now, however, she stared into Stick's eyes with innocence and sincerity, trying to convince him that he was more than a conquest to her. Cowboys were free. They were high spirited and untamed, providing Shelly with a great challenge. She didn't want Stick to learn of her great infatuation for them, that some driving force compelled her to break cowboys as they broke wild horses. Behind her, she had left a long trail of broken hearts, a danger she hoped to conceal from Stick. He was to be her next stepping stone. She'd not rest until his heart had been won.

Since the age of fifteen, she had been dating men in their twenties. Now, at twenty-one, she had probably left more men behind than most women twice her age, Yet, of all the men she had met, none challenged her more than Stick.

With men like Hardy Tillman, the cool confidence in their eyes was really nothing more than arrogance. But with Stick Slaton, it was different. His cold, steel blue-gray eyes revealed not arrogance or pride but a tempered type of confidence developed only through experience.

She heard her grandpa say that only the best trappers ever caught a three-footed wolf. Once a wolf had stepped into a steel trap and chewed his foot off to escape, he was unlikely to be caught again. Stick Slaton was such a wolf. Experience and real honesty dwelled in his eyes. Yes, he would be her greatest conquest yet.

Stick sometimes allowed his actions to contradict his reason. More than once, he had stepped outside his better judgment simply for the sake of satisfying his curiosity. Now was one of those times.

He had a notion that Shelly Tanner didn't know how to be honest. One minute, she seemed an innocent young girl, sweet and harmless; but the next, a manipulative, crafty side appeared, presenting her as a dangerous woman. His senses warned him that she had an ulterior motive for everything she did. *Was she even honest when she thought she was?* He doubted it. Common sense told him to say good-bye and head for the house, but his sense of adventure and excitement overruled.

He would enjoy the moment with caution. Who knew? Maybe this was just what he needed.

A half hour later, Stick held Shelly in his arms as they leaned against his pickup in the parking lot. The lights were turned off, but the full Texas moon illuminated the area, reflecting off the windshield of his pickup. Her face glowed, and her eyes glistened like the distant stars. Stick pulled her close and kissed her, and she rested her head against his chest and smiled. The twilight's obscurity couldn't conceal the victory in her eyes. She listened to see if his heart was beating more rapidly than normal.

"Stick," she whispered, "would you like some company while you're on the road?" She held him slightly tighter to emphasize her anticipation.

Stick quietly thought for a moment, and Shelly felt his chest fill with air. "If I know Dusty, he's already got Anna primed. He'll be planning to go," he said, trying to resist the temptation.

"Yes, but I'm talking about female company." She knew her persistence would be hard to resist.

"Shelly, it wouldn't work," he replied. "You'd get tired of it."

"Not as long as I'm with you."

"Believe me," he argued. "I know. It wouldn't work."

"What makes you so certain?" she asked. Shelly sensed something in his voice that told her she was losing this one.

"I've been through it before," he said, reflecting on the past. "Twenty years ago, when I was riding the circuit, I lost my wife. At first, it was exciting to her, but she soon got tired of it and wanted me to quit. When Becky left, we'd only been married a year."

"Well, I'm not Becky," she insisted. She was growing impatient. "It won't be like that with me."

"Shelly, you can't go. Didn't you hear me say, 'Twenty years ago?' I'm almost twice your age." This was where he would draw the line. "Let's drop the subject. I'll be leaving Monday morning. Maybe I'll see you when I get back."

"Monday morning," she echoed. "That's tomorrow." Sunday morning had begun two hours before. What was she to do? She felt him slipping out of her grasp. "When did you decide that?" she asked.

"Just now," he answered.

"Stick, I wasn't trying to run you off." There was a plea in her voice. How could she change his mind? Should she throw herself at him? Should she appear unconcerned, play hard to get? Throwing herself at him would most likely push him farther away, so she decided on the latter.

"Whatever you want," she reluctantly agreed. "But I hope you aren't making a big mistake. I hope no one comes between us while you're gone." She thought jealousy would be worth a try.

"It's best for everyone," he said, ignoring the threat. "Can I walk you to your car?"

"No thanks. I'm parked just over there," she said and pointed.

"Okay," he said and kissed her again. Only this time, Shelly didn't respond. Stick looked at her for a moment, then stepped into his truck and drove away.

Defeat darkened her appearance as Shelly watched him disappear. Unaccustomed to rejection, she scowled after his shrinking taillights until an idea suddenly changed her mood. "Good night!" She said with a smile and walked to her car.

The aroma of freshly brewed coffee crept into Anna's room, beckoning her eyes open. Her alarm clock was set for 5:00 a.m, but she preferred this method over its annoying buzz. Most mornings, however, she was wide-awake before the coffee even began to brew. It was TK who was responsible for her habit of morning coffee.

Time had not diluted her love for him. There were still moments when she would sweep her hand across his side of the bed, expecting to find him there, almost as if he had never left. Sometimes, she could even smell the scent of his hair on the pillow. She would always love him. He was tender, considerate, and very dependable. In ways, Stick was like him, but in other ways, they were totally opposite. Both, however, underestimated themselves and were really very humble. Anna enjoyed that character trait more than any other, although there were times when it seemed to hinder their ambition.

Anna vaguely remembered the mood she was in when her eyes closed eight hours earlier. It was one that was unfamiliar to her. She kept recalling the way that girl, Shelly, had looked at Stick. He was a bit naïve, she thought. He was a truly wonderful human being, a good man, but he didn't realize that about himself. What a great catch he would be for the right woman. But Shelly was most definitely not the right woman—or girl seemed the more appropriate word. No. Stick needed someone like, well, like herself.

What was she thinking? Why was there a hollow spot in the pit of her stomach? Suddenly, tears welled up in her eyes and trickled down her cheeks. She had cried more in the last month than she had her whole life prior, and she felt her world was in turmoil. She was confused—not so much mentally, but emotionally. She didn't understand the way she felt. It was as though she was irritated over some lack of control. But control over what?

nna's thoughts turned to Bobby. If only she could control his condition, but she was helpless. All she could do was pray, and she had spent many hours doing so. There were no words to describe her love for him. She had learned not to question God, but Bobby was her flesh and blood. She believed that God was sovereign, that He was absolutely in control, and there was a purpose for everything, but even her faith wouldn't allow her to see the rationale behind her son's affliction. The tears began to flow in a steady stream, and Anna no longer restrained the sobs.

It was nearly three a.m. before Stick climbed into bed, so even the Rhode Island Red rooster couldn't rouse him. Instead, it was the sound of Dr. Madison's car in the drive that raised his head from the pillow. Sunday house calls were a thing of the past, but the doc was a longtime friend of the family, so exceptions were made. Regardless of the reason, he enjoyed getting out on the ranch, since it in many ways reminded him of his childhood.

Sunlight shining through the window cast a short reflection on the floor, testifying that the sun had risen some time ago. This, coupled with the smell of overbrewed coffee, burdened Stick with a guilty conscience. He had never been able to sleep late. As a child, he had always been afraid of missing something, and now, as a grown man, he preferred the early morning hours. Besides, sleeping seemed like a great waste of limited time on earth, and thus came the guilt.

Stick knew that Dr. Madison was checking Bobby's symptoms in order to gauge the progression of the disease, a disease Stick couldn't even pronounce. The report would not be good, Stick was sure. Anyone could see that the boy was losing ground.

Being honest with himself, Stick had to admit that he was already witnessing some of the symptoms the doctor had described. Bobby was not as energetic as before, There was a certain discoloration of the skin, and even his eyes showed slight signs of fatigue. Suddenly, Stick was frustrated again.

He held his hands up and looked them over. They were strong. He had always been able to depend upon them. Why couldn't they deliver Bobby as they had himself so many times? He felt as though he was sinking, sinking in a pit of quicksand with nothing to grasp—no hope, only despair. All he could do was sit and watch while his child's condition gradually became worse. His child? Was Bobby really his? Maybe not biologically, but the answer was yes. Stick knew that he couldn't love anyone more. Bobby was most definitely his little boy. Suddenly, he realized that he must tell Bobby.

Stick would be leaving before daybreak the next day. He still had to pack his clothes, load the gear, make necessary arrangements, and determine a schedule. Did he really believe he could win? He couldn't answer that question, but one thing he did know: he had to do something to help, and rodeo was what he knew best. If there was another way to earn the money, a sure thing or just a way with less risks, he wouldn't hesitate to try. He had carpentry skills but could only use them to earn a wage. He could sell what cattle they had, but prices were low, and he'd only get a small portion of the money needed. He could sell his truck, the farm equipment, and the furniture out of the house. Keepsake was a good cutting horse and would likely bring five thousand. The gold nugget crossed his mind again. It had probably washed downstream from the hills on the back side of the ranch. It was a long shot at best. The Texas hill country wasn't known for precious metals. He might look for it for months without finding anything. Still, it might be a good plan B.

All in all, even if he sold everything they owned, they'd still only have half the money needed for the operation. Afterward, he would have no way of making a living. After all, transportation was a necessity, as were tools and equipment. No. The only thing he could do was gamble and hope for three sevens.

Stick wished God was more than an impersonal force, someone he could call on in times of trouble, someone with whom a man could truly have a relationship, someone who would hear and answer. Stick needed a God like that right now, a God who loved people, a God who could and would help.

"I can't do it myself!" Stick suddenly shouted. "I need help!" He looked toward the ceiling. "I need help."

Stick spent the rest of the day preparing for the trip. He entered the Lubbock Rodeo by phone and was told to be there early to pay an entry fee of two hundred dollars. The investment was going to be high. He only hoped the payoff would be much greater.

Shortly after Stick won the world championship, he and TK decided to have a dam built across Backbone Creek, which angled across the back corner of the ranch. Every year during the summer months, the drought dried up the creek, and they were forced to move the cows to another pasture. The dam would enable them to use the pasture all year long.

It took two months to complete the project, and soon after, the first freeze caused the cedars and the mesquites to go dormant, recharging the underground springs. It took only seventy-five days to fill up the area behind the dam. A beautiful, clear water lake formed, and the crystal spring water spilled over the dam onto the rocks below. TK said that it would have been a perfect place for a mill. Although it was never used for it, it became known as the mill pond, TK's favorite place on the ranch until the accident.

Two hours before sundown, Stick and Bobby rode Keepsake to the old mill pond. They went to the exact spot where TK had drowned, carrying fishing poles and a snack. Stick staked Keepsake in a thick patch of Bermuda while Bobby caught grasshoppers and crickets. Afterward, they sat underneath a large, live oak tree shading a large portion of the water.

"You know, Bobby," said Stick thoughtfully. "Nobody ever fished this pond after your dad passed away. I came here a lot right after the accident. I used to sit right here under this tree and talk to your dad. I guess I kind of figured he might still be hanging around or something. Anyway, it always made me feel better. I think he'd like for us to start fishing it again."

Bobby nodded. "Did my dad like to fish here?"

"You bet he did. He was a real thinker. He said he could get more thinking done while he was fishing than anything else. He spent a lot of time sitting right there where you're at, leaning against this big, ol' live oak. His favorite fishing spot was right over there on the dam." Stick pointed to a grassy spot where the dirt dam connected to the wall of the ravine.

"Uncle Stick, do you think he would've liked me? I mean, would I have made him proud?"

"Son," Stick said with a lump in his throat, "your dad would have been so proud of you that, well, I think he might've just busted wide open. You're just what he wanted in a son. You want to know something else?"

Bobby looked solemnly at his uncle. "Yes, sir."

"You're just what I wanted in a son too. I know that I could never replace your dad, but I couldn't love you more if I had been your real father. I kind of figure that…well, that you are mine."

Bobby turned his head and stared at the sun's reflection across the water. A smile slowly made its way across his face. He was happy, real happy.

"Uncle Stick," he said, still smiling, "I know I might die."

The statement caught Stick off guard. They purposefully avoided the subject while in Bobby's presence, so how much he really knew was left undetermined. Stick watched the brave little boy as the wind gently blew his hair into his eyes. For the first time in years, Stick wanted to cry.

"You don't have to worry though," Bobby continued. "If I die, I'm going to miss you and Mom, but I'm going to get to see my dad. Sometimes, I dream about him at night. He's all dressed up in the suit that he's wearing in their wedding picture, and he's real proud of me. And he's smiling. And he holds out his hand to me. And after we shake hands, he gives me a hug. And then he tells me how much he missed me. Sometimes, I feel like I can't wait to see him. So, if I die,"—Bobby looked seriously at Stick—"it's okay."

Suddenly, Stick was so proud that he felt a great, swelling pressure in his chest along with a lump in his throat. His vision became a blur. *How can such a young boy have so much courage?* Stick couldn't hold it back any longer. He felt tears rolling down his cheeks and onto his neck. He turned his head and looked away. Then, he heard TK's voice in a low whisper. "Cowboys ain't supposed to cry."

"Sometimes cowboys can't help it, brother," Stick returned softly.

"Uncle Stick, I need to ask you something," Bobby said in an urgent voice. "I need to ask you a favor."

"Name it, son," Stick said sincerely.

"If I die while you're gone, would you come back and take care of my mom? She'll be all alone. I'm afraid…she'll always be alone. Would you? Please?" he pleaded. There was desperation in his eyes.

"Of course I will, Bobby, but you quit worrying about that. You're not going to die. And your mother won't always be alone. Someday, she'll find someone who'll love her as much as your dad did. She'll get married again. You'll see." The intellectual level of their conversation was disturbing him. Bobby was much too young to be concerned with such things. He sounded like an older man getting his affairs in order.

"No, she won't marry again," Bobby stated flatly. "I heard her tell Brother Pug at church. She said her name would always be Anna Slaton, and she would never do anything to change it."

"Well," Stick said after thinking it over, "I reckon I can understand that." He had never considered it before, but if she married again, her name would change, and she probably would feel as though she was no longer a member of the family.

"Uncle Stick?" Bobby asked.

"Sir?" he answered. There was something else troubling his brow, another question the boy needed to ask.

"Do you love my mother?"

Chapter Nine

Stick had set the alarm before falling asleep, but it was an unnecessary act. With so much on his mind, he had slept very little. His time spent with Bobby at the pond had relieved some frustration and he'd enjoyed it, but in his mind still echoed that one shocking question.

"Do you love my mom?" Bobby asked.

Plucking a grass stem and grinding it between his teeth as a means for delay, Stick eventually answered the only way he could. "Of course I do, Bobby." The question had been pulled right out of the blue. What was the youngster thinking?

"I don't mean like friends," he continued. "I mean...you know...like my dad loved her?"

Stick nearly choked on the grass. "Why on earth do you ask a question like that, son?"

"'Cause…if you were to marry Mom, then you really would be my dad, wouldn't you? And her name wouldn't change, would it?"

"Well, yeah. I mean, no. I mean, I reckon so, but—."

"Do you love her?" he asked again, pushing for an answer.

"Well, Bobby, that's just something a man doesn't go around talking about. Your mom and I, we've been around each other a long time. I'm sure she thinks of me like a brother."

"I'll ask her," stated Bobby innocently.

"No!" jumped Stick. "No, son. You can't do that. That's not the kind of question you go around asking women, even your mom. Okay?"

"Why not?"

"It's just not. Okay? Promise me you won't do that."

"Okay," said Bobby reluctantly, "but I want you to be my real dad."

Stick sat on the edge of the bed and turned on the lamp, smiling as his gaze fell on a picture Bobby had drawn, now tacked to the wall. He shook his head and smiled. The boy amazed him, seeming to have so much figured out at such a young age.

Stick shut off the alarm clock to prevent it from sounding and slid into his jeans. His excitement about the upcoming adventure was slightly hampered by an increasing emptiness growing in the pit of his stomach. He wanted so badly to stay home near Bobby, near his family, but knew what needed to be done. Sure, it was a shot in the dark, but there always remained that small chance. Would Lady Luck now shine on him? The answer lay somewhere in the horizon. Stick slung his duffle over his shoulder and walked out of the room.

As he descended the stairs, his nostrils caught the faint smell of coffee.

"I didn't think you were ever going to get up," came Dusty's voice from somewhere in the darkness below. "We're burning daylight."

"You old coot, I was wondering if you were going." Stick was pleasantly surprised.

"I broke the news to Anna last night. She expected it, I think. She did agree that you needed somebody to take care of you."

"Is that coffee I smell?" asked Stick as he walked toward the kitchen.

"If you must go," came Anna's voice from just inside the kitchen, "you should probably take this."

Anna handed Stick a thermos of coffee, and for a moment, their eyes met. She was worried, knowing well the dangers of the rodeo life. She just knew the phone would one day ring, and Dusty or some unknown voice would tell her that Stick had been injured, perhaps killed.

Stick took the thermos and set it on the counter as Anna stepped close, sliding her arms around his waist. She pressed her cheek against his chest, and Stick hesitantly wrapped his arms around her. He hadn't held her this way since TK's funeral and could feel her heart beating rapidly through the cotton gown.

"Now, Anna," said Dusty, "it ain't like we're leaving you all alone. You've got four top hands to help out around the place."

Anna stepped away from Stick and walked to Dusty, embracing him quickly and kissing his cheek. Then, to avoid becoming emotional in front of them, she left the room without another word.

Stick nodded at Dusty, and the two men carried their luggage out the door. While Dusty threw the bags in the truck bed, Stick loaded Keepsake into the trailer, taking a final look around before opening the door. "What the—?" Stick exclaimed.

The interior dome light reflected off a tangle of blond hair, catching his eye. Shelly Tanner had been asleep on the seat until the light roused her. She lifted her head and looked at Stick through squinted eyes, smiling.

"What is this, Grand Central Station? What are you doing here?"

Shelly stretched her cramped muscles. "Well, you never actually said no, did you?"

Stick stared in unbelief, but his frown slowly softened. He looked through the cab at Dusty, who still stood at the passenger door. The old man shrugged his shoulders, smiled, opened the door, and got into the truck.

"For crying out loud!" Stick took a deep breath, exhaled, and shook his head. "Well, scoot over, but don't say I didn't warn you."

Dusty didn't really approve of the girl, but he couldn't help but admire her spunk. She reminded him of himself. He rubbed his hands together excitedly and patted the girl's leg. He had missed rodeo's adventurous lifestyle, and he couldn't blame anyone for hoping to tag along. Besides, the conversation normally slowed to a crawl between him and Stick after only a few minutes. This gal would undoubtedly help fill in the gaps, not to mention, provide a welcome change in scenery.

Stick started the pickup, wrestled it into gear, and pulled away from the house in a cloud of dust. "It'll take five or six hours to get to Lubbock. Might as well get some rest while you can."

After stopping for doughnuts and coffee in San Angelo, lack of sleep began to take its toll on Stick, so Dusty took over behind the wheel. Stick, with Shelly leaning against his shoulder, rested his head against the passenger door and quickly fell asleep.

After another hour, a road sign read, "Lubbock 5."

"Rise and shine, boys and girls!" Dusty shouted. "Lubbock's straight ahead, and I'm hungrier than a bitch wolf with fourteen suckling pups in the dead of winter trying to climb a forty-foot snow bank while dragging a number nine trap!" He rushed through the dialogue to keep Stick from interrupting.

But Stick allowed Dusty to finish this time. He knew Shelly hadn't heard all the old man's antics, and Dusty just loved to try them out on new people. Shelly laughed, and Dusty got his thrill.

Dusty pulled into the first café that had enough parking spaces for a truck and trailer. The trio got out and stretched their limbs, then entered the small restaurant and found a booth facing the street. Stick had a habit of watching his vehicle, especially when pulling a loaded trailer. They ordered coffee, bacon, eggs, and toast.

"What's the game plan?" asked Dusty.

"You and Shelly drop me off at the rodeo grounds," Stick responded thoughtfully. "Then you find us a place to stay the night. I'll pay the entry fee and see what the competition looks like. When you get back, we'll find a list of this year's shows and work up a schedule."

"You know," returned Dusty, "I've been thinking. The way I see it, you ought to stay with the smaller rodeos until you get back into the swing of things. The competition won't be so tough, and you'll stand a better chance of winning some money. It won't be that much, but it'll be better than nothing."

"Sounds good to me," Stick agreed.

An hour later, Stick surveyed a chart on the wall at the fair-grounds. The heading read, "Top Ten Money Winners," and in the number one position was Hardy Tillman with $11,560. The tenth man on the chart had $7,850.

"Guess I've got a ways to go," said Stick to himself. "But two thousand dollars ain't a bad start."

Stick stepped in line with a few other cowboys paying their fees in exchange for their identification number, which were stamped on a cloth and pinned to the back of the shirt

A middle-aged woman with a red cowboy hat waited on Stick. "Name?" she asked in a businesslike tone.

"Stick Slaton."

"Event?" she asked without looking up.

"Bull rider."

The woman filled out his paperwork and handed him his number and safety pins. "That'll be two hundred dollars."

Stick handed her the cash and put the pins in his pocket. He folded the number and put it inside his shirt. "What's the payoff this year, ma'am?"

"Two thousand for first, one thousand for second, and five hundred for third."

"Thanks. How about a schedule of all the PRCA rodeos this year."

"Which states?" she asked.

This was something Stick hadn't put a lot of thought into. "How about Texas, Oklahoma, Colorado, Wyoming, and New Mexico."

The woman ducked behind the counter and came up holding several pamphlets. She handed them to Stick, and he nodded his thanks.

"Good luck," she said.

"Thank you, ma'am," he returned and walked out the door.

Stick shoved the pamphlets into his hip pocket and stood for a moment, looking into the noonday sky. The sun felt good on his face. A slight breeze brought the scent of cattle to his nostrils as he faced the wind, inspecting a pen loaded with bulls. One bellowed and raked the ground with its hoof, clouding the air with dust and showering its back with debris. Stick smiled and stepped near the bull. "Dusting for flies, huh, fella?"

Stick leaned against the fence, allowing himself to see between the rails. The bull was a cross between Charolais and Brahman. It weighed at least a ton and didn't have any horns. Regardless, he was boss of the pen. The other bulls were younger and lighter. Some had horns, but were not interested in challenging his authority.

"You're a salty rascal, aren't you, big boy?" Stick commented.

The bull obviously did not like Stick being there. He snorted several times and tossed his head from side to side, slinging long streams of saliva. Twice, he bluffed by stepping toward Stick, an effective warning for anyone who might consider climbing into the pen.

"Don't worry, boy. I'm not coming any closer." Stick smiled. "I bet you're fresh off the pasture."

Dusty pulled the truck into the rodeo grounds and spotted Stick at the corral. Stopping the vehicle nearby, he and Shelly got out and leaned against the fence. Stick took the pamphlets out of his hip pocket and handed them to Dusty.

"Put that wise old knob of yours to work and figure us out a schedule. Our young friend, Hardy Tillman, is in first place. According to the chart, he's won eleven thousand five hundred and sixty dollars."

Dusty scratched the stubble on his chin and thumbed through the pamphlets. "The way I see it, with that kind of lead, you're going to have to hit five to six shows a month if you expect to catch him. You know he's going to burn the candle at both ends."

While Dusty studied the pamphlets, Shelly peered through the rails at the huge animals. "Are those bulls for the rodeo tonight?"

"Yes'm," Stick answered. "That's the bucking stock. I reckon this big Brahman cross is the roughest of the lot. Whoever draws his number is going to have his hands full."

Dusty shook the pamphlets to get their attention. "Okay. This is how we're going to do it. We won't hit any winner-take-all shows, only those that pay off first through third. That'll increase our chances. Then we'll only hit the small shows with the small payoffs. The competition will not be as great, and that'll also increase our chances. If we enter enough of them and place, I think we'll do good." Dusty grinned. "You just do the riding. Leave the thinking to me."

Stick winked at Shelly. "Looks like we're headed for trouble."

The trio left the rodeo grounds and went to the motel to rest. Shelly had emptied her savings account and buried the cash in her luggage, using a portion of it to pay for her room. Stick and Dusty took an adjoining room.

Dusty sat in a corner chair, poured a cup of coffee, and rolled a smoke, staring thoughtfully out the window. The main ingredients for riding a bucking tornado for eight seconds were skill and meditation, so he was careful to leave Stick time to contemplate. Stick was lying on the bed with his hands folded behind his head. While staring at the ceiling, he tried to concentrate on the ride—a task proving difficult to accomplish. His rebellious mind preferred other thoughts: the young lady in the next room; a sick little boy waiting back at the ranch; and Anna, whom Stick continuously reminded himself was his sister-in-law.

Stick thought of how Anna had felt in her cotton gown. He had felt her soft form against his chest as their hearts matched rhythm. Then he imagined kissing her moist lips, her eyes closed passionately, her breathing erratic, her body trembling.

Instantaneously, Stick bolted to a sitting position on the bed. What was he doing? What was he thinking? Sweat dampened his palms and forehead as embarrassment rushed over him for thinking of Anna in such a way, a way he had never before permitted. Why was his heart racing again? She was his brother's widow!

"Son, you look like that bull done got the best of you," acknowledged Dusty. "I believe you could use a drink."

"Yeah. Reckon so," answered Stick.

"You ain't getting the jitters, are you?"

"Naw. I was just…I guess I'm just ready to get this show on the road," fumbled Stick. He was glad Dusty couldn't read his thoughts. What a mess he was in. There were two women on his mind. One was half his age, and the other was his sister-in-law, or at least used to be.

Suddenly, the solution was clear. If he allowed himself to become romantically involved with either, the outcome would undoubtedly be disastrous. Besides, he was sure neither really cared about him in that way. Anna would not for a second consider him, and Shelly was just infatuated, just playing a game. No. Stick would not allow himself to think of either in a sexual way. For once in his life, he would do the wise thing.

Satisfied with his conclusion, Stick smiled and went to the restroom to freshen up before dinner. Afterward, he would find time to prepare himself mentally for the rodeo.

Dusty watched the door close behind Stick. Then got up and went to the window. Stick had always been an open book to Dusty, and he knew exactly what was going on. He wasn't stupid. Everything but the rodeo was demanding Stick's attention, and it would be up to Dusty to keep him focused.

CHAPTER TEN

U nfortunately for Stick, he did not draw the big bull for his ride. Instead, a local boy not yet eighteen years old rode the Brahman cross, bringing the crowd to its feet following the magnificent ride. He scored an 85, beating Stick by seven points. Of the twenty other cowboys in the event, only half managed to hang on for eight seconds. Rowdy Collins tied with Stick for second place, and they split the prize money for second- and third-place, netting seven hundred fifty dollars each.

The next few weeks carried Stick across four states, as he rode in rodeos from Big Spring, Texas, all the way up to Laramie, Wyoming. With a handful of first- and second-place finishes and as many thirds, his winnings now totaled $17,750, good enough for eighth place in the rankings. Ten thousand dollars had been sent to Anna's bank account, and the remainder was kept for expenses. Twice, he had crossed paths with Hardy Tillman and his cronies, losing both times to the younger rider. At Abilene Hardy gave his prize money to Bull and Phil, claiming he had already won enough to last the year. He turned to Stick and smirked, rubbing the victory in his face. But Stick could only smile back, nodding a congratulations.

Shelly was beginning to change. Previously she had utilized every opportunity to snare a younger cowboy's eye, futilely attempting to provoke Stick's jealousy. But she had given up such tactics, now appearing discouraged and distant. At Lubbock, she had stood near the chute and cheered for Stick, smothering him with hugs and kisses after the ride; but after Laramie, where he was bucked off and nearly trampled, she rarely watched anymore. At Steamboat Springs, Stick's spur was caught in the rigging, and he was tossed like a burlap sack as the clowns labored to free him. The crowds groans transformed to cheers when he finally hit the ground and ran, but Shelly was nowhere in sight.

When Stick found her later, she was still trembling and clearly had been crying. He held her for a while, and Dusty made his usual jokes to relieve the tension, stating that Stick would do anything for attention. Nonetheless, Shelly's cheerful smile began to fade, and she secluded herself, obviously bothered by something.

In Craig, Colorado, the bull flipped Stick over its horns, hooking his leg and slinging him into the air. Stick crashed down on the back of his head, momentarily knocking him unconscious. Two clowns distracted the bull, while two cowboys carried Stick through a gate. Had it happened a few weeks earlier, upon regaining consciousness, Shelly's face would have been the first object in view. But something had changed.

Stick began to notice a difference about himself as well. Twenty years ago, his condition improved the more he rode. He healed quickly, and his muscles grew stronger as they adapted to the repeated strain of riding. Soreness never lingered longer than a day or two, even after the most terrible wrecks. But now the pain was only compounded by each new day. His muscles and joints were stiff and always ached after traveling long distances in the truck. Almost everything hurt, and although he tried to conceal his condition, it didn't go unnoticed. Dusty's keen eyes didn't miss a trick.

Dusty was careful not to say anything but was wondering how much more Stick could take. Shelly was not as supportive as she had been, and Dusty was beginning to get tired. Day after day, traveling hundreds of miles, eating cold sandwiches, sleeping in roadside parks, and taking baths in truck stops was beginning to get old. The new had worn off. The honeymoon was over. All three were tired.

Stick quit his habit of meditation. His aching muscles wouldn't allow concentration on anything else. So he quit trying, and numbness took over. All he knew now was ride, sleep, eat, drive, rest, and ride again.

At Rock Springs, Wyoming, a bull catapulted Stick into the air, hyper-extending his arm before his grip broke loose. The elbow throbbed, as he had surely strained or torn a ligament, impeding his ability to effectively hang on. Without a speedy recovery, Stick's earnings would decrease drastically.

On the road to Grand Junction, Colorado, with Dusty driving and Stick asleep, Shelly stared thoughtfully out the window while the old man tampered with the radio. Over the past several weeks, Shelly had come to know Stick, learning his strengths and weaknesses. He was a quiet man, mostly keeping thoughts to himself and rarely carrying on a conversation. When he spoke, his statements were matter-of-fact or simple observations, requiring little or no response. Shelly couldn't help but wonder what went on inside his head and if he ever thought about her. He seemed to enjoy her company and offered frequent smiles, but he'd never made any advances. Night after night, she lay awake in her motel room, wondering if this would be the night he would come see her. But he never came. Why?

Something was happening to her. With new knowledge came change, and Shelly was slowly realizing that Stick Slaton was a man whom she would never control. He was too disciplined. She knew he wanted her, but he would never let himself go. For the first time in her life she couldn't have what she wanted, and it scared her. Sure, her pride was damaged, but that wasn't the root of her fear. Admittedly, this was no longer just a game to Shelly, and Stick was no longer just a conquest. Never had she loved a man...until now. She had fallen in love and fallen hard, and all she could do was cry.

Suddenly Shelly grew angry. Seeing Stick climb atop those terrible beasts frightened her, yet he continued week after week. They attempted to trample him and break him and gore the life out of him, but he still returned for more. Why? Couldn't he see what it was doing to her? Didn't he care? Weeks of this strain had heated her emotions to their boiling point, and she felt an explosion coming on. How much more of this could she take?

T he Grand Junction Rodeo, although not classified as a major show, was bigger than what Stick had been entering. Thirty cowboys had paid the three hundred dollar entry fee, making first prize in the vicinity of five thousand dollars.

Dusty drove into the fairgrounds long after the rodeo began. Stick, having entered the event over the phone, had only to pay his entry fee prior to drawing a bull. He wasted no time getting to the office to pay his fee. He was given the number two and would be riding in that order. Stiff from the long ride, he went immediately to the alley behind the press box and began stretching.

Shelly thought seriously about staying in the truck but, after more consideration, decided to find a seat in the stands. Anticipation of the coming event caused her to tremble. What made a one-hundred-and-seventy-pound man straddle a wild, two-thousand-pound animal?

The barrel racing event ended, and the bull riding was about to begin. The cowboys were loading the bulls into the chutes.

"Folks, let me have your attention," came the announcer's voice over the PA system. "Tonight's first contestant for the bull riding event is Topper Boudry. This young man is out of Casper, Wyoming. He's making a lot of waves this year in the PRCA. He's only three places out of the top ten money winners. This ride could put him on the chart. He's riding Gilligan."

Suddenly, the gate was pulled, and the bull burst out of the chute. He jumped into the air and landed on all fours with a jolt, then kicked his hind legs straight up. Topper Boudry lost his seating and slid down onto his hand and rigging. The bull spun right in a tight circle, slinging Topper to the left. Then the bull suddenly changed directions, spinning to the left, smashing a horn into the rider's face. Violently, Topper fell in a heap, and the clowns rushed in, ushering the bull from the arena. A deadly quiet encompassed the stadium, as several men rolled the cowboy onto his back. One man motioned for an ambulance.

"Folks, accidents are going to happen in a sport as dangerous as this. I'm sure this young man would appreciate your prayers," suggested the announcer.

The ambulance pulled through the gate and stopped near the group of men. They wasted no time putting the young man on a stretcher and lifted him into the vehicle.

"Let's give that cowboy a big hand, folks," shouted the announcer.

The crowd applauded as the men closed the doors to the ambulance, but Topper Boudry could not hear them. He would never hear anyone again. One of the cowboys who assisted looked up at the press box and shook his head. They had lost one of their own. The audience sensed the critical nature of the injury, and gloom came over them all.

Shelly Tanner sat quietly in a state of shock. She had lost her color, and if she'd had an ounce of courage left, she lost it too. Her heart was in her throat. She became dizzy and then nauseated.

Sometimes, an announcer's job was very hard. He had the burden of the show upon his shoulders. In times like this, he, above everyone else, must regain composure in order to lift the weight of depression from the crowd. He must set his emotions aside for their sake. "Our next contestant, coming out of chute number four, was once a world champion. He started riding before a lot of you were born. Put your hands together for Stick Slaton. He's riding Goliath, undefeated after thirty-two contests."

The crowd applauded while Stick adjusted his grip. The bull bellowed his disapproval.

Shelly felt faint. She thought about going to the truck but somehow couldn't bring herself to do so. She wanted to cover her face, but she didn't. Instead, with chest heaving, she stared at the arena below. Stick looked terribly small perched on the monster's back. She saw him nod, and the gate swung open.

The bull took one jump and immediately pivoted in counterclockwise circles, violently bouncing and twisting to rid himself of the rider. With each thrust, Stick fought for an inside position, and with each circle, the bull forced him out again. Goliath bellowed his defiance and swung in tighter circles, twisting his back in a way unsettling to most cowboys. All of this commotion and rage took place within a few feet of the gate, but Stick held true to his name and kept his seat.

Suddenly, the bull's rear slammed into the fence, bringing a sudden halt to the circles. This unseated Stick and forced him to the side, but he held on with all his might, hoping for the buzzer. His sore elbow throbbed and weakened, as it slowly lost feeling, but Stick would not let go. Little by little he slid down the bull's side, gripping the creature with his legs, squeezing like a vice. Stick's head narrowly missed the fence, and he knew he would soon be looking up at the bull's belly, waiting for a hoof to meet his face. With every ounce of strength he could muster, Stick held on, and finally the buzzer sounded. Stick released his grip and searched for the ground, discovering that his hand was stuck. Still parallel to the ground, Stick was slung in circles by his trapped hand. The clowns rushed in, and one collided forcefully with Stick's legs, while another met up with the bull's rump. The collision with the clown caused Stick to twist, and he helplessly watched the arena lights swirling above, expecting his final wreck at any moment. A blinding pain shot up his arm as a clown pounced on the bull's back, his painted eyes searching for the hung rigging. Shelly screamed and covered her face.

The clown found the rigging and frantically tugged. The heroic action sprang Stick from the snare. Another clown jumped dangerously close to Goliath's face in a self-sacrificing attempt to get his attention, allowing Stick time to roll away. It worked, and all three men made it to safety.

"Let's hear it for Stick Slaton, ladies and gentlemen, the first cowboy to ever stay on Goliath's back for eight seconds."

The crowd approved, and Stick made his way through the cowboys behind the chutes, headed for the first aid station. Several hands swatted his back as Stick passed, holding his wounded limb. Others congratulated him with a, "Good ride."

Dusty was waiting for him at the first aid station, a mobile doctor's office that looked much like a motor home. "Son, you're gonna give me ulcers. I wish you'd stop taking that double wrap with your rigging."

"Yeah," Stick nodded. "I intended to, but I pulled something in the crook of my arm the other day. I didn't know if I had the strength to hang on."

"You'll have to do something about that little gal too. She's over at the truck just bawling her eyes out. I don't know how much more of this excitement she can stand. Hell, I don't know how much more I can stand either." Dusty looked at Stick's hand. "Is she broke?"

"I don't know. Maybe."

"Well, that was one hell of a ride, son. You go on and get it looked at. I'll see how good the judges were to you."

Stick nodded, opened the door, and stepped inside the first aid station, where a lady in a white uniform waited. X-rays of his hand revealed a broken bone and a dislocation, while the elbow appeared fine. It didn't feel fine, though, so the nurse placed his arm in a sling, bracing the hands with a splint. "It'll be a few weeks before you'll be able to use that again."

Stick nodded. "Thanks."

"Uh huh, like you were listening," she complained.

He smiled and left the office. He was tired, real tired. All he wanted to do was find a bed and go to sleep. His right hand, right arm, and the whole right side of his body were hurting, and he may have pulled his left groin.

"Some cowboy you are," he said to himself, walking back toward the arena. "Probably won't even be able to get out of bed tomorrow." Stick found Dusty wearing all smiles. "You did it, son. You scored an eighty-eight. It'll take a miracle for one of these cowpokes to top that."

Stick nodded. "Judge treated me good, didn't he?"

"Treated you fair, I'd say," answered Dusty.

"Well, I'm ready to find a bed. Why don't you let the press box know and we can meet up with them tomorrow to collect."

"Tell you what," suggested Dusty. "I'll run you and Shelly to the motel, and then I'll come back and watch the rest of the show. I'll pick up your winnings when it's over."

"Deal," agreed Stick.

Stick was asleep as soon as his head hit the pillow, and he awoke in the same position he had last seen. Never could he remember resting so well, despite being a sound sleeper. There was a note on the night stand with five thousand dollars in cash under it. It read, "Took a twenty and went for breakfast. See you later."

Stick managed to pull himself out of bed. A stiff body and achy muscles compounded the growing number of physical problems. Perhaps a hot shower would provide a cure.

Shelly had the same idea. After the shower she intended to slip on her best dress and fix up her hair, touching up with perfume and makeup. Afterward, she would find Stick, and they would have a talk. No longer did owning his heart interest her; she only wanted to win it. She needed to tell him how she felt and convince him to give up this insanity, this suicidal sport called bull riding. The odds were against him. A man could only tempt fate for so long before he ended up like that poor boy, that Topper Boudry. Shelly couldn't stand the thought. Tonight, she would tell him that she loved him and beg him to quit.

After a long, hot shower, Shelly wrapped in a towel and blow dried her hair. A curling iron added body to her hair, and she applied makeup, choosing a bright red shade of lipstick. She examined herself in the mirror and liked what she saw.

Suddenly, there was a knock at her door. It was Stick. She had grown familiar with the way he rapped his knuckles against the door. "Shelly, you awake?" she heard him ask.

Shelly glanced once more at her reflection and then smiled. "Be right there," she answered. She went to the door and opened it, carefully standing behind it so that Stick couldn't see her. "Come in."

Stick stepped into the room. His hand was still bandaged, and his eyes tried to adjust to the dim light. "Dusty went down to the café. You want to go?"

Shelly stepped closer to him, still wrapped in the towel. "No thanks," she said in a sweet voice. "How's your hand?" She leaned forward and closed the door.

Stick lifted his injured hand and looked at her at the same time. He noticed her beautiful curves. "Uh, it's all right, just a little sore. Nothing to worry about," he managed.

Shelly stepped even closer and took his bandaged hand. She

pressed it affectionately against her cheek and then stared seductively into his eyes. He was searching her eyes like her grandfather's German shepherd used to do. The dog was a noble animal, but her actions confused him. He never knew if she was teasing or truly intended to toss him a treat. Stick was frozen in place. She could see he wasn't going to run. Now was the time.

She softly kissed the bandage and then took his other hand and placed it about her neck. She leaned against him and loosened the towel. It dropped to her feet.

"Do you love me?" she asked in her most passionate whisper.

Stick's hand slid down the curve of her back and pulled her until her firm, soft form pressed against him. She was so beautiful. He fully understood her intentions, and he held her for a moment as a war raged within, a war he desperately wanted to lose. He was tired of fighting. The truth was, he did want her. His heart was pounding, and a rush of adrenaline caused him to shake. Surely she felt his heart beating, since he could feel nothing else…nothing but her warm, soft body against his.

"Do you love me, Stick?" she asked again, this time placing her lips softly upon his neck.

It felt good. He closed his eyes to her touch, his heart now pounding in his ears. His will was fading. He would soon belong to her.

"Do you?" she pressed.

Suddenly, Stick knew the answer to her question. He doubted whether he had ever been in love, not even with the woman who left him so many years before. The only one he'd ever really cared about was Anna, but that wasn't really love either. *Or was it?* No, he didn't love this girl. Sure, he was attracted to her, but that wasn't love. Love is when you can't live without someone. Could he live without her? In his heart, he knew the answer was yes.

"No, Anna," he said, "I can't."

The words, "I love you," were forming on her lips when the sting of his voice stopped her. Shelly abruptly pushed herself away.

"Anna?" she echoed. "You called me Anna." She searched his face for the reason but couldn't find an answer. "Stick, it's me. I'm the one who's been with you all this time. *Me*. I'm standing here, offering myself to you, not Anna."

"I know. I'm sorry, Shelly," he apologized. He kissed her brow, pulled away from her, and opened the door. "Dusty's waiting," he said and then walked out. He took a deep breath of fresh air and shook the cobwebs from his clouded mind. He was still trembling. The man in him wanted nothing more than to swathe her sensual frame with his powerful arms and to taste the sweetness of her lips, but his heart stood resolutely against him. He could not contradict the truth by his actions.

Shelly's heart was broken, but not by some insensitive person only interested in entertaining himself. No. Those were her methods. Her heart had been broken by a good man who could have done with her whatever he pleased, a man who cared, a man who did not love her, a man for whom she would have done anything. *It serves me right,* she thought. Shelly knew that Stick would never love her. He wasn't the type to fake emotions, just to take advantage of her. She felt like laughing at the irony of her own misfortune.

"He called me Anna," she said aloud and repeated the name just to hear its sound. "Anna." Stick's voice didn't resonate as though he had made a slip of the tongue. It sounded more like he was actually speaking to Anna, as though he was facing her in his subconscious mind rather than Shelly. Had he been thinking about her the whole time? Why? The answer was painful, too painful. Shelly began to cry.

CHAPTER ELEVEN

H ardy Tillman had been closely watching the chart and saw Stick move into the top ten money winners, where he slowly climbed the ladder. With Bull Hawthorne and Phil McGrawe looking over his shoulder, Hardy studied the list hanging on the field office wall in Corpus Christi, Texas, noting that Stick needed less than ten thousand dollars to bump him out of first. "Lookie there," said Bull, "Ol' grampa himself done moved into sixth place."

"Yeah," Hardy answered. "But he ain't made a major show yet. He's got to be riding in six or eight shows a month to make that kind of money. Nobody can keep up that pace."

"You watch," Bull added. "First time he gets hurt, he'll quit."

Phil rubbed his chin thoughtfully, considering the impact of Stick's knuckles. "I don't know, Bull. He's pretty tough."

As much as Hardy wanted to dislike the man, he couldn't. There was just something about Stick Slaton, something that made Hardy take stock of his own life.

The past six weeks of bull riding had left their mark on Hardy, and he was half Stick's age and in excellent condition. Logic guaranteed Stick to be damaged and slowing, especially since he had ridden in twice as many events as Hardy, yet he seemed undeterred. Certainly ranch work had kept Stick in decent shape, but nothing prepared a man for the punishment received in bull riding except riding bulls. What unseen force drove this man? There was a certain quality about Stick that Hardy admired, a quality he knew was lacking in himself. Stick had nothing to prove to anyone. He had already won the world, so what brought him back to deadly bulls at an age when he should have been riding rocking chairs? He had been the champion, the best, number one. Why now, so many years later, would he try it again? Some driving purpose rested beneath the surface, a noble purpose forbidding Stick to quit, no matter how rocky the road. The man's determination was unnerving.

Hardy knew Stick respected him. He could see it in the older man's expression. It was a certain look, an acknowledgement, an admiration stemming from common experiences of difficulty. Hardy had competed directly against Stick twice in the past few weeks, beating him both times, but he knew it was luck of the draw. His bull had performed better. But Stick had made no excuses, clearly regarding Hardy highly, deeming him a worthy opponent. Although they were adversaries, they both were still bull riders. Suddenly, Hardy was tired—not physically or mentally. He was tired of himself. Everybody liked Stick Slaton, while he had no real friends of his own. Even Bull, if he was honest, would have to admit his admiration for the man. Of course, pride would never allow such an admission. Hardy knew that his two cohorts were not around because they enjoyed his company. On the contrary. They despised him, only tolerating him for the benefits he carelessly bestowed. They were much like the women, only attracted to the money and self-promotion. But Hardy was tired of meaningless relationships. He wanted more.

Strangely enough, Hardy began to think of the woman who had been with Stick the night of the dance. She was very attractive, even beautiful in a wholesome sort of way. Hardy had intended to use his boyish charm, his confidence, his charisma to entice her, but something in her expression had caused him doubt. She saw right through him. It was as though he had been stripped naked, leaving no mask to hide behind. He had felt totally exposed, and she had been unimpressed. And no wonder. In those few moments, she had probably compared him to Stick Slaton, leaving him with little hope. Who was the woman? What was her relationship to Stick? What was her name?

A nna sat on her bed, watching the sun go down. The window allowed a view of the northwest, and somewhere in that direction, Stick was preparing to ride in a rodeo. With her fingertips she traced the figure on the buckle Stick had given Bobby, as tears rolled off her cheeks, dripping onto the silver and gold prize. Crying again? Would she ever run out of tears? Why hadn't he called?

Fifteen thousand dollars had been wired to her bank account over the last several weeks, the latest coming from Grand Junction, Colorado. Although the money had paid for Bobby's tests and medications, the real expense was yet to come.

Suddenly, the knob on her bedroom door turned, and she heard it creak open.

"Momma," came a feeble voice, "Brother Pug is downstairs." Bobby stepped into the room. The effects of his illness were shocking even to Anna, as she had helplessly witnessed his slow decline over the last couple of months. Along with a loss of weight and appetite, his skin was terribly discolored, and obvious rings darkened his eyes. And his poor hair! The medication had caused it to fall out.

"Okay, son. Tell him I'll be right down."

She was glad that Pug Bond came to visit. He was a man of faith, and faith was what she needed at the moment. Pug had been pastor of Hillside Baptist Church for sixteen years, which TK had attended regularly until his death. Stick wasn't one to listen, but he once said, "If I was ever going to church, it would be Pug Bond I would hear preach." Anna and Bobby rarely missed.

Anna dried her eyes on the sleeve of her blouse, set the buckle in the window sill, and started out the door. She felt weak. The fact that Bobby was losing his appetite had taken away her desire to eat. She wouldn't cook just for herself.

Dressed in a dark blue suit, Pug sat at the kitchen table, smiling and cheerful as always. Folks found it easy to be around Pug, which made him unlike the majority of preachers. Most gave people a feeling of guilt, intentional or not, but Pug never did. He was born and raised in Cactus Falls, and everyone knew him. He had grown up just as rough as everyone else—working hard, fighting hard, riding hard, and now, preaching hard. He was the genuine article.

Anna recalled Pug from their days at school. He enjoyed pulling pranks and was generally mischievous. Because of that, he was in trouble a lot, receiving more paddlings than anyone in their class. After he graduated, it seemed that God boldly put forth his hand and touched the young man, changing him forever. Many of his friends waited patiently for him to return to his old ways, but it never happened. Whatever Pug experienced was permanent. He had become a very reliable person.

"Hello, Pug," said Anna as she entered the room. "It's good to see you."

Pug nodded a greeting. "Just wanted to check in on you and little Bobby. I've been thinking a lot about you lately. I heard that Stick was off chasing rodeos."

Anna took a seat at the table and folded her hands in her lap. "Pug, I don't expect that most people would understand. But, well, I think Stick felt helpless. The rodeo is his way of…of trying to help. He didn't know what else to do. He's always been one to take chances."

Pug smiled. "Don't I know it. I was just sitting here, thinking about the time I stuck that dead minnow in the band of his cowboy hat." Pug started chuckling. "He kept smelling this"—Pug laughed slightly harder—"this dead fish smell. You know how awful that can be. I was watching him." His laughing came even harder. "He started kind of cutting his eyes back and forth, and I could see his nostrils flare every time he would try to pinpoint where it was coming from." Pug stopped telling the story to wipe tears from his eyes. "When someone would walk by…he would…he would sniff them. Ha ha ha! Then he…he started smelling his armpits…and the inside of his shirt. By the end of the day…that minnow…it was…it was ripe. It was all I could do to keep from crying. Finally…ha ha ha…finally he comes up to me and says in kind of a whisper…'Man, somebody around here died! They stink like a dead fish.' Ha ha ha!"

Anna suddenly burst into a good, long laugh, and Pug leaned against the table, gasping for breath. Gradually, the laughter came to a stop, and Anna dried her eyes with a napkin, feeling much better. She needed that.

"When he found out what I did," Pug said, smiling, "he lit into me like a windmill in a West Texas wind storm. I was twice his size. I ended up sitting on top of him with my hands around his throat. I didn't think he was ever going to calm down."

"Yeah," said Anna. "TK said that you were the only one in school that could whip Stick."

"Yeah. I reckon that was so. Good thing for me too."

Anna and Pug sat quietly for a moment, reflecting on the past. It seemed like a long time ago. The memories were good.

"Anna, when are you going to get married again?" Pug asked with compassion. "It's not good for you to—."

"Grow old by myself?" Anna interrupted.

"Anna, you're a lovely lady. You've got a lot to offer. You're a wonderful mother. Why don't you find someone, marry him, and have more kids? It's not too late."

"Who?" she asked in order to make a point.

"I've got a notion," said Pug wisely. "But I'd rather not say."

"I'm a Slaton, Pug," she noted. "It wouldn't seem right to let that go. I just can't bring myself to . . . even consider it. Do you mind if we talk about something else?"

"Sure. I understand. Besides, that's not the reason I came out here. I'm here because I wanted you to know that I care and I wanted to pray with you. Would that be okay?"

Anna nodded and Pug knelt on the floor, taking her hand in his. "Lord, we come before your throne today with the knowledge that You are in control. We know that You love us and that Your foreknowledge is infinite. Therefore, we put all our trust in You. Lord, there is nothing we can do to help the situation that little Bobby is in, but we know that You can. We ask You, Father, to heal him. We ask that You would receive honor and glory unto Yourself, and we know that all things happen for the good. Lord, I ask that You would provide Anna with a husband, someone with whom she can share the rest of her life. You know who that man should be. These things I ask in Jesus' name. Amen."

Pug stood up and released Anna's hand. "I hope you don't mind my throwing that last part in."

Anna smiled and shook her head.

"Good," Pug allowed. "I'll continue to pray for you and little Bobby."

"Thanks," said Anna. "And thanks for coming out. You really cheered me up."

"That's what a brother is for," he said and walked out the door.

Bobby walked slowly into the room. "Mom, where is Uncle Stick?" he asked.

"I don't know, Bobby, maybe somewhere in Colorado. He sent money from there."

"Is he coming back?"

"Sure he is. And I bet he brings you something when he does."

Bobby looked sadly toward the floor. "I miss him real bad."

"Me too," she replied. "Me too."

Chapter Twelve

With his damaged hand resting on the steering wheel, Stick gazed thoughtfully at the road, considering his strategy for Hardy Tillman. The young man had just won first at Corpus Christi, extending his lead by another eight thousand dollars. The kid had a natural ability Stick couldn't help but admire. "Dusty, we ain't going to catch him unless we start entering the bigger shows. If he keeps winning, the gap between us will be so wide that we won't have a chance."

Stick was sure of it.

Dusty rubbed his chin. "You're getting pretty good, son. But the smaller shows are why you're in the top ten right now."

"Yeah," agreed Stick, "but the pace is wearing me out. We barely have time to eat, and I don't know how much more of this my old truck can take. Let's go for the big money."

Dusty opened the glove box and took out the schedule. "Well,

Santa Fe is in two weeks. But let's stay with the smaller shows until then, maybe give your hand a chance to heal. You're going to be using your left now, and that'll throw you off a bit, take some getting used to. What do you think, Shelly?" Dusty was watching her. She had been very quiet.

Shelly glanced at Dusty, offering an expressionless nod. She was clearly no longer happy. As her spoiled attitude had slowly been shed, Dusty had come to like the girl and enjoyed her company. But at some point over the past few days, an incident had occurred to bring despondency to her demeanor. It wasn't the long rides or the dangers of bull riding. It was something else. The thought caused Dusty to focus his attention on Stick.

But he was hundreds of miles away, staring through the side window at a little boy wearing a red cowboy hat. Pistols hung at his side, and he rode a stick horse. Clinging to the back of his neck was, of all things, a baby raccoon. Stick smiled reflectively. His mind was on Bobby.

T wo years ago, Lukey Flatt found a nest of baby raccoons in the barn and showed them to Stick and Bobby. They were hungry, as their mother had clearly been gone for days, introduced to some unknown misfortune.

Filling a box with old rags and straw, Stick and Bobby made a new home for the orphans, rearing them on bottles until they were old enough to eat solid food. Then Bobby began catching small frogs and minnows from the pond to feed them, and after two short months, the critters could no longer be contained. Anna found them in her kitchen cabinets, in the laundry, underneath her bed, in the closets, and even splashing about in the toilets.

Stick and Bobby built a large cage, cut a small tree, and fastened it to the center. They sat for hours watching the animals play,

Bobby laughing in that way Stick loved most. The creatures were more humorous than a circus full of clowns.

Bobby took a special liking to a small male whose coat was much darker than the rest. His tiny black mask was almost camouflaged by the equally colored fur, and his friendly nature assisted Bobby in choosing a name: Luke. Luke would climb up Bobby's shirt and onto the top of his head and then reach his little fingers into Bobby's ears. It must've tickled to the point of being unbearable. Bobby would allow the pet to continue until he could no longer take it, laughing so hard that everyone watching would join in.

After four months, Bobby determined that it was time to release his pets into the wild. He opened the cage, and the curious raccoons waddled their way to freedom—all but Luke. Stick watched him run straight to Bobby, climb up his pants leg and back, and then perch himself on top of the little boy's head as he'd done before. Immediately, the animal began sticking his agile fingers into Bobby's ears, again making the boy laugh hysterically. It dawned on Stick, as he watched, that the raccoon loved to hear Bobby laugh. He would stop tickling him, wait until Bobby quit laughing, and tickle him again. The two became inseparable. Luke followed Bobby all over the ranch.

Then, one day, tragedy struck the community. Big Tom Wiese was driving his tractor over a wooden bridge, which his father had built many years before, when a support gave way and his rear tire fell through. Tom fell to the dry creek bed only twelve feet below and would have survived, had the tractor not crashed down on top of him. He lived long enough to explain what had happened.

Little Tommy Wiese was Bobby's best friend. They were the same age and attended school together, and after the funeral, Bobby took Luke to Tommy's house, hoping to cheer him up. When he returned, the pet wasn't with him.

"What did you do with Luke?" Stick asked.

"He went to live with Tommy," Bobby said almost tearfully.

"Why?" queried Stick.

"'Cause," explained Bobby, "I used to think about my dad all the time—how I wished he was with me and how I wished I knew him. Sometimes, I was sad. When Luke came to live with us, I quit thinking about my dad all the time. He made me happy. Maybe Luke will make Tommy happy too."

Stick put his arm around Bobby, pulled him close, and fought to control his emotions. Bobby loved that funny little varmint more than any pet he ever had, but he must have loved Tommy more.

Luke lived with Tommy for more than a year. The boy kept him on a leash, bringing him to school often. More than once, Mrs. Wiese told Stick and Anna how much the pet had helped her son through the crisis.

One day, Stick drove to pick Bobby up from school. He waited for a long time in the parking lot, but Bobby never showed. The boy frequently stayed late to help his teacher with classroom chores but was rarely with her for more than thirty minutes. Stick became concerned. Finally, after an hour, he decided to check on his nephew. He got out of the truck and began walking across the school grounds toward the entrance to the building, where Bobby met him, red-eyed and sorrowful.

"Is everything okay?" asked Stick.

"Luke is gone," Bobby explained. "Tommy had him tied on the playground. When we got out of class, there was nothing left but his leash and the collar. He must've gone into the woods."

Stick put his arm around Bobby. "Have you been helping Tommy look for him?"

"No sir," was Bobby's answer. "Luke finished what he came to do."

"Oh." Stick nodded. "Then where have you been?"

"I was helping Tommy cry," the boy explained.

Stick remembered the compassion in his nephew's eyes. He could learn a lot from the boy. He smiled. It was time to call home.

F our hours later, Stick was straddling the back of Sidewinder, a
four-year-old Brahman cross, in Mineral Wells, Texas. With
his right hand of little use, a nearby cowboy assisted Stick in secur-
ing his left hand to the rigging. The feeling was awkward, but he
had ridden this way before, just a very long time ago. Knowing only
practice would acclimate him to the new grip, Stick nodded, and the
gate slung open.

Sidewinder was an ugly, spotted bull with thick curly hair and
sharp horns nearly a foot long. He sprang from the chute and darted
sideways, instantly dumping Stick to the ground. The clowns rushed
in to help, but not before the bull drove a crushing blow to Stick's
side, snapping his lower rib.

"That cowboy's hurt!" exclaimed the announcer. "Get him out
of there!"

Sitting in the alleyway with her back to the arena, Shelly jumped
to her feet and climbed the fence, watching as Dusty and three other
cowboys carried Stick to safety. "Somebody get a stretcher down
there," ordered the announcer.

Shelly forced her way through the crowd of onlookers and ran
up to Stick as four men, using a stretcher, carried him to the first aid
station. She caught his hand, and Stick looked at her and smiled.

"Nothing to worry about," he said through the pain.

They carried Stick into the first aid station and laid him upon a
table, where a doctor immediately listened to his breathing through
a stethoscope. A frown appeared on the doctor's face, as he shifted
the chestpiece to Stick's neck, then back to his chest. "Cowboy," he
said, "I hate to tell you this, but you're dead."

"Huh?" Stick replied. "Doc, I'm hurting too bad to be dead."

"Well," continued the doctor, "I'm having a heck of a time finding your pulse."

Stick appeared relieved. "Oh. I thought it was something serious. Doctors have been saying that all my life, that my pulse is really slow. Reckon it's my cold heart." Stick winked at Shelly.

"Are you okay?" asked Shelly, her voice trembling.

"Sure I'm okay. I just got the wind knocked out of me. That's all."

"I'm afraid it's a little more serious than that," said the doctor. "You've got a broken rib. Nothing much we can do about it, though. I'll wrap it up, but you'll have to take it easy for a while."

Stick winked at Dusty. "Doc, my pop used to say that pain comes from your brain and riding hurt is a simple case of mind over matter. If you don't mind, it don't matter."

"That may be so, Mr. Slaton, but a man's bones are what keeps him from being like one of those rubber wet suits that divers wear. If you keep breaking them, there'll be nothing left to hold your skin in the air."

Stick smiled. "I understand, Doc, but I reckon that's a chance I'll have to take."

Late that evening, Dusty drove the truck to a motel called The Boots and Saddle, and as usual, Stick purchased adjoining rooms.

Shelly slumped onto the edge of the bed and fell backward, staring at the ceiling and wondering why she stayed around. Was she hanging onto some thread of hope that Stick might change, that he might grow to love her as she did him? Of course. Because she certainly wasn't enjoying the rodeos. Perhaps she would give it another week or so.

Dusty stepped out of his room and took a deep breath of night air, intending to visit the lounge across the street for a nightcap or two…or three. Stick clearly wanted some time alone. The way he'd watched that little boy with the cowboy hat earlier could not have been more obvious. Stick missed home. He reluctantly picked up the receiver and dialed the phone. Why was he so apprehensive about this call? He knew the answer, even before the question came to mind. He was afraid he would get more bad news about Bobby and Anna would try to persuade him to come home. She would make perfect sense in her approach, and he would be riddled with guilt after refusing to comply.

Stick had always faced trouble head-on and would tackle a grizzly bear with a pocket knife if necessary; but when those he loved faced adversity, it shook him to the core. Standing helplessly by the wayside and watching had never come easily, even though oftentimes there was no other option. He hated hospitals and funerals, never sure of how to comfort the wounded.

A neighbor's home had once burned to the ground, destroying everything. As the family tearfully sifted through the rubble, Stick had been forced to walk away because he couldn't bear the sight of their pain. But what else could he have done? When others encountered trouble, guilt and heartache always spurred Stick into action, if there was anything that could be done. But was he using rodeo as an opportunity to help or an opportunity to escape reality? The question deserved serious thought.

Anna heard the telephone ring and somehow knew it was Stick. Her mother only called on Wednesday nights after church, while her five older brothers never did. She knew they loved her, but they had busy lives of their own, and she rarely heard from them. In fact, the last time they had all been together was at TK's funeral. She thought it a shame that it took a tragedy to bring a reunion. So perhaps it was a process of elimination rather than woman's intuition that told her who was calling. Regardless, she excitedly dried the dishwater off her hands and moved toward the phone.

Bobby also knew that it was his Uncle Stick who was calling. After all, the telephone hadn't rung since Brother Pug had called, promising to call again next week. So Bobby, although weak, ran to the extension and answered.

"Hello." His voice shook.

Stick was aware of the noticeable difference in Bobby's condition after the one word, but he couldn't help smiling. The boy's voice was like fresh rainwater on the desert floor. "Hey, partner. How's it going?"

"Uncle Stick, where are you?"

Anna picked up the kitchen extension and listened.

"We're in Mineral Wells."

"Are you coming home now?" asked Bobby with anticipation.

"No. We're going to Santa Fe, New Mexico, next. Then, right after that, we're going to Houston. Do you think your mom would drive down to meet us?"

"I can ask her," exclaimed Bobby.

"Okay, but first tell me how you're doing."

"I'm fine. I'm just not ever hungry, but I try to eat anyway because it makes Mom feel bad when I don't."

Stick remembered Dr. Madison's words and knew the disease was progressing. "How's your mom doing?"

"She's okay I guess. I think she's kind of sad though. She misses you. I do too. When are you coming home?"

"Well, Bobby, I'm not sure. I'm in the top ten right now. That means I can go to the national finals. But I miss you and your mom real bad."

"Uncle Stick, I'm afraid that something is going to happen to you. I have bad dreams at night. I'm afraid you're not coming back."

"I'll be back, partner. Don't you worry about that." Stick wanted to change the subject. "Now, what I want you to do is take care of yourself. You've got to eat so you can keep up your strength. Okay?"

"Yes, sir." Bobby hesitated. "Uncle Stick?"

"Yeah, partner."

"I love you."

"I love you too." Stick struggled to choke down the emotion that was swelling in his throat. "Now put your mom on."

"Yes, sir. Bye."

"Bye, son."

Bobby put the phone down, and Anna immediately spoke up. "Hi, Stick."

"Hello, Anna. How are you holding up?"

"Okay I guess. How about you? How many broken bones do you have?"

Stick glanced at the bandage on his hand. "Oh, you know, nothing serious. Just the typical bull-riding stuff. What about Bobby? He sounds pretty weak."

"He is, Stick. He's lost his appetite. And he's lost so much weight you'll be shocked. His skin is discolored. Dr. Madison said we can't wait much longer. Bobby needs an operation within the next forty-five days. The doctor said that when he operates, he'll know if the disease is isolated to the one kidney or if a transplant will be necessary."

"Anna, I wish I could be there with you. The truth is, as much as I hate to admit it, I'm too old for this stuff. But I just can't quit. I—."

"Stick," Anna interrupted, "I don't want you to quit. I've been doing a lot of thinking, and it might sound selfish, but I'd give my life for Bobby. And I know you would too. The money you sent has been a big help. And I want you to know that I would never put the value of money above your life, but if that's what it's going to take to save my son…" Anna hesitated.

"That's okay. That's exactly the way I feel. If a few risks are necessary for even a fraction of a chance to save Bobby's life, then I'm willing to take them."

"The operation is going to cost a hundred thousand dollars, and we've got to have a good portion of it right away," she acknowledged.

"Yeah…well…I guess our only hope is the national finals."

"Stick," Anna said desperately, "Please … don't quit. I don't know what else to do. We need you to win."

"I will. You can count on it. Will I see you and Bobby in Houston? I need to see you."

"Yes. We'll be there. I think we'll leave a few days early and stay with Mom and Dad. It's been awhile since I've seen them."

"Good. That'll make them happy." Stick was feeling much better. "Anna, it'll be really good to see you."

"Bobby and I'll be looking forward to it. And there's something … I feel I must tell you."

"Go ahead," Stick said.

"I will … when I see you in Houston."

"Okay … in Houston," he agreed.

"Stick," Anna said with apprehension, "I want you to know that … I … appreciate you very much."

"Heh … it's my pleasure," he returned. "Goodnight," he said and eased the phone to the hook.

Anna held the phone to her bosom and fought her emotions. That was not what she wanted to say. She wanted to say much more, to tell him exactly how she felt. She wanted to tell him that she loved him. Yes, she loved him. With all her heart, she loved him. But how could she say such a thing? He was her ex brother-in-law. They had to live in the same house. What if he didn't feel the same way? There was no reason for her to believe he did. To make that mistake would be a catastrophe.

Anna put the receiver on the hook and sat down at the table, releasing a long sigh. She just wanted a normal life … a complete, healthy family. Instead, turmoil seemed to hover overhead, awaiting the opportunity to dive into her life. And she was tired, so very tired.

Chapter Thirteen

Hardy Tillman increased his lead by another six thousand dollars. His back was stiff from what could have been disaster in Las Vegas, New Mexico. Perhaps his mind hadn't been fully focused on the ride. Regardless, the bull had turned quickly to the left after going airborne and landed hard on his front hooves. His hindquarters were twisted to the side, unsettling Hardy. The sharp turn caused him to lose his grip, and he fell quickly to the ground, the bull's hind leg landing in the center of his back. He failed to place.

Prior to that, he had placed first in Tulsa. The win had given him enough of a lead to take a break after being injured in Las Vegas. So, although still sore, he was prepared for Santa Fe. During registration, a quick glance at the list of contestants told Hardy that Stick Slaton would be there. He was glad. Why? He wasn't sure.

Hardy had been keeping close watch on the charts. Stick Slaton remained in sixth place, while Hardy had extended his lead by winning over twice what Stick had won. He heard that Stick had failed to score in his last three rides. With just three weeks until the finals in Ft. Worth, Hardy could coast and probably not lose his position. But he wasn't one to coast.

The Santa Fe Livestock Show and Rodeo had thirty contestants in the bull-riding event. The rodeo would last three nights, with ten cowboys riding each night. Hardy drew the number eight spot, so he would be riding the first night, a position he did not prefer. Stick had drawn number twenty-four and would be riding the final night. Ironically, both cowboys drew the same bull, a magnificent brute called Sudden Impact. He was infamous in that he was undefeated and was known to have injured several cowboys. One was paralyzed.

Stick would have the advantage. The draw gave him the opportunity to study the animal while Hardy rode. There were more than likely other cowboys present who had attempted to ride the bull in the past. Hardy would nose around to see what he might find out. Among the contestants were three other cowboys who held top-ten positions. Hank Gilpen was in second place with $32,480. Frank Hysler was in seventh with $22,450, and Chris Shockley was in tenth with $21,250.

Hardy had kept his eyes open but had not yet spotted Stick Slaton. The sixth cowboy had already ridden, and Hardy was getting prepared. He had spent the last hour behind the bucking chutes in the alley, stretching his limbs and trying to work the soreness from his back. The bruise had left a large knot in the muscle on the right side of his spine.

Hardy eased down onto the back of Sudden Impact. He gripped the rigging and took a wrap. Somewhere in the fog of his mind, he could hear the announcer's voice and the applause of the crowd, but it was all indistinguishable. His sixth sense told him that if he was to ride this animal, it would require total concentration. Hardy's sudden feeling of discomfort was more than stiffness from the injury. It was as if an inner voice was telling him not to ride. He had looked square into one of the bull's black eyes before climbing the fence and saw his own reflection, noticing a red glow in place of his eyes. Hardy shrugged. Perhaps it was the arena lights.

Two cowboys had ridden the full eight seconds. Chris Shockley scored a 78 and a local, Ben Stanton, scored a 79. The press box was paying the top five positions.

Hardy jammed his black hat over his ears, set his head rigidly between his shoulders, slid forward, and nodded. The gate flew open. The bull became a sky rocket, flying into the air from within the chute. The sudden impact, when all four hooves hit the ground, jarred Hardy to the bone and made him aware of how the bull got his name. The enormous beast bellowed his fury and jumped twice into the air, twisting his body. He began to whirl to the left. Each time, his rear made an exaggerated swing until his body formed a U shape.

With each swing to the left, Hardy was forced to the right, but he kicked and fought to retain his position. Each time, an agonizing pain gripped his back, almost paralyzing him. Hardy felt himself losing the fight. Finally, the bull jumped into the air and swung left, and Hardy lost his grip and fell against the bull's rump just as it swung around. The two connected, and Hardy became a human projectile. He landed on his hands first and then the top of his head before flipping onto his back. He tried to rise, and then lightning struck and all went black.

When Hardy came to his senses, he was being half carried and half dragged by cowboys on each side of him. Sudden Impact was still on the rampage, and the clowns worked hard to keep him at the opposite end of the arena. Hardy realized the two men had seized him at great personal risk and rolled his head back to thank his saviors, expecting to see Bull and Phil.

Blood clouded his vision, but he was sure that he looked into the smiling face of Stick Slaton. "Hey, grampa," he whispered and passed out again.

Hardy Tillman received a concussion as well as two black eyes. The ambulance transported him to the hospital for x-rays, where he stayed for the night. It was peaceful. The soft bed and pain killer offered him a much-needed rest.

By the end of the second night, Hank Gilpen was in the lead with an 81, Ben Stanton and Frank Hysler were tied for second with 79, and Chris Shockley and Tyrone Fenton were tied for third with 78. Stick got his second look at Sudden Impact hospitalizing another cowboy.

Stick was infatuated with Sudden Impact. The bull was a hatred-driven killer, and Stick was certain he sought to do harm each time he entered the ring. The bull made him nervous, and Stick knew what that meant—he was afraid. Stick became automatically angry with anything that caused him to fear. He had been afraid of things in the past, and he was driven to master each of them. He would have to master this one also before his turn to ride.

Stick went to the corral where Sudden Impact was kept and stood on the first rail of the fence as the bull watched him closely, pawing dirt in warning. Stick fixed his eyes on the bull and climbed the fence, despite a snort of disapproval. He gently eased himself to the ground inside the pen, staring into those dark eyes. Sudden Impact slung his massive head from side to side, tossing strings of slobber. A minute went by, and then two. After five minutes, Sudden Impact seemed less aggressive. Stick took a step forward, and the bull's ears pricked. He raised his head in defiance. Stick held his ground, his eyes trained on the animal.

Again, five minutes went by. Sudden Impact took his eyes off Stick for a moment and glanced side to side. He was losing confidence.

Stick took another step.

Sudden Impact lowered his head, preparing to charge.

Stick spoke softly. "Me and you have got to understand each other."

Sudden Impact raised his head, ears pricked again.

"I'm going to ride you, and you might as well get used to the idea. There's a little boy back in Texas who's depending on it, and I ain't going to let him down."

Again, the bull took his eyes off Stick. He glanced to his left and then back at Stick. Slowly, he began backing away. Stick smiled at the bull. There seemed to be something going on behind those black eyes. Stick deliberately turned his back and walked to the fence. Once there, he looked back. "See you tomorrow," he said and then climbed the fence and walked away.

Sterling Slaton had taught Stick that trick when he was a boy. He told his son that many a battle could be won before it even started. All it took was a faceoff, like two boxers standing toe to toe, glaring into each other's eyes before the match began. The truth could be seen in the eyes. No matter what had been said, the eyes would reveal the facts. If one was looking into the eyes of his master, he knew it. If one was looking into the eyes of his subordinate, he knew it. The subordinate would lose heart while the master would gain confidence. Sudden Impact had seen his destiny. Stick wondered if he would remember.

The third night began with three local riders hanging on for eight seconds, but scoring low. As Stick climbed the chute, Anna was on his mind. He heard her voice over and over again telling him to win. Never before had he wanted something so bad. He had never cared anything about being anyone's hero, but he wanted to be her hero. "Lord," he said quietly, "if you'll just let me ride…I'll…I'll…" He stopped and shook his head, trying to push the thought of praying from his mind. He remembered something Pug said one Easter Sunday when he accompanied the family to church. The preacher asked, "If you don't need God, then why pray to Him when you're in trouble?"

"Awe…hell. Who am I kidding?" Stick growled.

What kind of deal was he about to make, anyway? How would he have finished the sentence? God didn't need anything. He owned everything already. God only wanted one thing from him. And there was really only one thing he had to give. "God, I'll not be making any deals. I probably wouldn't keep my end of the bargain anyhow. But if you can hear me and if you see fit, I'd sure like to ride tonight."

Stick climbed the chute with Dusty at his side. The two looked at Sudden Impact and exchanged glances.

Dusty whistled. "He's a rank one, son. You up for this?"

Stick smiled but offered no response. He eased onto the bull. "You remember me, boy?"

Dusty pulled the rigging underneath the bull and handed it to Stick. The cowboy took a grip and pulled it tight. "You remember now, boy. You and I have ourselves an understanding."

Stick wrapped it once around his left hand, settled into position, raised his right arm, and nodded. Stick was promptly reminding himself of the bull's pattern as Sudden Impact sprang into the air and came down on all fours outside the chute. Stick was ready, and he absorbed the shock. The bull jumped again and again, then whirled left. Stick compensated with counter thrusts. Never before had he been on such a merry-go-round. The crowd was a blur. The arena lights appeared as one large, circular light. He could feel the bull's power, and he felt himself giving in to the centrifugal force. He was sliding to the side. Suddenly, the bull sprang into the air, but Stick held his grip, straining against the force. Christmas came quicker than those eight seconds. Where was the bell?

Suddenly, the horn sounded, and the crowd went wild. Stick fought to stay on. He was in a bad position. He couldn't thrust himself away from the bull, and he was not in a position to use the bull's motion to catapult himself out of harm's way. He was going down. He had no alternative but to let go. And let go he did.

Stick fell underneath Sudden Impact. He attempted to roll to one side, but the bull's enormous leg came crashing down onto his ankle. Stick heard it snap, and agony scarred his face. Sudden Impact turned with head raised defiantly and glared at his opponent. Stick held his ankle and looked at the bull. The animal pawed the ground and snorted, but Stick didn't move. The bull lowered his head, and Stick angrily returned the stare. Two clowns jumped about frantically, one waving a hat, the other waving a red handkerchief; but Sudden Impact wasn't concerned. He was watching Stick, his massive head shaking, his hide quivering. Then he turned, and as suddenly as it began, it was over. The dreaded bull ran through the gate.

Dusty was immediately at Stick's side. "Heard her snap all the way over to the chute. I swear, son. You're like one of them snowballs rolling down hill. Once you start breaking things, they get bigger and bigger as you go. What's next?"

"How about a hospital," suggested Stick through clenched teeth.

Resolution sobered Dusty's appearance. He understood what this injury meant. He hung his head sadly. "Reckon that's all she wrote, son."

Someone called for the ambulance, and a gate was opened at the opposite end of the arena to allow it in. It was driven to where Stick was lying, and two men jumped out and opened the back doors. They rolled the gurney out and placed it on the ground beside the injured cowboy. Stick assisted as they lifted him up and placed him on the stretcher. For the first time, Stick became aware of the audience. They were applauding.

"Stick Slaton takes the lead with an eighty-eight!" announced the press box.

The roar of the crowd intensified, and Stick stopped the men who were carrying him to the ambulance. He sat up, looked about the arena, took his hat off, and waved to the crowd. Suddenly, the applause became deafening. The crowd came to their feet. Everyone was clapping, whistling, and yelling.

Dusty looked about the arena. Hundreds of people were there, but not a soul was sitting down. Water blurred the old man's vision, and a tear toppled down his cheek. These people loved Stick. The courage and mental toughness he displayed was characteristic of a champion and a tribute to the American cowboy. Stick was deserving of their admiration.

Stick managed a smile through the pain, still waving his hat as the crowd applauded. Then he leaned back onto the gurney and placed the hat on his chest. The ovation continued. The two ambulance drivers were proud to be a part of this as well, smiling as they rolled Stick into the ambulance. With the back doors closed, one of the young men waved to the crowd as if it was he they applauded.

The other young man turned on the flashing lights and drove the vehicle slowly through the gate. Hardy Tillman stood, applauding with the rest of the audience. His head was bandaged, and his eyes were black, but a smile was on his face. He admired Stick Slaton. Maybe he did have an advantage, but the cowboy was good, real good. Phil McGrawe stood at Hardy's left, whistling loudly, and Bull stood slightly behind them, defiant and scowling.

It took three hours for the doctor to x-ray, set, and build a cast for Stick's leg. The cast covered his foot and extended to just above the knee so as not to allow much movement. He was given a pair of crutches as well as strict orders to stay off his feet. A nurse seated him in a wheelchair, propped his injured leg on a rest, and pushed him toward the waiting room. Stick was in deep thought. His heart was burdened with a tremendous responsibility, and a broken ankle made it worse.

Dusty and Shelly were seated on a couch. They saw Stick being wheeled toward them and stood to meet him. Dusty tossed an envelope into Stick's lap.

"Here," he said. "Maybe this'll cheer you up."

Stick opened the envelope and pulled out a check for eight thousand dollars. He stared blankly at the paper, still deep in thought. He knew that it wasn't enough.

Shelly stepped forward, rubbing her hand along the cast. There was peace in her eyes. She wore a look of contentment, glad it was finally over. She was ready to go home. She wanted Stick to be as far away from rodeo as he could get. It was obviously his first love, her only real competition, as she had convinced herself that Anna posed no true threat. No. It was rodeo—a deadly female who was not beautiful but dangerously attractive, not glamorous but viciously exciting, not seductive but shamelessly inviting. How could she defeat such opposition, especially when the one she loved seemed addicted to danger?

Dusty patted Stick on the shoulder. "You moved into third with that ride, son. First time that bull had ever been ridden." He shook his head thoughtfully. "You sure took your share of the undefeated. Too bad it's over."

A furrow appeared in Stick's brow. He looked soberly at his old friend. A world of thoughts became visible in the bull rider's eyes. Dusty saw a resolute glare that had not admitted defeat. What was he thinking?

"It is over, isn't it?" Shelly asked with a plea in her voice. She saw the same thing as Dusty.

Stick studied her face. "Shelly, the doctor said that it was a clean break and that it would heal quickly. There's no rule against riding with a cast. I think I've got a good chance at the finals." He was remembering his promise to Anna.

"Heck of a chance, I'd say," exclaimed Dusty with a smile and newfound enthusiasm.

"No!" shouted Shelly. She glared at Dusty. "You're supposed to be his friend!"

Dusty shamefully averted his eyes and looked thoughtfully out a window. He could not respond to her logic. In a way, she was right. He should try to discourage Stick from continuing, but this wasn't about a title. It was about a family. On the other hand, Stick would be no good to them dead.

"It's got to stop here," she continued, "before you get your crazy self killed. The next time, it could be your neck."

Dusty looked down at Stick and put a consoling hand on his shoulder. "Maybe she's right, son."

Stick leaned back and gazed at the ceiling. He wiped his brow with his good hand. "Look," he said, "this is about a sick little boy and his mother. They're counting on me. I told them I wouldn't let them down, and by George, I'm not going to. As long as I can still function, as long as I've got the breath, as long as I have the opportunity, I'm going to ride." Stick looked at Dusty. "To tell you the truth, Dusty, I'm hurting all over. If all I had to think about was myself, I'd be headed for the house. But I don't want Bobby to give up no matter how bad he feels. Now how can I ask that of him if I'm willing to quit because of how bad I feel? I'd die before I quit. Now, with or without the two of you, I'm going to finish what I started. What's it going to be?"

A tremendous smile wrinkled Dusty's face. "If you're waiting on me, son, you're going backward. I'm heading for Houston."

Both Stick and Dusty looked at Shelly, awaiting an answer.

Her chin quivered with absolute frustration. "All right! Fine!" she responded finally. "Go ahead. But if you get on another one of those killers, don't expect me to watch. I don't know how much more of this I can stand."

Stick took her hand in his. "Shelly, remember a few weeks ago, before all this began? I told you that this was no life for a woman. Remember? But you said that you could handle it."

Shelly began to cry. "Well, I was wrong. I can't stand to see you torture yourself like this. I don't care who you're doing it for. You can't keep it up."

Stick squeezed her hand. "You've got to understand, honey. As long as I'm physically able, I won't quit."

Stick handed the check to Dusty. "Dust, take this and cash it. Wire six thousand back to Anna, give five hundred to Shelly, and hang on to the rest."

"Shelly," Stick said turning to her, "I want you to take the five hundred, and any time you feel like you can't stand anymore, you buy yourself a bus ticket and head back to Cactus Falls. Dusty and I will understand."

Shelly nodded but was too upset to speak.

CHAPTER FOURTEEN

A huge Ferris wheel marked the location of the Houston Livestock Show and Rodeo. People came from hundreds of miles to enter the world-famous Houston Coliseum.

Stick had never seen so many people gathered in one place. Twenty years earlier, the sport didn't attract such a following, but now it was madness. All contestants were allowed to park closer to the arena, but it was still a long walk. Dusty saddled Keepsake so they could tie their gear to the horn while Shelly gazed at the crowd.

Dusty led the gelding while Stick, using crutches, hobbled behind, making his way through a crowd of trucks, trailers, campers, horses, and onlookers. Many of the folks recognized Stick. His growing popularity became apparent at such a large gathering, as fans shouted greetings and waved. He, on the other hand, knew very few of them, although some were vaguely familiar.

They found a comfortable place near the arena opposite the bucking chutes, where it was quiet and bothered by less traffic. Stick took his gear off the horn and eased into a sitting position to stretch.

"I'll see if I can't rustle us up something to eat," said Dusty.

Stick nodded and watched Dusty disappear into the crowd. He looked up at Shelly and noticed that her countenance had brightened. The activity served to distract from her emotional pain. "Shelly," Stick asked, "could I get you to run ahead and get in line for me at the registration office? With all the contestants, the line is bound to be long. I don't know how long I can stand before my leg starts throbbing. I'll catch up in a bit."

Stick dug into his pocket and pulled out enough money for the fee and handed it to Shelly. She took the money without saying a word and followed Dusty into the crowd. Stick pulled his hat down over his eyes and attempted to rest.

Twenty minutes passed, and although Stick didn't actually sleep, he was able to relax. He managed to get on his feet by leaning against the crutches and started toward the registration office.

"Hey, grandpa," came a familiar voice.

Stick looked up and recognized the egotistical mug of Bull Hawthorne. He was eyeing Stick's cast.

"Getting a little slow in your old age, aren't you?" the big man growled.

"Fast enough," Stick replied with a tired smile.

"I saw your pretty little granddaughter strut by a while ago. What's wrong? You getting too slow for her too?"

Stick hadn't the patience to deal with Bull at the moment. Broken leg or not, if the big man wanted another shot at Stick, he could have the opportunity. Stick grinned in a way that Bull remembered very well. "Unless you got other ideas, I'm kind of busy."

Bull's smile faded. He knew Stick was inviting him to jump anytime he felt froggy, but now wasn't the time. He watched as Stick continued on his way. Then, he cupped his hands over his mouth and shouted, "Reckon we won't see you at the finals after all huh?"

Stick stopped and turned once again toward Bull. "Don't count your chickens, son."

Stick left the big man staring at his backside. Bull was obviously confused about Stick's intentions. Could he be thinking about riding with a busted leg? He didn't know exactly what Stick was going to do, but one thing was for sure: If the older man was figuring on being at the finals, Bull was going to do everything within his power to keep that from happening. Hardy had been mighty generous lately, and Stick Slaton was not about to mess that up.

Stick searched the crowd for Shelly. He followed signs leading to the registration office and suddenly ended up face to face with Anna. Their eyes met, and she smiled so sweetly. Stick stood, momentarily soaking in it. That smile was something he had longed for over the past few months. "Hi, Anna," he said. "You're a sight for sore eyes."

She looked him over, her eyes stopping once on the bandaged hand, then the cast. "Just typical bull-riding stuff huh," she said sarcastically but still smiling. "Dusty said that you've broken your hand, your rib, and your ankle, and you've torn a ligament in your elbow."

"He did?" Stick mocked. "Well, that's way out of proportion. The torn ligament is merely speculation. When did you talk to him?"

"Don't worry," she laughed. "He hasn't been calling in reports. I saw him just a moment ago. He told me where to find you. I left Bobby with him at the concession stand."

Stick instinctively looked in that direction, hoping to see Bobby.

"I wanted to speak with you first, Stick. I wanted…"—Anna looked away—"to prepare you."

"For what?" asked Stick.

"For you to see Bobby." Anna focused on the ground. "He doesn't look good, Stick. You'll be surprised. In fact, we can't stay to see you ride. He's too weak. He wanted so badly to see you, and I was afraid…" She hesitated, unable to finish the sentence. "Dr. Madison said it would be okay, if we only stayed for a minute. He came with us. So did Lukey Flatt."

Stick limped closer to Anna. He was becoming distressed. "Anna, where is he? Take me to him. I want to see him now."

"He's so excited to be here," she said, trying to keep her bottom lip from trembling.

"Uncle Stick! Uncle Stick!" came an excited but weak voice, a voice Stick barely recognized.

Stick turned, and Bobby hurried toward him. Dusty and Dr. Madison followed while Lukey limped behind. They stopped several feet away to watch. Stick tried to kneel but couldn't, so he dropped the crutches, balanced on one leg, and lifted Bobby effortlessly to his chest. The boy was rail thin. Tears immediately filled Stick's eyes as he felt Bobby's frailness. His hands and arms were tiny, his eyes hollow and dark, and only a few patches of hair remained. Stick was afraid little Bobby would break if he held him too tightly. His clothes hung loosely about him, and his skin displayed a yellowish shade.

Dusty walked away from the scene. It was too much for him, and he knew nothing good would come from losing control of his emotions. Stick savored the child's embrace and looked sadly at Anna. Her lips trembled. Reality had finally hit home, and she knew her precious little boy was about to die. Stick had refused to think about it. He had refused to believe it. It was as if the whole thing was just a...a what, a figment of someone's imagination, a mysterious vapor, present all the time yet so indistinctive that he was willing to shrug it off, set it aside?

Bobby lifted his head and looked into Stick's eyes. "Uncle Stick, I've got to ask you something."

"What's that, partner?" Stick returned and cleared the lump in his throat.

Bobby pulled a card out of his back pocket. "My friends at school sent this to me. Jenny Fischer brought it to the house."

Stick looked at Anna.

"That's the little girl he likes," she explained.

"Oh. I see," acknowledged Stick. "She's your girlfriend. Does she know how you feel?"

"I'm scared to tell her," Bobby said. He opened the envelope and pulled the card out.

"Why is that?" meddled Stick.

"Because. What if she doesn't like me back?"

"Hey, partner," Stick advised. "You'll never know unless you go. You have to tell her. Don't ever be afraid to tell someone how much you care."

Anna shamefully looked away. It sounded like good advice, but could she apply it in her case? Some things were more easily said than done.

Bobby opened the card and showed it to Stick. "Everybody in the class wrote something on it. See. Even Mrs. Simms wrote, 'Get well soon,' but they all just signed their names, except for Jenny. She wrote that she misses me, and she signed it, 'Love, Jenny.' Do you think it means she likes me? I mean, do you think she wants to be my girlfriend?"

Stick smiled. "That's the way I read it."

"Uncle Stick," Bobby asked, "What does that mean? Do I have to give her something?"

"Well," Stick thought, "I reckon it means she wants to be around you all the time. She enjoys your company. She likes to look at you…and talk to you…and touch you. She likes to have fun with you. You don't have to give her anything but yourself."

"Oh." Bobby hung his head.

Stick could read the boy's mind. He pulled him close and hugged him tight. "Don't you worry, Bobby," he whispered. "You're going to have an operation, and everything will be just fine."

"I'm afraid of having an operation," he admitted softly. "What if I don't wake up? Jenny will feel bad."

"I know," Stick whispered, "but you tell Jenny how you feel about her anyway. You hear? It'll make her real happy. Okay?"

Bobby nodded, leaned back, and looked Stick in the eye. "What happened to your leg?"

"The bull was faster than me," Stick replied with a teary-eyed smile.

"Does it hurt?" Bobby worried.

"Naw. Not much at all."

"Did you cry?" wondered Bobby sympathetically.

Stick shook his head. "You know," he said with a shaky voice, "cowboys ain't supposed—." He almost choked on the words. He looked at Anna through solemn eyes, knowing that he was a living contradiction. "They ain't supposed to cry."

"Oh yeah." Bobby nodded.

Anna stepped near and took Bobby from Stick's arms. "Uncle Stick can barely hold himself up." She put Bobby on the ground and picked up Stick's crutches. "Bobby, why don't you go with Dusty while Uncle Stick and I talk."

"Okay," said Bobby.

Stick watched Bobby until he caught up with Dusty. Anna handed the crutches to him, and he placed them under his arms.

"Stick," she said, stepping closer, "I want to confess. When I first heard your idea about riding again, it sounded…well, it sounded foolish to me. I didn't believe it was possible. I mean, after all this time…I'm sorry. I just didn't…"

"I know," Stick interrupted. "You thought maybe there's a little too much water under the bridge, huh?"

"Well, I thought it was a sport for twenty-year-olds. I know now that I was wrong. Again, I'm sorry. I guess I just didn't want you to leave, and I refused to see the good in it."

"No," replied Stick, "you weren't wrong. It is a sport for twenty-year-olds. I think maybe when I started out I didn't know that, at least not for sure. I always did have to learn things the hard way."

"Well, regardless, you've proven otherwise. If it weren't for you, Stick, we would have a mountain of medical bills. I'll never doubt you again."

"Hang on a minute," said Stick, holding his bandaged hand into the air. "This is Stick Slaton you're talking to. Remember me? I'm not worthy of that kind of trust. Heck, I don't even trust myself."

"Stick, there was a time when you did what you wanted when you wanted. But you didn't have commitments back then. You didn't have responsibilities. Since TK died, you've never put yourself first. You've thought about doing things that might have been irresponsible, but you never did them. When it came down to it, you always did what was right. And you did what was right this time too. I'm sorry I couldn't see that. I just want to thank you for…for giving me hope. I believe that Bobby may actually have a chance, a chance to lead a normal life, a chance to live."

"Yeah…but he looks so sick," acknowledged Stick.

"Yes, but the doctors say that if he has the operation things could change rapidly for the better. Dr. Madison says we're racing against the clock. I'm just praying time doesn't run out before they admit him."

"When will that be?"

"Soon as they find a donor. It won't be a simple operation now, Stick. He needs a transplant," she admitted.

Dr. Madison stepped forward with hat in hand. "Stick, both kidneys are infected. All we need is a donor and twenty-five thousand dollars. Then they'll operate. With the six thousand you wired last week, you've got nineteen to go. Anna suggested that you might be able to get the rest if you started selling things."

"Maybe, but I hope that won't be necessary," Stick said, but he was willing to try anything. "Doc, about that transplant. What about me? Can I be a donor?"

"No, Stick," Dr. Madison shook his head sadly. "Neither you nor Anna have the right blood type. We'll just have to wait for the right one to come along."

Anna put a consoling hand on Stick's arm. "Stick, I just want you to know that I see what rodeo is doing to you. I know I asked you to keep riding, but … I don't want you to trade your life for Bobby's. I'm sorry if I made it sound that way." Anna took a deep breath and closed her eyes. "What I mean is … it's okay to come home."

"That's all right, Anna. You don't have to ask it of me. I'd do it in a heartbeat," Stick returned.

Tears of compassion were streaming from underneath Lukey Flatt's wire-rimmed glasses. They made a trail around the crook of his mouth and dripped off his chin. He had listened quietly to their whole conversation. Dr. Madison draped a caring arm across his shoulders, and they walked away.

Stick watched them go and nodded thoughtfully to Anna. "Is that what you meant when I was on the phone with you in Santa Fe, when you said you had something to tell me, that it's okay to come home?"

"No," she said almost shyly. "Not exactly."

"There's something else then?" he asked.

Anna stepped closer and held Stick's broken hand, looking deep into his eyes. "There's something that I feel I need to … I must tell you—especially after what you said to Bobby. You see, I've come to realize that … that I—."

"The registration office said all contestants have to ride in the grand entry," interrupted Shelly.

How long she had been there, Stick did not know.

She stepped closer and took Stick by the crook of the arm. She stared at Anna, showing no emotion at all.

Anna released Stick's hand and stepped away from him. She was bewildered. Her mind was racing. What was that girl doing here? How long had she been with them? Did Stick approve of it?

"You drew number three," she continued. "You'll be riding tonight."

"Which bull?" asked Stick.

"Hammerhead," Shelly replied.

"What's the payoff?"

Shelly pulled a paper from her pocket and looked it over. "Thirty thousand for first place, fifteen thousand for second, and seventy-five hundred for third."

Stick nodded. "Thanks, Shelly. Would you mind leaving my number with our things? I need to talk to Anna."

Shelly's jealousy was apparent. She looked through her brows at Anna and released Stick's arm. She didn't want to go. Reluctantly, she turned and walked away.

"When did she get here?" asked Anna uncomfortably. She wasn't sure it was any of her business.

"She was waiting in the truck the morning we left," replied Stick.

"You mean," queried Anna as realization surfaced in her mind, "that she's been with you all these months—Wyoming, Colorado, New Mexico, the whole time?"

Stick nodded. "Yeah. She's a might persistent, but she's changing. When we started out, I told her that this was no place for a woman. But, to tell you the truth, she's stuck with it a lot longer than I thought she would. Now, what were you going to say?"

Anna searched Stick's face, hoping for some truth about his relationship with Shelly. Did he love her? She looked in the direction Shelly had gone. The girl loved Stick, or at least thought she did. That was obvious. Anna's mind began to wander as she allowed her imagination to take control. Had they been together? She thought the answer was obvious and felt emotion rising in her cheeks. Her eyes filled with tears. She tried to fight, but she was losing.

"Anna, what were you going to tell me?" Stick asked again.

She shifted her eyes to the ground, afraid to look at him. "It wasn't important," she managed. It didn't matter how she felt. Her heart sank. She suddenly realized what had kept her going. It was her hope in a future relationship with Stick, and that had just been destroyed. She needed to cry. She wanted to cry. "I've got to go," she said glancing momentarily at him. "I promised Dr. Madison we would only stay for a minute." Then she hurried after Bobby.

In the instant she looked at him, Stick saw the tears in her eyes and the emotion in her face. He saw the weight of the world robbing her joy, and it bothered him, although he wasn't sure what to do about it. He wished he could just take her in his arms and make it all go away, make everything different, better. But he could only watch as she disappeared into the crowd.

"Dinner's getting cold," said Dusty, interrupting his thoughts. "Anna took Bobby. They went home."

Stick shook his head. "I was hoping they could stay longer. Reckon I'm not much help."

"Sure you are, son," commented Dusty. "Your problem is that you're blinder than a bat."

Stick looked at Dusty with a question in his eyes. "Huh?"

"Take that little gal, Shelly, for instance," Dusty explained.

Stick rolled his eyes. "I know. You're going to tell me she's too young and immature and playing schoolgirl games. Well, don't bother. I knew that from the beginning."

"Yeah," agreed Dusty, "I figured so, but that ain't all of it. Fact is, somewhere along the way, that little gal fell in love with you. At first, she was just tickling her fancy, but then she got caught in her own trap. Now she's afraid and jealous."

"What are you talking about?" Stick was in an irritable mood. "I know she's afraid, but bull riding is nothing to be jealous over."

"I'm talking about Anna, you thick headed bumpkin. I think your brain is full of stump water. Even that little gal could see."

"See what?"

"Son, are you going to make me spell it out for you?" Dusty's frustration was causing him to boil. "I could crunch pecans between my toes right now."

"What are you getting so hot about, you old sidewinder?"

Dusty threw his hands up. "Anna loves you, son. And I ain't talking about no schoolgirl kind of love, and I ain't talking about no sister-like love neither."

Stick's frown slowly disappeared. He stared blankly at Dusty. "You been drinking?"

Dusty's face turned red, his eyes bloodshot. "That's neither here nor there. What I'm telling you is the truth. Anybody with a pair of eyeballs can see it."

Stick was genuinely shocked. Realization slowly set in. The additional burden on a broken leg unsettled him, and he stumbled backward, catching himself just before falling. "But she's TK's wife," he whispered.

Dusty put his hand on Stick's shoulder and calmed down, realizing the cowboy's sense of honor wouldn't allow him to think such thoughts. "TK is dead, son. She's an incredible woman, and she needs a man. Why do you think she ain't never took no callers up on their invites?" Dusty watched Stick through narrow eyes. "And I've got a notion you feel the same way about her, only you're too dumb to know and too scared to admit it if you did."

Stick was consumed with more consideration than he cared to tackle. How much truth was there to what Dusty said? Was that just an old man's imagination running away with him? Honestly, Stick had to admit that those thoughts had crossed his mind a time or two. But he was entering a forbidden area. He had always forced the thoughts away. Why did Anna have to go?

Anna helped Bobby into the passenger side of their vehicle, buckled him in, and got behind the wheel. She was visibly upset. Dr. Madison and Lukey lagged behind, fighting a thick crowd.

"Mom, do you want to be around Uncle Stick all the time?" Bobby asked innocently.

Anna leaned over, put an arm around her son, and began to weep softly.

Bobby patted her on the back. "Me, too," he said.

Stick and Dusty found their way back to their gear without saying a word.

Suddenly, determined to make one final attempt, Dusty grabbed Stick by the arm. "Who the hell do you think she's waiting on…Prince Charming?"

"Okay, Dusty. I get the picture." Stick looked around at his gear and his expression changed. "Where's my saddle?"

Dusty quickly scanned the area. "It was here when we left."

Stick rapped the corral fence with his crutch. "What else can happen?"

Dusty picked up some papers that were lying with the remainder of their things and scanned through them. "Well, if you really want to know, I'll tell you what else can happen. Shelly left. It says here that she's tired of competing for you. She's going to take a taxi to the bus station, and from there she's headed back to Cactus Falls. At the bottom it says, 'P.S. Somebody has stolen your saddle.'" Dusty looked at Stick. "How about that?"

Stick shook his head and eased to the ground, leaning against the corral fence. "I have a good idea where my saddle disappeared to, but I'm sure it's long gone by now."

"Sounds like a trick someone might use to get your mind off the ride," suggested Dusty.

"As if it was necessary," added Stick sarcastically.

CHAPTER FIFTEEN

Hundreds of cowboys and cowgirls paraded the arena during the grand entry, while the American and Texas flags led the way. They halted in mid-arena as "The Star-Spangled Banner" echoed across the coliseum and a young female vocalist led the audience. After a prayer, there was a deafening applause.

Stick was mounted on Keepsake, using a borrowed saddle. A tremendous energy could be felt by everyone present, and excitement filled the air. With the finals only three weeks away, each contestant was clearly focused on their event, as every ride was detrimental to their reaching the championship. Who would win? Who would be crowned world champion? The title carried with it the assurance of endorsements and contracts worth thousands of dollars. Wrangler, Stetson, and Tony Lama were sure to offer tempting amounts.

Bull Hawthorne and Phil McGrawe watched Hardy ride by, circling the arena. A minute later, Stick rode by, eyeing them knowingly, and Bull offered a wink and a grin.

"Let's get this show on the road," shouted the announcer over the PA.

The contestants rode out of the arena, and Stick immediately stepped down and unsaddled Keepsake. Dusty slid the tack off the horse's back and set it before a fourteen-year-old barrel-racer. Stick limped close to her. "Thanks for letting me borrow your saddle, Tina."

"Oh. Anytime, Mr. Slaton." The starry-eyed girl smiled.

Stick winked at her, and the two men returned to their place. Stick sat down, took out his pocket knife, and cut a grove around the cast just six inches below the knee.

Dusty watched anxiously. "I hope you're not messing up, son."

"Reckon we'll find out," asserted Stick.

Two hours later, Stick eased himself onto Hammerhead, positioning himself slightly to the left to compensate for the cast. Although a large portion had been cut away, it still weighed a considerable amount, and Stick intended to use it as a counter-weight. He just hoped the bull wouldn't spin to the right.

Each of the two cowboys riding before him had managed to score: Terrel Stetson an 82 and Jamie Hendricks an 80. Both cowboys were from Mesquite.

Dusty assisted with the rigging, pulling a tight wrap after Stick gathered a good grip with his left hand. "Hope I don't have to run for my life," said Stick.

Try as he might, Stick couldn't concentrate on the upcoming ride. It was critical. If ever he needed to win, the time was now, but he couldn't stop thinking about Bobby and Anna. Dr. Madison's words about money echoed in Stick's mind: *"You've got to get it somewhere. It's his only hope."* Bobby's life depended on it. Sure, they could sell things, but they would be fortunate to get twenty-five cents on the dollar—any more and it would be charity, people paying out of the goodness of their hearts.

Raising his right arm and sliding forward, he gave a nod, and the gate flew open. Hammerhead hesitated for a second, forcing Stick to spur him with his left heel. This got the bull moving, as he jumped forward, stumbled, and immediately began to fall. It was obvious that the big animal was going down, so Stick tried to jump clear, but was too late. Hammerhead crashed to the right, landing on Stick's cast, momentarily pinning him beneath the bull. Agonizing pain wrenched his face as clowns and two cowboys dashed in to help. The bull scrambled to his feet, kicking Stick twice more before charging away, and the cowboys helped Stick quickly through the gate.

The judges offered Stick another ride, but he was in no shape. The money for the entry fee was lost. Dusty drove Stick to the hospital for an x-ray, where the doctor confirmed the bone was still intact and didn't need to be reset. Before allowing Stick to leave the hospital, the doctor forced him to endure a lecture on the severity of the injury.

Lukey Flatt sat quietly next to Bobby in the backseat of the car, as Dr. Madison drove them back to Cactus Falls. He watched his young friend through pain-filled eyes, studying the frailness in Bobby's limbs, the thinning of his hair, the discoloration of his skin. The dark circles under his eyes presented a lifelessness, a look furthered by Bobby's lethargic movements. Lukey studied his own crippled limbs, vaguely remembering life before the accident. Thinking came slowly now and only after great effort. Never again would he run and play. Why was Bobby slowly dying from this terrible disease, this unseen force, when he had survived an accident that should've easily killed him?

Lukey tried to remember the day he had chased the cat into the street. Only brief flashes of light, intermittent visual clips, tires squealing, and lots of screaming came to mind—except, that is, for something very strange.

The cat belonged to the lady next door and had been missing for several days. It was all she had, and the old woman was terribly upset. Lukey remembered the car. It was headed straight for the animal, and Lukey rushed into the street, lifting the cat into his arms. Then the strange part happened. He floated, watching the scene from somewhere above, watching his brother James cry as he hovered over some boy's body. The lady next door was also crying, holding her cat, blankly stroking its fur. Over and over people told James that it was no use, to give up and let go. But he refused. Finally the little boy was loaded into the ambulance, and James went too, leaving Lukey to watch it speed away. Then something even more confusing occurred.

Lukey Flatt could see a hundred miles as he floated above the ground. He felt happy. He was glad to be there, wherever he was, and didn't want to leave. It was as though, for the first time in his life, he was experiencing true love, cradled in invisible arms. He began rising toward the heavens. That's when he heard the voice.

It said, "Do as I have done."

Then, as suddenly as it had begun, it was over.

Lukey woke up in the hospital, surrounded by a team of doctors and nurses, all wearing masks and working frantically. He remembered their eyes and how confused they seemed when he asked for his brother, who was watching from behind a window. "He's back," sounded a feminine voice.

Soon after Lukey was released from the hospital, he noticed a profound change within himself. The compassion he held for others was overwhelming, and his level of sensitivity had risen to extreme heights. He actually felt everyone's pain, whether physical or emotional, and he could not remember being so acutely aware of such things prior to the accident.

Now, Lukey Flatt was not afraid to die. He didn't know why he was alive but figured it was for good reason. He knew for certain that there was life after death and that death was nothing more than separation from his earthly body. He never tried to tell anyone his story. He didn't think he could explain it, not even to his brother.

Once outside the doctor's office, Dusty helped Stick into a wheelchair. "Those sawbones are busier than a long-tailed cat in a room full of rocking chairs thanks to you," he commented playfully, attempting to make light of their situation.

"Yeah, and I'm starting to believe they don't appreciate me," Stick said sarcastically. "Well, at least I didn't re-break it."

Dusty pushed Stick down a long corridor, passing an elderly nurse headed in the opposite direction. She smiled at Dusty but continued on her way. He tipped his hat and turned to focus on her hips, never stopping the forward progress.

"Look out, ol'-timer!" shouted Stick. His leg served as a battering ram to scatter a group of people. "You get your driver's license at a garage sale?"

Dusty took hat in hand. "Pardon me, folks." He blushed and quickly pushed Stick toward the entry. "Reckon we can still make San Antone if we hurry."

San Antonio was ninety miles from Cactus Falls and was almost like home to Stick. It would be the closest he had been to home since the day they'd left, and Stick considered visiting the ranch but knew it wasn't possible. Following his ride in San Antonio, he would have less than twenty-four hours to get to Amarillo for the next rodeo. He was anxious to spend more time with Anna and Bobby, but their need for money dictated his every move. Amarillo would be the last rodeo before the finals. As far as Stick knew, he was still ranked in the top ten, although this depended largely on how well those close behind him had competed at Houston. One good score from each would knock him out of the runnings, shattering his hopes at the finals. So much rested on his success in these next two events.

Dusty's words about Anna weighed heavily on Stick's mind. Did the old man know what he was talking about? It all sounded too good, too simple, too unrealistic, as Anna's behavior did not confirm Dusty's claim. She was the same Anna he had always known, and despite their closeness, he couldn't sense her love. Stick certainly loved her, but if his love was more than brotherly, it had been so for a long time.

Stick leaned against the passenger window and stared at distant lights, remembering things long forgotten. Years ago, he had allowed himself to dream upon occasion, thinking how wonderful it would be to hold Anna, to kiss her, to love her. He dreamed of marrying her, but it was an unrealistic fantasy. Eventually, the dreams became farther and farther apart until he no longer allowed it. Until recently, he managed to suppress them. If she really loved him, why didn't she tell him? Why didn't she show it?

H ardy Tillman had ridden the third night in Houston, fighting victoriously for an eight-second-ride but failing to place. Although still plagued with soreness and aches, he was healing quickly and hoped to be near full strength for the finals. But he had one more show in mind first: Amarillo. A win there would guarantee him first place going into the finals.

Hardy expected to see Stick Slaton in Amarillo after having bumped into Shelly Tanner in the parking lot at the Houston rodeo. She seemed very distraught and didn't feel like talking, but Hardy coaxed her without much effort. During this brief chat, one of his previous suspicions about Stick had been confirmed. A little boy was in need of an operation, which explained why Stick had returned to bull riding after so many years. Perhaps Hardy would consider helping, after he won the title.

Shelly was no longer traveling with Stick, he learned, as she mentioned that Stick and some other woman had loved each other for "no telling how long," and, "Why didn't they just admit it and get on with it and save everyone else a lot of trouble?" Hardy didn't understand the situation, but evidently, Shelly felt rejected. Surely it was a first for her.

Hardy started to offer her a ride, as they would be traveling near Cactus Falls on the way to Amarillo, but decided against it. She didn't seem to be in the mood, and he didn't want depressing company. He could get that from Bull and Phil.

Bull had been acting strange, as if hiding something, keeping a secret, which Hardy felt probably concerned Stick Slaton. When Stick had fallen that first night in Houston, Bull wore a sinister smile that suggested he knew something no one else did, as though he had something to do with Stick's being tossed. And come to think of it, Stick had seemed a bit preoccupied. Also, a man had given Bull several one-hundred-dollar bills, an issue Hardy hadn't raised. What did Bull have that was worth that kind of money?

Hardy was weary of the two men. There were only using him, and no real friendship could ever exist. Phil was a drunkard, and Bull was just plain mean. Hardy began to notice that his association with them was producing a number of raised eyebrows. And why not? A man is known by the company he keeps. After Ft. Worth, Hardy would have to reconsider their relationship.

Stick and Dusty made it to San Antonio in time to register and get his name in the hat for the draw. It was another three-night rodeo with thirty-six contestants in the bull riding. Stick drew the tenth position and was scheduled to ride another undefeated bull. His name was Billy Bad, and this was the bull's first PRCA rodeo. None of the cowboys knew a thing about him. Stick would be going in blind and depending totally upon his skills.

Stick and Dusty had a few hours to kill but only enough to reach Cactus Falls and turn immediately back around. Traveling seemed to take a lot of energy, and Stick was having difficulties concentrating.

His thoughts kept going back to Anna and Bobby and how important placing in this rodeo was to them. Stick tried to call them, but there was no answer at the ranch. Dusty saw what Stick was going through and suggested they tour the Alamo to get things off their mind. Stick agreed. He couldn't remember the last time he had been there.

Stick knew a lot about the old mission. He enjoyed Texas history, and the Alamo was a key factor in establishing the Republic. Stick admired the men who had been willing to give their lives for something they believed in. They had not been willing to compromise. He was kin to a man who had died in the siege.

While touring the adobe structure, Stick found an old diary written by a colonel in the Mexican army. It had been discovered by a University of Texas graduate student in the Mexico archives in 1974, giving a detailed account of the battle from the colonel's point of view. He wrote about the heroism of the Texans they fought. Stick found it interesting that Hollywood portrayed Davy Crockett dying within the mission's walls but the diary gave a different account of the hero's death. It seemed that Crockett and six other men were captured after running out of ammunition. The Mexican soldiers overpowered them and took them back to Santa Anna, who was in San Antonio, which was then Bexar. The general was so embarrassed by the fact that one hundred and eighty-six men killed nearly two thousand of his troops that he ordered their immediate execution. The soldiers had so much respect for the seven men that they disobeyed the general's orders. Finally, a new patrol arrived that was not present during the battle. In an effort to gain favor with the general, their commander ordered his troops to bayonet Crockett and his comrades. The diary said that Crockett died without uttering a word.

Stick read the letters of Commander William Barrett Travis, written from within the Alamo. "God is on our side," the letter said.

"Wished he was on mine," uttered Stick in reply.

Stick read other accounts of how the men had gathered together and prayed. He agreed with Pug on that score, thinking it hypocritical for men to pray when their back was against the wall, while they refused to acknowledge God's existence any other time. Stick had basically done the same thing and felt shameful for it, although he *had* placed first…breaking his ankle in the process.

Travis's letter stated that the Mexican Army's victory would be worse than a defeat. The Texans had known they were destined to die there, but they stayed. Stick thought that Travis knew and understood the impact of his own prophetic words. The battle must have taken the wind out of Santa Anna's sails, because, shortly thereafter, a small group of Texans defeated the whole Mexican army at San Jacinto. General Sam Houston burned the river bridge after his men crossed over to the battle, so there would be no retreat, and routed the Mexican army. The land where the famous battle had taken place was owned by more of Stick's relatives.

Somehow, the tour had spoken to Stick. How? He wasn't exactly sure. The inaudible voice seemed to carry some kind of spiritual significance. There was a deep conviction, a directing force upon his soul. What was it saying? He sensed that he should listen carefully, for whatever it was saying was important.

Soon, it was Stick's turn to ride, and he hoped for a mean bull, as five of the nine men before him had managed to score. Although his hand felt better, his ankle throbbed with every movement, and his rib made its presence known with every breath. His wounds wouldn't permit much stretching, which threatened to add more injuries to the list. The elbow was the worst, however, and Stick knew it would take many months to heal. Instinct declared the ligament torn, leaving him with no choice but to continue riding with his left.

Stick ignored the pain. "Mind over matter, right, Pop?" he mumbled, although he couldn't help wondering if his father had ever hurt like this.

Stick climbed the chute and directed his attention toward Billy Bad, the undefeated bull. The animal was smaller than average, weighing about fifteen hundred pounds, but that only made him quicker and more athletic. Slinging his head, he raked the fence rails with blunt horns about ten inches long.

"Better keep a close eye on this one," said Dusty, as he handed Stick the rigging.

Stick eased onto the bull's back and slid both legs down his side. He desperately needed to place. His back was against the wall. As he gripped the rigging with his left hand, he considered the men of the Alamo and how they had stood against unbeatable odds. Should he pray? No. He couldn't stand hypocrites. Taking a sturdy wrap, Stick scooted forward, leaned back, and nodded. The gate flew open, and Billy Bad was quicker than Stick had thought.

The bull whirled to the right with such speed that Stick slid immediately to one side, gripping the rigging and hoping for a miracle, unable to effectively squeeze with his cast. He could feel himself losing the fight, slowly; a few more spins would throw him to the ground. But the bull suddenly changed directions, and Stick's head collided with a horn, splitting his brow. He fell limp beside the bull, blood flowing freely across his face, as Billy Bad bucked away. Dusty was immediately at his side. "Well, you did it again," said Dusty, handing him a handkerchief. "Now they'll have to sew up your noggin." Dusty grabbed Stick's hat and helped him to his feet. The crowd applauded, but Stick was oblivious to it all.

Dusty studied a chart while the medic gave Stick a local anesthetic and twelve stitches in his left brow. Afterward, he applied a large bandage over an antibiotic salve and told Stick how fortunate he was to still have an eye.

"Thanks," Stick offered painfully.

Dusty and Stick walked slowly back to the alley behind the bucking chutes. Stick dropped to the ground and leaned against the fence. He wasn't one to become discouraged easily, but he was beginning to believe the situation was hopeless.

Dusty read his face and kneeled quietly beside but there was nothing he could say.

"Hello, boys," came a vaguely familiar voice.

Stick looked up and recognized the friendly eyes of Pug Bond. "Howdy, Pug. Did you witness that fiasco?"

Pug nodded and shook hands with them both, appearing more serious than usual. "Pull up a pulpit, preacher," invited Dusty. "You always did shake hands like you was clubbing a snake," he joked.

"I came to talk to the two of you," said Pug matter-of-factly.

"Huh?" queried Stick with interest.

"It's little Bobby. He's in bad shape, Stick. Anna wanted you to know, so I volunteered to find you."

Stick tried to stand, but dizziness along with his other injuries drove him back down. Panic was in his eyes. He looked at Dusty and back at Pug.

"When they came back from Houston," Pug continued, "Bobby's fever started to rise. Doctor Madison said that it was a sign that the infection was taking over. His temperature was over a hundred and four when they admitted him to the hospital. They're doing everything they can to force it down."

"What can they do without a donor?" asked Stick.

"Stick." Pug's voice broke. He was fighting the need to weep.

Stick looked him in the eye and watched tears roll down his face.

"I've got something to tell you." Pug wiped the moisture from his nose. "As long as I live…I'll never see the like again." Pug began to weep.

"What is it, Pug?" Stick's own eyes began to water as he watched the big man's shoulders heaving.

Dusty put an arm around Pug, glanced at Stick, and shook his head sadly. "Easy, son," he said to Pug.

"It makes me feel so…so…I don't know…unworthy I guess," said Pug as he cried.

"How's that, Pug? It ain't your fault," Stick stated flatly.

"The pride is…so strong…in my chest. I feel like I'm going to bust. Never on this earth have I known such a man." Pug buried his face in his hands and cried harder.

Stick threw a perplexed look at Dusty. "Pug...what are you talking about? What happened?" he asked.

"The love...that must have filled his heart." Pug shook his head in total disbelief.

Stick reached forth a strong hand and turned Pug's face toward him.

Pug wiped his red eyes. "Lukey Flatt," Pug said. "He's dead."

"What?" Stick's heart sank. "How the *hell* did that happen?"

Pug blew his nose on a handkerchief. "Greater love has no man than this." Pug wiped his nose and then returned the handkerchief to his pocket. "That a man should lay down his life for his friend."

"Huh?" Stick frowned and glanced at Dusty with confusion. The older man shook his head, beginning to realize what must have happened.

"After the trip to Houston," explained Pug, "he walked into Dr. Madison's office and said he was there to help his friend, Bobby. Knowing his simple way of thinking, no one considered what he meant." Pug looked at Dusty and then stared deep into Stick's eyes. He started to cry again. "If I only had that kind of courage."

"What happened?" asked Stick with a quiet voice.

"He stepped into the restroom. The nurses heard a shot. And...they found him slumped over on the floor."

"What? Why?" Stick fought the tears. The muscles in his face began to twitch. His insides were churning. He felt he would soon explode. Emotion choked him.

"Aw...no," said Dusty sadly and hung his head.

"Poor kid," Stick whispered.

"Stick," Pug said sadly, "Dr. Madison said they were a perfect match." Pug shook back the tears. "Lukey only had one kidney left. He couldn't have known anything about blood types, but he did know that he could never help his friend while he was alive."

Stick could hold it in no longer. He buried his face in his hands and began to cry. He didn't know how to feel. It was all so wrong and all so right at the same time. What a wonderful person was this Lukey Flatt, whom he had known all his life. There was certainly no greater love than that.

Stick wiped his eyes and looked at his longtime preacher friend. "Imagine that," he whispered.

Pug's forehead became a mass of wrinkles. "That ain't all, Stick."

Stick leaned closer to his friend, who was whispering now.

"I found out two weeks ago." His lips tightened. He fought to control himself. "I am…I…" He stammered and then shook his head. "I'm also a…match for Bobby's blood type. I just didn't have the courage to do anything about it." With that out, Pug cried. "I didn't have…the courage."

Stick stared in quiet shock. The guilt that was plaguing his friend seemed unbearable, and Stick lifted a hand to Pug's head and pulled him close. The preacher wept in great, gut-wrenching sobs.

Stick looked at Dusty through red eyes. "We'd better head back to Cactus Falls," he suggested sadly.

Pug cleared his throat and dried his eyes. "Stick," Pug confessed, "Bobby is unconscious. He won't even know you're there. They can't do anything until they control his fever. Anna wanted me to tell you not to come. She said the operation is what Bobby needs. It's going to take money."

Stick glanced desperately from Pug to Dusty and shook his head solemnly. "Lukey finished what he came to do," he said, remembering Bobby's words. "Guess it's my turn."

Dusty placed a hand on Stick's shoulder. "I didn't want to tell you this, son, but you dropped to ninth after Houston. Now, after tonight, you may not even be in the top ten. I'm afraid if you don't place in Amarillo, you won't be going to Ft. Worth," Dusty acknowledged.

Stick felt his blood pressure rise. He was frustrated. He was angry. If this was only something he could fight, if he could get his hands around it, he would choke the life out of this problem. Until now, he had depended upon his hands, but they were useless now. Stick looked at Pug and slumped against the fence.

"You were the only one in school that could whip me, Pug," he stated with resignation.

"Still can," Pug forced a smile through the tears.

Stick looked at the man. He had a thick neck and broad shoulders. Stick smiled. "Guess you can," he agreed. "Wish you could whip this problem for me." Stick surveyed Dusty's face. "Wish I was rich, old-timer."

Dusty nodded.

"You are rich," said Pug, the preacher in him beginning to resurface, "and when you figure that out, maybe things will start turning around for you."

Stick smiled, but Pug's seriousness changed his expression. A question appeared in Stick's eyes. "I'm rich?"

"The ransom of a man's life *are* his riches," Pug said convincingly. "Proverbs, chapter thirteen, verse eight."

Stick made no reply but stared blankly at Pug, letting him know that the statement needed an explanation.

"A ransom is what you're worth to someone else. In other words, if you were being held hostage, the ransom is what someone would pay your abductor to set you free. How much could the abductor get for you?"

"Maybe I'm a little dense here, Pug, but I'm not following you," admitted Stick.

"The ransom of a man's life are his riches. How valuable are you to your friends? How valuable are you to Anna, to Bobby, to Dusty here? You're worth everything to them, everything they've got. What about all your friends back in Cactus Falls? How much are you worth to them? A lot, I would say."

"Okay, Pug, but how does that help me now? Maybe those folks would give me the shirts off their backs if that was all they had to give, but how does that get little Bobby the operation he needs?"

"Well," Pug explained, "if your pop was a billionaire and you were worth everything to him, how much would *you* be worth?"

"A lot I reckon, but my pop wasn't a billionaire."

"No," agreed Pug, "but God is. How much are you worth to Him? Think about it."

Stick smiled. "Very little, I'm afraid."

"Wrong, Stick. You're worth everything to him. You were worth the life of his Son. So how rich are you?"

Stick stared thoughtfully at the ground. "That's certainly a lot to think about," he said at last.

Pug nodded. "I've got to be going. I'll be praying for your family."

"Pug," said Stick sincerely, "thanks for coming. I appreciate it."

"Glad to do it. Chew on what I told you. If you come to realize how rich you really are, I think it'll make all the difference in the world. God is for you, Stick." Pug turned and left the men staring after him in silence.

Chapter Sixteen

L ights from oncoming traffic illuminated Dusty's face as he drove the old truck. Stick was attempting to rest on the passenger side with his head against the window. His eye was almost swollen shut.

"When I said to keep your eye on them horns, I didn't mean to try to poke one of them out," said Dusty jokingly.

"Got any aspirin?" asked Stick.

"The only pain killer I've got is this," said Dusty and shoved a beer in Stick's face.

The cowboy took the beer and pressed it against his swollen eye. Then he popped the top, and drank several swallows. "How's our expense money holding out?"

"Let's see," thought Dusty. "With the doctor bills, the entry fees, hotel rooms, gas, another saddle, feed for Keepsake, and food for us, we're near busted. We'll be lucky to have a dime left after we pay the Amarillo entry fee."

"And Pug says that I'm rich."

"Naw," replied Dusty, "You ain't rich, just free."

Stick watched the headlights coming toward them in the opposite lane. He wasn't sure that he understood all of what Pug said, but he did trust the man. Pug had earned Stick's respect years ago. He was honest and hardworking and had once been as rough as they came. The year after Stick had won the championship, Pug had nearly won the title for steer wrestling. And Dusty was right: the man had a grip like a vice.

"How do we get to Amarillo from here?" Stick asked.

"We keep heading west on I-10. When we get to Junction, we'll take a right on eighty-three and go up to Abilene, turn east on I-20, then north at Sweetwater. And so on. You get some sleep, and let me worry about it. I'll have us in Amarillo by morning."

The sky was glowing bright orange on the eastern horizon, and the sun was on the verge of peeking over the distant plain. Dusty's eyes were heavy. He yawned and drove the truck past a sign that read "Amarillo City Limits."

"Hey, you black-eyed cripple, wake up," said Dusty with a raised voice, attempting to be jovial during the trial they were facing.

Stick opened his eyes and peered ahead at the city lights. He sat up and tried to stretch, realizing he was sorer than the previous night.

Two hours later, Stick stood in line at the registration office, watching Dusty study the top-ten chart. He appeared disturbed, but Stick didn't ask what he already had assumed. A middle-aged man standing behind the counter handed Stick a white cloth with the number 13 stamped on it.

"Last time I wore this number, I won two thousand dollars," Stick stated.

"Well," said Dusty, "let's hope it's your lucky number. Look here." Dusty handed Stick the top-ten chart.

One quick glance told Stick that he was no longer in the top ten. Hardy Tillman dropped to second, and Hank Gilpen was now in first. Amarillo would be Stick's last chance to make it to the finals. He dropped the paper to his side and frowned as Hardy, Bull, and Phil entered the room.

"Mind your manners, Stick," Dusty whispered. "You ain't in no shape to handle any trouble."

"Okay," Stick agreed.

"Well," needled Bull, "if it ain't grandpa and great grandpa. You two look like you've been on the road all night." Bull winked at Hardy and Phil. "We flew in yesterday," he lied. "Been staying at a fancy hotel at the airport. You can do that when you're winning, you know." Bull stepped closer to Stick, wearing a wide smile. "What did ya'll ride in on?"

Stick could smell Bull's bad breath, and he was in no mood to patronize the big man. He was dangerously close, and Stick sensed that he was looking for a fight. Bull looked first at Stick's cast and snorted. Then he looked at the bandage on Stick's head and, finally, his black eye. He laughed, trying to coax Stick into throwing the first punch. Stick was determined that it wouldn't work.

"I know one thing," said Bull, leaning closer. "You didn't ride in on your horse because the way I hear it, you done lost your saddle. Ha ha ha!"

Suddenly, with lightning speed and all the strength he could muster, Stick swung a powerful left cross to Bull's nose. The big man flew backward, striking the wall with the back of his head and sliding unconscious to the floor. Stick turned on Hardy and Phil.

"I was wondering when you were going to do that," Dusty said with delight. "I thought that feller was fixing to get embrangled with my fists."

Phil quickly threw both hands in the air, letting everyone know that he wanted no part of the action. Hardy looked at Bull lying peacefully on the floor, then watched Stick limp out the door. He noticed Phil trembling ever so slightly. Then he smiled, stepped over Bull, and walked to the counter. "Need to register for the bull ride," he said.

"What now?" asked Dusty once outside the registration office.

"You were right about the money," returned Stick while rubbing his knuckles. "I've got twenty bucks left after paying the entry fee. How much have you got?"

"Twelve."

"Well," said Stick sarcastically, "let's put things in perspective. I'm no longer on the chart, I can't even climb the chute without help, Bobby is in the hospital, and we ain't even got enough money for gas to get back to Cactus Falls."

"That's about the size of it, son." Dusty stepped closer and put a hand on Stick's shoulder. "Guess there ain't but one thing left to do."

"What's that?"

"Win," stated the old man emphatically. "There ain't but sixteen thousand between the first- and tenth-place money winners. All you have to do is place, and you'll be back in the hunt. We'll be Ft. Worth-bound. Which bull did you draw?"

Stick checked the paper in his pocket. "Same one that broke my rib in Mineral Wells: Sidewinder."

Dusty rubbed his grizzled jaw and looked at Stick through his brows. "All right then. There you go. You already know his moves. I reckon it'll be a cinch."

Stick glared at Dusty, then started toward the truck. Dusty followed. Once there, Stick rummaged around in the pickup bed. Finally, out of a tool box, he withdrew a keyhole saw.

"What're you doing with that?" asked Dusty.

Without answering, Stick moved to the tailgate and sat down. Then, he began to saw the cast. "See if you can find a couple of ace bandages, old timer. I'm going to need them once I get this thing off."

Dusty nodded and took off for the first aid station.

It took thirty minutes for Stick to saw through the cast. Once completed, he found his leg to be badly bruised and slightly swollen. Dusty returned with the bandages, and Stick carefully wrapped his ankle with both. Afterward, he took off his shirt and removed the bandage around his ribs.

"I don't want anything constricting me tonight."

Dusty nodded. "It's do or die."

Suddenly, Stick remembered the men of the Alamo and what he had read about them. "Dusty," he said, "I need to be alone so I can get my head screwed on straight."

Dusty grinned. "Well, I'm so hungry that my belly thinks my throat's been cut. Reckon I'll find something to eat. I'll call home while I'm at it."

Stick slid into the bed of the truck and leaned against the cab. What was it they were trying to tell him, these men at the Alamo? What was he supposed to learn? Why did he feel that there was some special significance about their situation in relation to his? He began to consider the possibilities.

First of all, their backs had been against the wall, and so was his. The odds had been against them, just as they were now against him. The lives of others, as well as the independence of Texas, had depended upon their performance, just as Bobby's life depended upon Stick's. The men had been willing to pay the price for Texas with their lives, and Stick would do the same for Bobby.

"Pay the price," Stick mumbled.

Texas was worth a lot, everything those men had to give. Suddenly, Stick understood what Pug Bond had been trying to tell him: Bobby was worth a lot, everything Stick had to offer. It all became perfectly clear.

Pug kept telling Stick that he was rich because God owned everything. Stick was worth a lot, everything God had to give. That's why the men of the Alamo, when their backs were against the wall, began to pray.

That's what Travis meant when he said, "God is on our side." That's what Pug meant when he said, "God is for you."

"God is for me," whispered Stick. "God is for me."

Suddenly, Stick was sorry about a lot of things. He was sorry he always considered God an impersonal force, not willing to get involved in the lives of people. He was sorry he didn't measure up. He had always been independent, self-reliant, confident in his own ability. He had always felt that depending upon someone else was a weakness. He never considered that it could be a strength. How strong could a man be if God was on his side? Like at the Alamo, strong enough to defeat two thousand with only one hundred and eighty-six.

"God," Stick unexpectedly found himself praying, "I guess you know how I feel then. I would trade my life for Bobby. He means that much to me. If I really mean that much to you, would you help me? Would you be on my side? I can't do it myself."

Stick sat quietly for a moment, feeling much better about the situation, as he tried to remember Sidewinder, the bull he had ridden in Mineral Wells. The name was the most memorable thing about him, that and the impact of his horn with Stick's rib. He remembered sitting on his back and looking at the thick curly hair between the animal's horns. He was a spotted bull, a Brahman cross. His horns were less than a foot long and very sharp. As he recalled, they hadn't even been tipped.

Sidewinder, rather than jumping, seemed to spring into the air with all fours. This resulted in a bone-rattling impact. Other bulls would jump into the air and usually land on their front hooves, unseating the rider and causing him to slide forward, sometimes flipping him over the animal's head.

If Stick's memory was correct, the bull whirled to the left and swung his head a lot. Suddenly, Stick recalled being underneath Sidewinder as the animal slung its head, attempting to hook Stick with its horns. Stick thought that it would be better to ride the bull straight up rather than leaning forward over his head due to the way he sprang. Then he would lean inward, to the left, in preparation for Sidewinder spinning left. Hopefully, the centrifugal force would not be more than Stick could stand with all that was broken. The bull would score high. Stick had no doubt the animal would do his part. Stick had only to hold on for eight seconds. He would have to fight too. He would spur with his left, pulling himself to the inside with every thrust. Suddenly, it was settled. Stick was not going down this time. He was sure of it.

It was to be a three-night rodeo, with twelve bull riders each night. Stick would be the first rider on the second night, and, once again, Hardy Tillman again had drawn the same bull as Stick. He would ride Sidewinder on the third night. Drew Ferguson, from Oklahoma City, would ride him on the first night. First place paid twenty thousand dollars, second place paid ten thousand, and third place paid five. Any one of them would put Stick back in the top ten.

"You got your head screwed on straight yet?" asked Dusty as he handed Stick a hamburger.

"I ain't going down this time, partner," replied Stick. "How's Bobby?"

"No answer at the ranch. I reckon they've got him in one of them big hospitals in Austin. They know how to get in touch with us though. We'll hear from them if there's any change."

Stick unwrapped the hamburger and took a bite. He wondered how Bobby was doing and how Anna was holding up. How would everything turn out once this was all over? Would they ever again lead normal lives?

Anna was sleeping, slumped over the foot of Bobby's bed. She had napped every few hours, sleeping about thirty minutes at a time, checking on Bobby constantly. His fever still burned, and he was dehydrated. The doctors were feeding him intravenously. Someone knocked at the door, and Anna woke immediately.

"Come in," she whispered.

Pug Bond opened the door and stepped into the room. His smile gave her instant encouragement. He slid a chair next to Anna and put an arm around her. "How's he doing?"

"There's been very little change," she said sadly.

"Well, that's good," he offered. "Things aren't any worse. You watch. Bobby is going to be just fine."

Anna smiled. "Thanks, Pug."

"Now, how about you? How's Anna holding up?"

"I'm kind of tired," she replied. "Did you talk with Stick?"

"Yes, and he was going to come, but I told him what you said. He looked pretty beat up. I watched him ride. I didn't want to tell him about Bobby until afterward. He had a bad cut above his eye. It took several stitches."

"I'll be so glad when he comes home. Do you think he's all right?"

"Anna, I think the man is just about flat on his back, but I'd say that was good. Because when you're flat on your back, there ain't but one place to look, and that's up. Stick is about as close to looking up as I've ever seen."

"I'm just so afraid for him. I'm afraid of…of losing him."

"Why don't you tell him the truth?" queried Pug.

"I told you why. That girl has been with them the whole time. He must care for her. He might even love her. I saw the way she looked at him and the way she looked at me. She loves him. I'm sure of it."

"I don't think she's with them anymore, Anna. I really doubt that Stick loves her. Besides, what difference does it make? That doesn't change the way you feel, does it?"

"No. I've thought about it, and I guess I'd love him no matter what. Sometimes I feel like I'm the only one who really knows him. He's really not so different from TK. He thinks he is, but he's not. Beneath the surface, deep down, they're a lot alike. TK was more conservative. Stick has a quicker temper, and he's more apt to react on impulse. He's even stubborn. But I like that. He's got a good heart. And I believe I can always count on him to do what's right."

"Then tell him, tell him what you told me, that you think you've been in love with him for a long time. You'll never know unless you do."

"Maybe I will." She offered a trembling smile. "He'll be in Ft. Worth in a few days. Maybe I'll see him there if Bobby's doing better."

"I don't know, Anna. I talked with some fellows from town, and they said that Stick dropped out of the top ten. If he doesn't place in Amarillo, he won't be there."

"He'll place then," she said with confidence. "That's when Stick does his best."

Pug smiled. "Yeah. In high school he was always the one we wanted at the plate when it was two outs in the last inning and we were down. I don't think he ever struck out."

"He'll be in Ft. Worth too," assured Anna.

Stick was situating himself on the back of Sidewinder, preparing for what could end up as the most important ride of his life. Sidewinder had thrown Drew Ferguson the first night within a second of leaving the chute. The bull stayed true to form, springing forward and spinning left, sending Drew off on the right on the first circle. Chris Shockley had scored a 79 on a heavy black Brangus bull, and Terrel Stetson and Jamie Hendricks, partners from Mesquite, had scored 80 and 82. Ben Stanton was tied with Chris, but no others had managed to score Stick couldn't get his boot over the bandages, so he wore an extra large sock for more protection. He eased down onto the bull's back but kept his broken ankle elevated to keep the animal from mashing it against the fence. He looked at Dusty with serious concentration in his eyes. "It's our last shot, Dust. Do or die. Right?"

Dusty handed Stick the rigging. "Do or die," he repeated.

Stick took a grip with his left hand and wrapped the rope around it once. Afterward, he glanced quickly at Dusty and took another wrap. Dusty looked Stick in the eye and nodded his approval. Stick set his head rigidly between his shoulders and slid forward. "Remember the Alamo," he whispered between clenched teeth, and then, "God help me," and he nodded his head.

The gate was pulled, but before it was opened all the way, Sidewinder rammed it with his horns. The gate struck a cowboy on the outside and knocked him to the ground. The bull sprang into the air as was his custom and then began to whirl in circles to the left. Stick fought furiously. With each thrust, Sidewinder made to the left, Stick kicked with his left boot and forced himself to the inside. Suddenly, the brute did something unexpected. He stopped spinning and jumped into the air, landing on his front hooves. Stick was too far forward. He folded onto the back of the bull's neck. The bull jumped again, and Stick flew backward, slamming his head against the animal's rump. Without warning, Sidewinder shifted directions, spinning to the right. Stick had trouble kicking with his broken ankle, but he continued to force himself inside.

Finally, the horn sounded, but Stick was in trouble. He was falling to the left, crudely perched on top of his hand, unable to free it. The bull turned sharply, and Stick flipped off its back, flying parallel to the ground with his hand hung in the rigging. The clowns rushed in, desperately pulling at the rope and dodging the sharp horns. Stick's body crashed into one wearing giant short pants with red suspenders, and the blow knocked him into the dirt. With athletic agility, the clown scrambled back to his feet and worked his way in. Then, as quickly as it began, it was over. Stick's hand was free, and he was rolling head over heels in the dirt. The clowns taunted the bull, coaxing him away.

The crowd roared with excitement. Stick tried to get up but couldn't. Dusty was quickly at his side, pulling him to his feet. He placed Stick's right arm over his shoulder and began helping him to the fence. The audience screamed with pleasure. Whistles, yahoos, clapping, and stomping filled the air. Stick waved his hat.

"Son, I'm too old for stunts like that. Are you trying to kill me or something?" Dusty pretended to be angry.

"Do or die, partner." Stick smiled.

Dusty half carried Stick through two gates and eased him to the ground in the alley behind the chutes.

Stick leaned against the fence, closed his eyes, and smiled. "Thanks, Lord," he whispered under his breath.

"And the judges grant Stick Slaton an eighty-seven for that ride. That's good enough to put you in the lead, cowboy!" shouted the announcer.

The crowd came to their feet and continued their applause.

"Maybe thirteen *is* your lucky number," shouted Dusty over the uproar.

Only three other cowboys scored on the second night. Dale Thomas was awarded an 84, Boots Laird scored a 78, and Stub Hoffman took an 82. One cowboy was disqualified, and the seven remaining were thrown from their bulls.

Stick sat quietly in the alley with his eyes closed until the bull riding was over. He'd just about made up his mind to sleep in the bed of his truck when he heard someone walk up. He opened his eyes and saw Hardy Tillman standing before him with his hand outstretched.

"Good ride, gramps," he complimented.

"Thanks," Stick said cautiously and shook his hand.

"Where're you staying?" Hardy seemed curious.

"Maybe right here where I'm laying or maybe in the bed of my truck if I can make it that far." Stick was none too friendly. "I'd have money for a room, but I had to spend it on another saddle."

"That's why I'm here," said Hardy. "But first, I just wanted to tell you thanks for dragging me out from underneath that bull. That was you, wasn't it?"

"You're welcome," Stick replied dryly.

"Well, anyway, I just wanted you to know that I didn't have anything to do with your saddle," Hardy said sincerely.

"Uh huh." Stick grunted.

Hardy dug into his front pocket and pulled out a roll of bills. He peeled one back and handed it to Stick. "Here's a fifty. It's a loan against that ride you just made. Why don't you get a room? You can pay me back in Ft. Worth."

Stick looked thoughtfully at the fifty-dollar bill and smiled indecisively. Finally, shifting his eyes to meet Hardy's, he shook his head. "No thanks."

"Okay," admitted Hardy. "Maybe, indirectly I am responsible for your saddle. Come on. Take the money. It's the least I can do."

"All right," Stick said, accepting the cash. "Pay you back in Ft. Worth."

"Tell you what," said Hardy. "After I win the title, you can keep it." Hardy started laughing and then waved and left.

Stick watched him walk away. The young man showed promise. If it wasn't for the fact that Stick needed to win in Ft. Worth, he might pull for Hardy. There was good hidden somewhere below his artificial surface, which was finally beginning to work its way out. Stick's Pop had always said that cream rises to the top. Maybe Hardy just needed a chance to grow up.

Stick thought about the hotel room. It sounded good. There wasn't an inch of his body that didn't ache. His left arm took a severe wrenching after his hand had been caught in the rigging, and both

AMARILLO BY MORNING

sides were sore, especially the broken rib. Surprisingly, his ankle didn't seem to be any worse for the wear, nor his hand. His forehead was mighty tender around the stitches.

Yes, he could use a soft bed and a good rest. Matter-of-fact, he would stay in bed the next day until time for Hardy's ride. Maybe he would soak for a while in a hot bath. Hopefully, three days would be enough time to recuperate.

H ardy was in an excellent position. He had drawn the last spot, allowing him to view everyone before his turn to ride. He knew exactly what he had to do and had watched Side-winder two times. The advantage was his if there was one to be had. Stick Slaton was the man to beat, and Lou Cooper was in second place with an 85. Hardy had an opportunity not only to win but to beat Stick on the same bull. He liked the older cowboy, but it would be very gratifying to defeat him head up, same rodeo, same bull.

"Coming out of chute number three, ladies and gentlemen," shouted the announcer, "is Hardy Tillman riding Sidewinder. This bull is one for two, batting fifty percent. Good luck, cowboy."

Hardy slid forward and gripped the rope with his right hand. He took a tight wrap and pounded his gloved fingers with his left hand. He knew exactly what the bull would do. He would spring out of the gate, turn four circles to the left, stop, jump into the air, jump again, and then spin right. Somewhere in there, the horn would sound, and Hardy would win. All he had to do was make the ride look better than Stick Slaton's. He would do that with a flying dismount, landing on his feet with hat in hand, waving to the crowd. The judges would love it.

"He's all yours," said Bull as he helped Hardy with his preparations. "Show grandpa how it's done."

Hardy nodded his head. Stick had ridden the animal straight up, and Hardy would take the same approach.

The gate flew open, and the bull sprang forward. Sidewinder once again didn't give the handler time to open the gate, this time coming down against the railing, leaving no room to spin. Instead, Sidewinder jumped into the air, kicking his hind legs high about Hardy's head. The cowboy was still in a straight up position when the bull landed on his front hooves, the shock forcing Hardy forward. He flipped onto the bull's head and lost his grip. Instead of spinning, the animal then thrust his head into the air, launching Hardy airborne. He landed hard in the dirt, and Sidewinder followed, lowering his head and hooking Hardy in the rear as he scrambled to stand. Airborne again, Hardy flew several feet before skidding across the dirt on his belly. The clowns claimed Sidewinder's attention and gave Hardy time to get away.

"Yeehaw!" shouted Dusty. "That bull just won you first place and twenty thousand dollars. I think I'll find him and give him a kiss."

Stick smiled at Dusty. "Back in Cactus Falls, you said, 'Pardon me if I don't kiss you,' and now you want to kiss a bull?"

"Yeah. Ol' Sidewinder is a lot better-looking than you. Yeehaw!" he shouted again.

"Dust, we need to wire nineteen thousand to Anna. If there's enough left over, I'd like to get a temporary cast put on my leg."

"Well, let's go collect and find us another sawbones. Unless they find something else busted on you, we'll be in Ft. Worth tomorrow evening."

Chapter Seventeen

The popularity of the Ft. Worth PRCA World Finals had grown to reach phenomenal proportions. Television cameras, news crews, radio disk jockeys, movie stars, and country music celebrities were in attendance. It was a momentous occasion. Patriotic country music played continuously over the PA system, blending with screams from the roller coaster, children laughing, cattle bellowing, automobile engines, guns, and carnival sideshows yelling, "Step right up!" Red, white, and blue banners were draped over fences and hanging from guy wire. Flags were flying. Mechanical bulls, carnival rides, sirens, dances, small bands, and clowns added to the racket.

Old pot-bellied cowboys, young people wearing giant belt buckles, red skirts, ten-gallon hats, Indians, ropes, and rhinestones were a common sight. Popcorn, cotton candy, beer, and soda pop were sold on every corner. The smell of cigarette smoke, horses, goats, pigs, and cattle mixed with the more desirable scent of perfume, caramel apples, and freshly roasted peanuts. An audience gathered at the arena laughed at three small monkeys riding stock dogs as they herded sheep into a pen.

Conestoga wagons, red lipstick, teased hair, and tight-fitting jeans helped define the character of the western atmosphere. Colorful helium balloons floated about. Spurs jingled. Couples walked hand in hand.

Stick tried to recall the finals of the early years. It was nothing like this. Things had certainly changed. Somehow, media had overly dramatized rodeo, ranching, and cowboys in general, portraying them as glamorous and romantic. The prize money was at least ten times better though, and the endorsements offered to winners could pay off even greater.

It was easy to get caught up in the excitement. Somehow, all this activity made people forget reality. They forgot about their jobs, their struggles, their debts, and their responsibilities, losing themselves in a world of make-believe. Reality was placed on the backburner, and a difficult way of life was displayed with a deceitful shine, like the rhinestones everyone wore. Ranching was hard work. A cowboy's life was filled with hidden dangers and unrest. He was constantly battling the elements, weather, disease, and the economy. Yet, everyone here was wearing cowboy hats, boots, bandanas, shiny belt buckles, and the like, giving reality a false covering.

It was very hard for ranchers to make ends meet. Cattle rarely turned their owners a profit. A cowboy had only to let his guard down for an instant and he would be selling his stock at floor price just to pay the feed bill. The factors bringing disaster were always waiting for an opportunity to strike so that, even in an unusual year when profits were made, one couldn't afford to spend. He must save for the next drought, the next disease, the next drop in cattle prices, or the next increase in feed. He was constantly battling grasshoppers, fire ants, rats, and sometimes rabbits and deer. Of late, coyotes could be added to the list.

Stick smiled. Everyone should have to experience this glamorous life. They should try farming and ranching just once before they passed on. They should cut and stack a cord of firewood in a day; haul five hundred bales of hay from the field to the barn before dark in one hundred-degree heat; cultivate and harvest two hundred acres of corn; help a dozen heifers have calves over a three-day period, watching them night and day. No, it was certainly not glamorous.

There were times few and far between when Stick thought it a bit romantic though—late in the evening after a hard day's work, sitting on the porch with a million stars lighting the sky and as many fireflies appearing and disappearing in the darkness. The smell of fresh rain on a dusty crop always brought a smile to Stick's face. He couldn't help but laugh when young calves bounced around their mothers, chasing one another with tails held high in the air. He enjoyed the deep green glow of a fertilized pasture and fat cows grazing in knee-high Bermuda. He liked watching horses kicking at the air while running about the field, burning up excess energy. He liked listening to the bleating of newborn kid goats and waking early to a rooster crowing. Stick liked seeing his old hound dog stretched in the sun on a cool spring morning. He liked the feel of his sun-warmed fur. He could sit for hours, watching pigs playfully tugging at one another's ears and hens chasing insects—now that was entertainment. Yes, perhaps everyone should experience this life. It could change them for the better.

The evening flew by, and Stick was soon seated upon Keepsake in the center of the arena with the other contestants. With hats in hand and heads bowed, someone in the press box prayed.

"And, Father, we ask that you charge your angels with the task of keeping every cowboy and cowgirl safe tonight as they participate in these events. All these things we ask in accordance with your will and in Your Son's name. Amen."

Immediately after the amens, the crowd cheered and the contestants galloped in a circle and then out of the arena. Stick rode Keepsake through the gate behind the cattle pens to his truck. He dismounted, favoring his broken ankle, and then unsaddled the horse.

Dusty stepped up and patted Stick sympathetically on the back. "Look what I've got," he said and handed Stick a chart.

Stick took the poster and looked it over.

"From no place to first place!" Dusty exclaimed. "You're the number-one bull rider in America right now. You're favored to win. There's a news crew that wants to interview you."

"Huh?" Stick was shocked.

"Yeah. I told them I'd bring you over. You're going to be on TV, cowboy. This is a big deal."

"No," Stick said with unbelief. "I can't do that."

"Sure you can, son. Come on. It'll be fun." Dusty frowned. "You ain't scared, are you?"

"Heck yeah I'm scared. I don't want to be on TV. Why did you tell them I'd do that?"

"Well," reasoned Dusty, "it's kind of your responsibility. You're number one, a celebrity. You owe it to the people."

"Owe it to them? Look at me. I'm broken up and bruised, and I've got a black eye."

"Yeah," agreed Dusty. "You look like a bull rider. Now quit being a sissy, and go over there with me."

The camera crew was set up near the corrals, using a pen full of wild bulls as the backdrop. The anchor person was a pretty strawberry blond woman in her early thirties. In the spirit of the affair, she wore jeans, boots, a yellow western blouse, and a white cowboy hat. Her eyes brightened with interest when focused upon Stick.

"Stick Slaton?" she asked with an extended hand after recognizing Dusty from their earlier meeting.

"Yes, ma'am," he answered and shook her hand.

"I'm Jo Anne. Have you ever been on TV, Stick?" she asked smiling.

"Not hardly," Stick laughed.

"Okay," she explained, "I'm going to ask you a few questions, and all you have to do is answer them."

Stick nodded and then frowned at Dusty. The old man stifled a laugh.

"Let's get started then." She looked at the cameraman. "Roll it," she ordered and faced the lens. "Hello. I'm Jo Anne Reaves, live from the Ft. Worth PRCA World Finals Rodeo. I'm standing here with a former world champion bull rider who happens to be the number-one bull rider in the country today. His name is Stick Slaton, and I understand that he's forty-two years old."

Jo Anne turned to Stick. "Mr. Slaton, what makes a man of your age get back into such a dangerous sport after almost two decades?"

Stick looked timidly toward the camera. "Money, I reckon."

"I understand that the reason you need money is because you have a nephew in need of an operation. Is that right?" She pushed the microphone toward him.

"Reckon so," he answered, feeling a bit uncomfortable with the question.

"Can I ask how you came by that black eye?" she asked, smiling again.

"San Antone," he replied without explanation.

"Yes, and I understand you broke your leg in Santa Fe, your rib in Mineral Wells, and your hand sometime before that," she stated.

Stick unconsciously ran his index finger down his mustache and nodded. "I reckon I've broken most everything but my back at some time or another."

"Stick, can you explain to us how the judges determine a winner at the world finals?" Again, she shoved the microphone toward him.

"Well," he began, "the top ten money winners ride once a night for three nights. Their score for each night is combined, and the highest total score is the winner."

"In which position do you ride?"

"Since I'm in first place, I get to ride last each night. Frank Hysler is in tenth place, so he rides first each night."

"What can you tell us about the bulls?"

"They're the best bucking stock of the year. No bull will be ridden twice. That way, nobody gets an edge on anybody else by watching the bull's moves. They've got thirty bulls here. Some of them have never been defeated."

"Defeated?" she asked.

"Yeah. Nobody has ever stayed on them for eight seconds."

"What's it going to take to win here?"

Stick shrugged. "It's anybody's guess. If a few bull riders happened to score all three nights, it'll probably take two hundred and forty points or better to win. If all the riders only score twice, a hundred and sixty-five points could win."

"What do you think it'll take?" she pushed.

Stick smiled. "I think that anyone who scores three nights will win."

"So, what you're saying is that you think everyone will be thrown at least once?"

"More than likely," he nodded. "These bulls are tough."

Jo Anne faced the camera again. "Well, folks, there you have it. This is Jo Anne Reaves with champion bull rider Stick Slaton at the Ft. Worth PRCA World Finals."

The cameraman dropped the camera to his side, and Jo Anne faced Stick again with an extended hand. "Thank you, Mr. Slaton, and good luck."

Stick took her hand, glanced again at Dusty, and then turned and walked away. He was amazed by all the attention.

Skinny Fuller had been invited to narrate the bull-riding event. He loved the sport, and it was evident in his zeal to serve. It was his job to announce this year's contestants, and he was more than pleased to call Stick's name from the list.

"Ladies and gentlemen, may I have your attention?"

The crowd grew silent.

"I'd like to introduce to you, this year's finalists in the bull-riding event. In first place is veteran bull rider and the world champion from twenty years ago, Stick Slaton."

The audience applauded.

"In second place is last year's world champion, Hank Gilpen. In third place is an upcoming new star Hardy Tillman. In fourth position is Chris Shockley. Fifth is Tyrone Fenton. Sixth is Terrel Stetson. Seventh is Ben Stanton. Eighth is Drew Ferguson. In ninth place is Jamie Hendricks. And in tenth place is Frank Hysler."

The crowd continued to applaud for several moments. Finally, Skinny's voice brought an end to the ovation.

"Bull riding is the most dangerous sport in the world. These men will be competing for this year's national bull riding title. The highest combined score will determine the winner. This year's world champion will receive a check for one hundred thousand dollars from the Professional Rodeo Cowboy Association. Now let's get this show on the road. Our first contestant will be Frank Hysler, riding Hammerhead."

The gate flew open, and a large, white bull burst out of the chute, spinning circles to his right. Frank Hysler could not hold on. He fell to the left and scrambled out of the way.

Frank's effort set the tone for most of the following rides. The bulls were quick and athletic. The cowboys called them a salty lot. Jamie Hendricks received a concussion and was taken to the hospital. Drew Ferguson managed to score a 78. Ben Stanton was thrown just before the horn sounded. Terrel Stetson was stepped on and acquired a broken foot. Tyrone Fenton was thrown forward, catching a horn in the mouth. He lost two front teeth and received four stitches in his bottom lip. Chris Shockley scored a 79.

Hardy Tillman sat on Nightmare, a small, black, Brangus bull that had no horns. Bull Hawthorne, sporting a bandaged and broken nose, was in an irritable mood. He helped Hardy with the rigging.

Hardy had never seen the bull and had no idea how to prepare for his ride. He took a tight grip and shouted, "Let him go, boys."

The bull was released. He jumped out of the chute and continued jumping to the center of the arena. Hardy spurred, but Nightmare refused to spin. He did spring high into the air, however, twice coming down almost perpendicular to the ground. The horn sounded, and Hardy allowed the bull's upward thrust to catapult him into the air. The cowboy landed with hat in hand, waving to the crowd. It was an impressive move.

Hardy walked back to the corral, dusting himself off. The audience acknowledged their approval.

"The judges say seventy-nine, Hardy," shouted Skinny Fuller over the PA.

Hank Gilpen was next. The gate was pulled open, and Brown Sugar spun out like a west Texas dust devil. Halfway into the ride, Hank lost his grip. He bounced high into the air and landed hard on his back. The clowns helped him out, but it was several minutes before he could catch his breath.

Stick climbed the chute and carefully positioned himself on UFO. He had used the keyhole saw once again to remove the cast, wrapping his leg with bandages. Suddenly, Dusty leaned close and ripped the number from off his back.

"Hey!" worried Stick. "What are you doing?"

Dusty threw the old number to the ground, unfolded a new number, and taped it to his back. "By special request," he smiled.

"Stick Slaton," announced Skinny, "now wearing number thirteen, will be coming out of chute number two on UFO."

"Thanks, Dust," Stick offered and then whispered a prayer. "Lord, this is for Bobby." He gripped the rigging, pulled it tight, slid forward, and leaned back. "Okay!" he yelled.

The gate came open, and UFO charged from the chute. He bucked; turned; twisted; and then, true to his name, began to fly. Stick couldn't recall riding a bull that jumped so high. Stick's performance was also true, and he stuck to the bull's back. The horn sounded, and Stick allowed himself to be bucked off. He landed on his left leg and rolled onto the ground, protecting his broken ankle.

Dusty was quickly at Stick's side and helped him to his feet. The audience applauded, and Stick waved his hat. "Good ride, son, but I'm afraid it won't score very high," Dusty noted. "That bull wasn't much help."

"Yeah, but I'll take what I can get right now," replied Stick.

Dusty helped him through the gate and eased him to the ground in the alley. Stick leaned against the fence while propping his leg over the gear.

"The judges say that ride was worth seventy-seven points, Stick," announced Skinny. "That's good enough for fourth place. And that concludes the bull riding event tonight, ladies and gentlemen. After the first round, Hardy Tillman and Chris Shockley are tied for first, each with a seventy-nine. Drew Ferguson is in third with a seventy-eight. And Stick Slaton is fourth with a seventy-seven. Right now, it's anybody's ballgame."

The ride was what Stick would call non-eventful. Although the bull hadn't been terribly hard to ride, Stick managed a score, and he wasn't sore from the contest. It was a soft landing, and he was pleased. There was still time to score more points, and Stick felt sure that three eight-second rides stood a good chance to win.

Shelly Tanner had seen the interview on TV, and she watched the results of the first night on the late-evening news. Stick Slaton was the talk of the town. Perhaps she had been hasty and shouldn't have left him. Stick hadn't really given her reason to believe that the two of them couldn't eventually have a serious relationship. He hadn't said he was in love with Anna, a conclusion Shelly had made on her own. Maybe her imagination had run away with her. Maybe there was really nothing between him and Anna after all.

With the PRCA finals concluding in two days, rodeo would soon be over. Stick would be going back home, and she would no longer have to compete with bulls, injuries, and the road for his attention. Her competition would be cut in half. And, if there was nothing between Stick and Anna, she would have no competition at all. Stick would eventually grow weak and give in to her enticing. After all, he was just a man.

Her new rationale constituted a trip to Ft. Worth, a trip that would pave the way for the future. She had not yet been defeated.

T he second night of competition began much like the first with the first three riders being thrown. Frank Hysler, Jamie Hendricks, and Drew Ferguson failed to score, but Ben Stanton held on this time and scored an 80 while riding a bull called Fatal Attraction. Terrel Stetson's broken foot, a painful wound with heavy swelling, forced withdrawal from the competition. Tyrone Fenton attempted to ride after losing his two front teeth but was disqualified when his free hand touched the bull. Chris Shockley was thrown at the sound of the horn, and, after much deliberation by the judges, they decided he'd missed scoring by a fraction of a second. Hardy Tillman straddled an enormous bull named Terminator Two. The animal was slow but very fleshy and hard to ride. He began to spin the moment he came out of the chute and continued through the duration of the ride. Hardy made it look good. He spurred the bull and fought his way to the inside each time the brute circled. After the horn, he dismounted with a jump and landed with hat in hand once again, waving at the crowd. The judges were pleased and awarded him an 81.

Stick felt better than he had in days. He carefully climbed the fence, easing into the chute and onto the bull named TNT. It was said that dynamite comes in small packages, and TNT was certainly no exception. The bull was as salty as they came, and he bellowed his disapproval as Stick lowered onto his back. The bull attempted to turn and hook Stick in the thigh with his sharp horns. TNT was a cross-bred animal, half Texas Longhorn and half Brahman. He was small and agile.

Stick took the time to remind God that he needed help and that Bobby and Anna were counting on him, then slid forward and nodded. The gate was pulled, and TNT exploded out of the chute with a burst. He jumped and twisted; spun to the right, one, two, three, four times; and then jumped again. Stick showed himself to be a strong fighter. Each time he felt himself sliding to the outside, he would thrust his body inward and cast his free arm to the opposite side to regain his balance. The bull began spinning to the left, twisting his body to unsettle the rider. Suddenly, the horn sounded, and Stick released his grip. The bull bounced once more, and Stick flew into the air and landed on his feet. The shock brought considerable pain to Stick's healing ankle, but he didn't fall. The crowd roared, and Stick hurled his hat into the air. This was the greatest ride yet.

Dusty fetched the hat and helped Stick to the gate. "Now that was a ride, son. If the judges ain't blind, that'll put you in the lead."

Stick smiled through the pain. He hoped the landing hadn't re-injured his ankle. It was hurting worse as he tried to walk. "Dust, I think I need some ice for my ankle. That landing was a little too much."

"Okay," agreed Dusty. "You just sit down and prop your leg up. I'll be back in a flash."

Dusty helped him to the ground, propped his leg on the gear, and quickly left. Stick leaned against the fence and closed his eyes.

"Stick Slaton takes the lead with a ninety-four, ladies and gentlemen," shouted Skinny with excitement. "His combined score is a hundred and seventy-one. Hardy Tillman holds second with a hundred and sixty points. Ben Stanton is in third with eighty. Chris Shockley has fourth with seventy-nine, and Drew Ferguson is fifth with seventy-eight. That concludes the second round. You folks come back tomorrow night. It's anybody's guess who's going to be this year's world champion bull rider."

Stick smiled with satisfaction and released a sigh. "Thanks again," he breathed.

Dusty returned carrying a bag of ice and immediately began to pack it around Stick's ankle. "There. Maybe that'll keep her from swelling."

Bull Hawthorne watched the two from an unseen position several feet away. One hundred thousand dollars split three ways was still a handsome sum. He could do a lot with thirty-three thousand dollars. Hardy didn't need the money. He would certainly share it. He might even let Bull and Phil split the whole amount. Bull smiled. Fifty thousand dollars was even better.

Stick Slaton was the only man standing between Hardy and the championship, the only man standing between Bull and perhaps fifty thousand dollars. Bull was counting on the older cowboy's injuries to eliminate him from the competition, but it didn't happen. Somehow, he would have to offer some assistance.

A series of creative thoughts, mostly illegal, began to bounce around in Bull's head. He must be careful not to get carried away. He didn't want to press his luck by taking anything else belonging to Stick. No. Stick's emotions would have to be the target. But what would he use? What about the old man? If something was to happen to him, Stick would most certainly be distracted. What about their truck? Four flat tires might do the trick.

Hardy was good, but Stick Slaton was better. Bull had seen that the first time they rode against each other. He wasn't a better athlete, but his experience gave him the edge. Hardy and Phil couldn't see it. They ignorantly assumed that there was a chance for Hardy to win, but Bull couldn't stand idly by and watch. He would make sure of Hardy's success.

Chapter Eighteen

Skinny Fuller sat in front of the microphone in the press box, wearing a white western suit and string tie. "Welcome to the third and final night of the world finals bull-riding competition," he announced. "Stick Slaton leads with a hundred and seventy-one points while Hardy Tillman trails by eleven. These are the only two cowboys who haven't been thrown, which serves to show that the cowboys aren't the only professionals here. These bulls were hand-picked from this year's bucking stock. Frank Hysler will be starting the show in chute five, riding Thunderbolt. Give him a hand, folks."

The crowd encouraged Frank Hysler as he prepared to ride. Stick and Dusty sat in the alley, near their gear, awaiting their turn.

GLEN STEPHENS

A nna heard the announcement from a distance, as parking had been difficult to locate. Bobby was with her in a wheelchair, and she eased him through the crowd and into the arena. Remarkably, the youngster had grown much stronger after his fever broke, something for which the doctors were hoping. He was excited to be there, although still weak and terribly sick. He had watched Stick on TV while at the hospital and wouldn't quit until Anna promised to bring him. The doctors consulted with one another and decided that it might give him opportunity to gain more strength before the operation. Anna paid the down payment, and they scheduled the operation. Everything was set.

Bobby carefully pushed himself out of the chair. "I'm going to see him, Mom."

"Okay, but go slow," she warned.

Bobby headed eagerly toward the alley where he was sure to find Stick, leaving his mother to maneuver the empty wheelchair through the crowd.

Stick and Dusty moved down the alley, away from their gear, in order to get a better view of the bull riding. Bobby entered from the opposite end and recognized Keepsake tied nearby. Two unfamiliar men knelt beside the horse, searching through his uncle's gear. He moved closer, tired from the long walk.

Bull rummaged through Stick's gear while Phil watched. "I don't like this, Bull. It ain't right. What if somebody sees us?" he complained.

"Shut up, Phil," Bull snarled. "Grandpa is going to cost us a lot of money if we don't do something. It don't take much to make him lose focus." Bull laughed. "All it took was a saddle in Houston."

Phil shook his head. "So it *was* you."

Bull looked up. "Yeah, and he couldn't concentrate after that. Wonder what it'll take this time." Bull looked through the gear. "How about this?" he asked, holding Stick's rigging in his hand.

"I don't know, Bull," Phil said reluctantly.

"Watch this," Bull said and tossed the rigging into a pen containing a huge bull named Migraine. "Let's see Stick Slaton get his rigging out of there." Bull patted Phil on the back, and the two walked several feet away, stopping to watch.

Bobby saw the big man throw his uncle's gear into the corral. He didn't understand why they did such a thing but knew it was wrong. His uncle needed the rigging for his ride. Weak as he was, Bobby crawled under the fence, using every ounce of his energy. He cleared the bottom rail and pushed himself to his feet, trembling as he glanced over his shoulder. The two men were talking, but they hadn't seen him. Bobby started toward the rope lying in the center of the pen.

Suddenly, Migraine spotted his victim and began pawing the earth. He bellowed loudly. Bobby heard the bull blow and froze, staring fearfully into the animal's eyes. He hadn't the strength to run.

"Hey, kid! Get out of there!" shouted Phil.

Stick heard the commotion and looked toward the pen, recognizing Bobby immediately. "Bobby!" he shouted. Then, ignoring the broken ankle, he ran to the fence, vaulting over it in one fluid motion. The impact sent a sharp pain through his ankle and up his leg, but he pressed on. In two steps, he was at Bobby's side, and Migraine charged. Stick pulled Bobby into his arms and stood as Migraine bore down, head lowered, horns focused, aiming through his brows.

Just before the bull struck, Stick saw Hardy Tillman jump the rail, and he pitched Bobby toward him, absorbing the blow from the furious animal. Pinned against the fence, Stick felt great relief when Bobby safely reached Dusty's arms, despite the despair of his own situation. Migraine tossed Stick into the air as if he was no more than a feather, and Stick crashed down hard, only to be thrown again. The bull enjoyed it.

Hardy slapped him on the rump, and Migraine turned with head lowered and charged. "Get him out of here!" yelled Hardy.

Phil jumped the fence and shoved Stick's limp body under the bottom rail. Hardy dodged the bull with remarkable quickness, distracting Migraine until Stick had been dragged to safety. Then he made good his own escape.

"Get an ambulance!" he yelled from on top of the fence. "Get an ambulance!"

Phil didn't hesitate. He knew that the ambulance would be at the gate entering the arena, and in a matter of seconds, two paramedics came sprinting down the alley. A crowd began to assemble, and Anna broke through, taking Bobby from Dusty's arms. "What happened?" She panicked. "What happened? Stick!"

Dusty knelt beside Stick as the paramedics examined him. "It's going to be okay, son. It's going to be okay." Blood filled his nostrils and flowed freely down the side of his face.

At the sound of Dusty's voice, Stick managed to open his eyes. Try as he might, he could not focus. Dusty's face was a blur, blending with the bright lights beyond his head.

"Let me down, Mom. Let me down," Bobby pleaded with his mother. Anna eased him to the ground and moved over to his uncle.

Stick recognized Bobby's form standing over him, and a weak smile quivered his lips. He saw Hardy Tillman standing nearby. "Thanks," he whispered brokenly and tried to offer his hand.

Hardy nodded and took Stick's hand. Stick focused on his eyes. Hardy's grave expression told Stick what the numbness of his body prevented. The injuries appeared very serious. The ambulance backed into the alley and stopped.

"All ... she ... wrote," Stick said in broken English. "Summer's over."

Stick's hand slowly dropped to the ground, and his head rolled to the side. One paramedic placed a stethoscope on his chest. "Cardiac arrest," he whispered to his partner. "Start CPR. I'll get the gurney."

The second paramedic began, pumping Stick's chest. Everyone watched in fear.

"Come on, son," whispered Dusty. "Aw. No ... Not him."

Anna couldn't believe her eyes. Falling to her knees beside Stick, she began to weep bitterly. "No!" she sobbed. "No! You can't! I love you. I love you, Stick. I love you."

The paramedic continued CPR for several minutes. Again, they used the stethoscope to check for signs of life. The paramedic looked up and sadly shook his head. "Let's go," he said.

Dusty knelt beside Anna and placed his arm around her. "I loved him, Dusty," she cried. "I loved him."

"I know, honey. I know you did, and he knew it, too." Dusty whispered. He was stricken with unbelief.

Bobby stepped toward Dusty and buried his face in his collar as the old man pulled him close. Bobby's heart ached. "Uncle Stick promised he would come back home," he whispered. "He promised he would come home. He promised."

Dusty looked at Bobby and nodded sadly. The boy was holding his breath, struggling against his emotions, so Dusty held him tighter. "It's okay, son. Let it out. It's okay."

Bobby pushed himself away and looked Dusty in the eye. His lips were trembling. He closed his eyes, fighting to speak. "But," he uttered, "cowboys … ain't supposed … to cry." Then his tears flowed freely.

The paramedics placed Stick's body on a stretcher and covered him with a sheet. They placed him into the ambulance and closed the doors.

"I'll ride with you," said Dusty.

"Sir," said the driver, "there's really nothing you can do, and we don't have enough room. Besides, your family needs you."

Dusty nodded slowly and backed away, taking Anna by the arm and lifting Bobby. They walked to a vacant office nearby. It was a place where they could think more clearly, a place where they could determine what to do, a place where they could cry.

N ews of the accident reached Skinny Fuller only seconds before Hardy Tillman's turn to ride. During his many years of experience, he'd witnessed hundreds of tragedies, but none had ever hit so close to home. He stepped away from the microphone and fought back tears. Could it be true? Stick Slaton was a man who seemed immortal. Maybe there was some mistake. Maybe it was a rumor. No official word had been spoken. He gained control of his emotions and stepped back to the microphone.

"Ladies and gentlemen," he began, "word has reached the press box that our first-place bull-riding contestant has been severely injured and will not be able to ride. Stick Slaton was hurt when a bull charged him behind the alley. I'm not sure about the extent of his injuries but...please pray for him."

H ardy Tillman carefully straddled the bull's back, his face a screen of mixed emotions. Anger, sorrow, aggravation, and sympathy struggled to claim control. His heart was no longer in the business. He wrapped the leather around his hand and pulled it tight, as the crowd remained hushed in a sympathetic lull. The arena held an eerie silence.

Skinny Fuller's voice lost its former excitement. "Ladies and gentlemen, this young man is the only remaining rider with a chance to ride three bulls. He can beat Stick Slaton's score of one hundred seventy-one points. All he has to do is hang on for eight seconds to win the National Championship. Coming out of chute number seven is Hardy Tillman, riding Peaches 'n Cream," he announced.

"Let's do it!" Hardy shouted angrily.

The gate flew open, and the bull jumped through, spinning to the left and bucking. He bounced to the center of the arena, but

Hardy was in total control. When the bull twisted, Hardy turned. With every move the bull made, Hardy countered with a move of his own. He couldn't be shaken. Then, suddenly, as the horn was about to sound, Hardy released his grip. The bull bucked him into the air, as usual, and he landed on his feet. His head hanging sadly, he began walking back to the chute.

A deathly calm gripped the arena. Slowly, a cloud of confusion began to clear until it became obvious what Hardy had done. No one moved. Even the bull eased quietly away.

Then one member of the audience began to clap, the sound echoing across the dome. Another joined in, then another. One at a time, the observers stood to their feet, and the applause became increasingly louder. Hardy stopped in the arena, watching the thousands of people. The applause turned to cheering, and cheering to screaming. Hardy took off his hat and waved it in a circle, and a thunderous eruption exploded from the awestruck multitude. Hardy smiled.

Skinny Fuller brought the ovation to a halt with his announcement. "Ladies and gentlemen, Stick Slaton is your new PRCA world champion bull rider."

The ovation resumed. Hats began flying into the arena. The mob went wild.

Hardy Tillman sailed his hat into the stands and jammed his fist passionately toward the sky. He gave a nod, walked to the chute, and climbed out of the arena. Phil was whistling, and he could whistle very loud. Bull was quietly staring into space. He hadn't intended for the outcome to be so extreme. It had been an accident. How could he have known the kid would go in after the rope? Still, Stick Slaton had beaten him—not by strength and ability but by something completely intangible, something that continued to linger even after the cowboy was gone. It was his worth to other people. It was Stick's character that so soundly defeated Bull.

Stick had given everything to reach the finals, to offer Bobby a chance. Dusty and Anna knew that he would want them to stay for the finish. There was nothing they could do for him but accept his prize. Necessary arrangements could be made shortly thereafter.

At the awards ceremony, in the center of the arena, thirty minutes later, Hardy extended a hand to Dusty in front of an emotional crowd. The old man's gray eyes stared deep into Hardy's as he shook the cowboy's hand. The young bull rider then stepped toward Anna.

"I'm sorry, ma'am."

Anna sadly accepted his condolences.

Skinny Fuller leaned toward the microphone and began to speak. "Ladies and gentlemen, rodeo is the most dangerous sport in the world. Because of this, tragic accidents are common." Skinny couldn't hide the shaking in his voice. His words began to break. He tried to stifle a cry. "Tonight…a man I've known…for a long time…was…"—he couldn't say killed, but chose rather to avoid such heavy and eternal language—"injured while saving a little boy's life." Skinny's sorrow of heart became more evident in the sound of his voice. "Stick Slaton won the world championship twenty years ago, and tonight, he won again. Long may we remember him."

The stadium erupted in thunderous applause. The sound reverberated across the parking lot to the ears of Shelly Tanner, who had arrived only a few minutes earlier. She had hoped to see Stick and persuade him of her love. Now she knelt near a bus and sobbed uncontrollably.

"Dusty Briggs," announced Skinny, "Stick's longtime friend, will accept his trophy. Bobby Slaton, Stick's nephew, will accept his solid gold belt buckle. And Anna Slaton, Stick's sister-in-law, will accept a check for one hundred thou-

sand dollars. Ladies and gentlemen, instead of applause, please let's have a moment of silent prayer for World Champion Bull Rider Stick Slaton."

The stadium obediently grew quiet. Even the animals seemed to approve the show of respect, as everyone in the arena bowed their heads. Then, slowly, Bobby lifted his eyes and focused on the arena gate. He blinked several times, unable to believe what he saw. He rubbed his face and looked again.

"Uncle Stick," he whispered. He glanced up at his mother and gently tugged her blouse, then returned his focus on the gate. A smile appeared on his face. "Uncle Stick?"

"Look over there," yelled someone in the crowd.

Dusty and Anna lifted their heads, looked at Bobby, and followed his gaze to the arena gate. Anna gasped and leaned against the platform for support. Dusty half fell into a chair.

Stick Slaton limped into the arena with a new bandage around his head and his right arm in a sling.

"What the heck?" exclaimed Dusty.

Stick stopped before them and smiled painfully. "You think you're surprised. You should've seen the guys in the ambulance. When I sat up with that sheet over me, I thought they were going to bail."

The assembled spectators began to cheer.

"Just because you can't find my pulse…it doesn't mean I'm dead," Stick said and looked intently into Anna's glossy brown eyes.

Totally confused, everyone in the arena began to exchange glances. Hardy Tillman started to laugh.

Stick limped close to Anna and took her by the hand. "Was I dreaming," he asked, "or did you say you loved me?"

The tears in her eyes reflected the arena lights. She couldn't believe Stick was standing before her. She watched the crowd as they proclaimed their great esteem and admiration. She smiled. "Richard Stick Slaton, I love you with all my heart," she said.

Stick looked deep into her eyes. "And ... I love you too ... Anna."
His smile suggested some obscure idea.

"What?" she asked, joyfully.

"You won't even have to change your name," he replied.

"Then ... the answer is yes," she stated.

Stick leaned close and met her beautiful, full lips with his, as
her soft form pressed against him. Her heart beat rapidly against his
chest, and he tasted her pleasant sweetness in a long, tender, savoring
kiss. It was all he had hoped it would be. It was perfect.

Bobby watched them, smiling contentedly. He walked over and
put his arms around Stick's leg.

"Let's go home, Uncle ... Dad," he said.

Stick looked down at his adorable son and winked. Pug was
right. He was a rich man. A very rich man.

LIVE

listen|imagine|view|experience

AUDIO BOOK DOWNLOAD INCLUDED WITH THIS BOOK!

In your hands you hold a complete digital entertainment package. In addition to the paper version, you receive a free download of the audio version of this book. Simply use the code listed below when visiting our website. Once downloaded to your computer, you can listen to the book through your computer's speakers, burn it to an audio CD or save the file to your portable music device (such as Apple's popular iPod) and listen on the go!

How to get your free audio book digital download:

1. Visit www.tatepublishing.com and click on the e|LIVE logo on the home page.
2. Enter the following coupon code:
   307c-770b-2a49-44dc-e989-db5b-40d3-8665
3. Download the audio book from your e|LIVE digital locker and begin enjoying your new digital entertainment package today!